BEACON GROVE
book one

CALLING
QUARTERS

USA *TODAY* BESTSELLING AUTHOR
JEN STEVENS

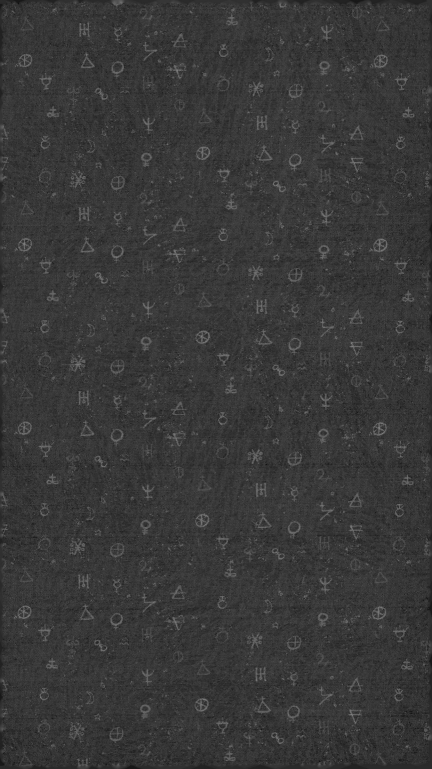

BEACON GROVE
book one

CALLING
QUARTERS

USA TODAY BESTSELLING AUTHOR
JEN STEVENS

MAP OF BEACON GROVE

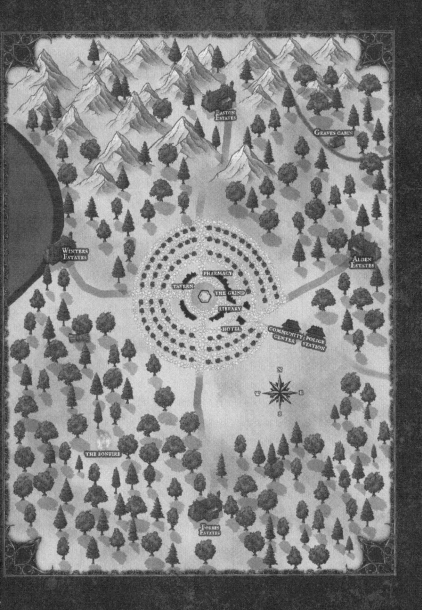

CALLING THE QUARTERS

Calling the quarters is a ritual used by magical practitioners at the start of magical or spiritual work. It involves calling on the five elements and their corresponding cardinal direction of the compass to bring these energies into the magical circle to protect and strengthen the practitioner. For the purpose of this novel, the following correspondences are made:

North — Earth

East — Air

South — Fire

West — Water

Center — Spirit

BEACON GROVE

Location: Beacon Grove High Priest: None
High Priestess: None
Elections held: every 3 years
Mayor: None
Sheriff: Kyle Abbot

THE MOVEMENT

A political regime with the goal of removing the
Quarters of Watchtower Coven

Founder: Rayner Whittle
Second-In-Command: Demi Kade

THE QUARTERS OF WATCHTOWER COVEN

NORTH - EARTH
Current: Lorenzo (Enzo) Easton
Elder: Andrew Easton
Counter: Unknown

EAST - AIR
Current: Lux Alden
Elder: Drake Alden
Counter: Unknown

SOUTH - FIRE
Current: Rhyse Forbes
Elder: Silas Forbes
Counter: Unknown

WEST - WATER
Current: Remington (Remy) Winters
Elder: Rowan Winters
Counter: Storie Graves

CALLING QUARTERS
PLAYLIST

Monster – Imagine Dragons
Dreams – Gabrielle Aplin, Bastile
Fallingforyou – The 1975
Little Talks – Of Monsters and Men
Kiss Me – Ed Sheeran
The 30th – Billie Eilish
Wolves Without Teeth – Of Monsters and Men
Seven Devils – Florence + The Machine
Shivers – Ed Sheeran
Deep End – Ruelle
Devil's Playground – The Rigs
I Put A Spell On You – IZA

PROLOGUE

D eep in the heart of the pacific northwest, nestled into dense forest and tall, reaching mountains, lies a town most have never heard of. It doesn't follow the same set of rules as anywhere else. It only infiltrates the minds of those who have been blessed with the knowledge of it once a year, when they're invited in. One by one, their cars trail in through the singular winding road, unaware of the important role they play for this sacred time.

This town is packed with ancient magic and a powerful coven of witches. But it was built on a strong foundation of secrets and lies. Its inhabitants are fiercely protective over one another, though distrust spreads among them like wildfire. They don't take kindly to nosey outsiders and they keep their skeletons hidden deep.

I was never meant to return. My own family gave their lives to ensure that was the case. They kept this place from me for nearly my entire life, raising me to believe I was just as painfully average as every other child I went to public school with in the city. But they weren't here anymore to discourage my instinctual need to dig into the past, and I owed it to them to find answers about their mysterious deaths.

To get back to my roots.

This town goes by the name of Beacon Grove, and it's the home I never knew existed—the family I desperately craved.

CHAPTER ONE

STORIE — FOUR YEARS AGO

I could hear Aunt Ash arguing with someone downstairs. The soft rumble of a man's voice vibrated through my bedroom floor. Their hushed, aggressive whispers were clearly in disagreement over something. I opened the door and tiptoed to the top of the stairs, listening.

"It's time, Asher," the man said, his tone icy and detached.

"But she's still in high school. She's not ready for this. She has a life here... one that shouldn't be disrupted. You haven't even let me warn her," Aunt Ash replied in a desperate plea. I imagined the crease between her brows had deepened the way it always did when she was concerned.

With careful, calculated steps, I navigated down the stairs quietly, avoiding all the spots that groaned or squeaked. I'm not sure it would have mattered. They appeared to be too engrossed in their argument to notice anything else.

"Don't make this harder on yourself. You knew the terms when you took this on. You shouldn't have grown so attached. Haven't you learned that yet?"

"She's my family, Rayner. The last of it that I have left. You were once considered her family as well. Why do we have to uphold this silly agreement, anyway? She's unwanted there. They'll only come after her if she returns."

"Because this is the way. They need her. You know The Movement won't allow anything to go too far. You have no right to question how things are done, especially when you've hardly done your part." He turned his back to her then, black eyes scanning the mantle that was filled with pictures of me and Aunt Ash along with protective crystals littered in between with disinterest.

Until they landed on me.

His brow slightly twitched before he straightened his features again. Back to the mask of indifference. He continued to stare, though.

He was oddly dressed. Black dress shirt, black slacks, shiny black shoes, all covered by a black floor-length trench coat. It made no sense in the middle of June.

"Storie," Aunt Ash breathed my name out in a panic. "I didn't realize you were home." She quickly strode across the room to place herself between me and the strange visitor. "Rayner is an old friend of your father's. He was actually just leaving."

He still hadn't released me from his intense stare but took the hint and placed the black fedora he'd been holding back onto his head. With a silent warning nod toward Aunt Ash, he walked himself out and slammed the door behind him.

"He was odd," I finally said, breaking the tense silence. "What did he want?"

Clearly, it had something to do with me.

"We were just discussing some unfinished family business." She made her way back into the kitchen, a strained smile stretching across her features. "How did your finals go?"

I stood back as she gathered random ingredients from the pantry, stacking them into her arms as if she were in too much of a rush to make multiple trips. Once she was satisfied and her arms were full, she dumped the pile onto the counter and pulled out a large pot from the cabinet.

"I think they went pretty well. Not that it matters, though."

I'd already been accepted into State, despite some pushback from Aunt Ash for applying. She didn't want me to go away for college, but there was no way I was staying here. So long as I didn't bomb this final semester, I was basically done bothering with high school the moment I received that acceptance letter. I think I did well enough to fly under the radar and get by.

That's typically how I handled most of my high school career, anyway.

Aunt Ash was too distracted to respond. She'd grabbed her tattered grimoire from the shelf across the room while I spoke and was hunched over the counter, manically flipping through the handwritten pages in search of something. I hated when she was like this. It had been a while since she needed the book for a rite or spell. She'd memorized all the ones she used regularly.

I've never believed in the witchy voodoo she practiced, but it brought her comfort, so I didn't say anything against it. At least, until she tried to push it onto me. That had resulted in some nasty fights between us through my formative years. For some reason, she thought it was important that I knew this useless stuff. I just always had better things to do.

"Just the basics," she had argued, practically forcing me away from my schoolwork to practice with her. I spent countless nights copying basic spells into my own leather-bound notebook by hand while cursing her under my breath.

"Keep pouring negative energy into it and you'll get nothing but negative energy back," she always warned, disappointment lacing her soft tone.

Eventually, I gave in to her and memorized a few of the spells. To this day, it's been a waste of time.

But something was bothering her, and it clearly had to do with the man who just left. I shifted to look over her shoulder at the page she finally landed on. It appeared to be a heavy protection spell. One we'd never used before that required a lot more ingredients than what she kept in the pantry.

"What did that guy say to you?"

She was mumbling something under her breath. Something that clearly wasn't English. "Hm? What guy?"

I reached out to grab her hands in mine, forcing her to look at me. "Aunt Ash, talk to me. What is going on?"

The panicked look that her eyes held when I first came down the stairs still hadn't left. She was keeping something from me, and I had no idea why. We told each other everything. It's always been that way.

I watched the conflict dance in her eyes as she warred with herself over what to say. How much to reveal. Eventually, she gave up. Her shoulders fell as her head hung between them, eyes cast down to the floor.

"I've failed them."

"Failed who? You're not making any sense."

"Your parents." She pulled her hands out of my embrace and turned back to face the pot on the stove, then threw a handful of rosemary in. "It doesn't matter. They were going to come either way. Resistance was futile. I told your father that."

It was clear she wasn't going to explain any further when she began chopping up sunflower stalks while mumbling in that horrible foreign language again.

This was why I needed to get out of here. My presence was only a burden on Aunt Ash, and it had been for two years now. The day I turned sixteen, we'd gotten into a car crash. Nothing serious, just a few bumps and bruises. But Aunt Ash began acting weird after it happened—more protective of me and our home. Like she thought the crash was intentional.

That was also when she started pushing her practices on me and fighting the idea of college. I'd just figured it was because of the close call. Like, maybe she didn't want to lose the last bit of family she had left. But now, it seems like there was more to it than that.

I left her alone, dragging my feet up the stairs.

CHAPTER TWO

STORIE — PRESENT

T he two-lane road curved around mountains and in between large, ancient-looking trees. It was terrifying and
exhilarating to weave around the natural landscape. Any exhaustion that I'd built up from the previous day of driving was
slowly wiped away with each sharp turn.

I felt like I belonged there, in the trees. It was a foreign feeling
to me—one I'd never had growing up in the big city with Aunt
Ash.

Just as the road narrowed and I was sure it was about to come
to an end, dumping me into the woods with no cell phone service or way out, the smooth pavement transitioned into gravel
that was only wide enough for one vehicle. I checked my GPS
for the thousandth time, hoping it would give me any idea as
to where I'd ended up, but it continued circling, attempting to
calculate a route and failing miserably.

The sky had darkened overhead, and the trees provided a
green canopy that made me feel even more claustrophobic. The
only option was to turn back and find a different path around
this hauntingly beautiful forest, though turning around was
going to be next to impossible. With my mind made up, I slowed
to a stop and shifted into reverse.

I hadn't noticed the headlights when they neared me or the
flashing red light until it was right beside me. I was halfway
through my attempt to turn around when the officer appeared

at my window, unbothered by the constant rocking of my car as I tried to shimmy myself in a circle.

He knocked on my window three times, then stepped back and placed his hand on his weapon.

"Ma'am, are you lost?" His low, authoritative voice rumbled once I rolled my window down halfway, still not completely convinced he was real. I hadn't seen a soul around here for hours before he seemed to have appeared out of nowhere.

"Y-yes, actually. I was trying to find my way into Beacon Grove, but I think I may have taken a wrong turn somewhere. This road doesn't lead anywhere, does it?"

That was a dumb question. Clearly, it led to wherever he'd just come from.

His face shifted at the mention of Beacon Grove. Gray eyes narrowed in on me, then bounced around the car in search of something. I took the chance to survey his appearance, sizing him up in case he gave me any issues.

He was tall and lanky, his arms a little too long for his body. His hair was peppered with gray strands that matched his eyes perfectly and only made the onyx color of the rest of his hair pop even more. His name tag read, "Abbot."

"What's your name, Miss?" the man asked skeptically, finally returning his gaze back to me.

I debated not telling him. Why would he need my name, anyway? If he were a real officer, he'd have asked for my license and registration and gotten that information himself. We stared each other down for a long, heavy moment before eventually, I caved. He was the only living soul I'd seen for nearly 24 hours and there was nothing he could do to me by simply knowing my name.

"Storie Graves."

Recognition flashed across his features. He took me in once more, this time more unapologetically. "It can't be..." he whispered in disbelief.

Somehow, this strange man had heard my name before. He knew me, though I was certain we'd never met. His stony eyes softened then, the crow's feet loosening just a tad. Something shifted within him. He dropped his hand from his gun and took a step closer.

"I'm just going to keep trying to turn around. I think I can find another way. Sorry to bother you, officer."

"No!" he shouted, startling me. When he saw me jump, he lifted his hands, palms out. "I'm sorry. I just mean, this is the only road you can take to get to Beacon Grove. You won't find another way around."

"Oh, okay, thank you." I pressed the button to roll the window back up and he reached his hands out again, placing his fingers on the edge of the glass. It completely ceased movement at his touch, as if he were strong enough to stop it from going up any farther, though he didn't appear to be using any effort.

His voice dropped. "Who sent you here, Storie?" he demanded.

"What? No one sent me..."

I needed to get out of here. This man was clearly unhinged, and he was coming more undone as each minute passed.

His head shook. "I don't understand. You weren't supposed to come back. Unless... oh no, Asher... Is she okay?" he rambled, holding one hand on the window glass as he raked his fingers through thinning, black hair. His eyes looked tortured.

"How did you know Aunt Ash?" I asked before thinking. I shouldn't have been entertaining this mania. It was getting weirder by the minute.

Who was this random man and how did he know so much about me?

As far as I knew, Aunt Ash didn't have any remaining friends or family, especially from Beacon Grove. In fact, she'd spent so long drilling into my head that it was just her and me that I completely skipped over holding any sort of memorial service for her. There was no one to call and notify of her odd, tragic passing and no one left to guide me through the harrowing process of getting back onto my feet after losing a loved one.

A voice on his radio interrupted his response, snapping him back to reality. He quickly pulled himself together and stood up straighter, glancing into the woods.

"Beacon Grove is that way, Ma'am," he pointed his finger down the road, past his vehicle. He then dropped his voice back down to a whisper. "If you're smart, you'll turn around now and forget this place ever existed."

"I can't do that," I found myself explaining.

He huffed out a breath and shook his head at my stubbornness. "Then don't trust a single soul you encounter there," he warned. With that, he took a few steps back and turned toward his vehicle, calling over his shoulder, "I'll lead the way."

Beacon Grove was just as beautiful as the forest surrounding it. Officer Abbot was right, there didn't appear to be any other way in or out of the sleepy town aside from the dirt road we were on. His police cruiser led me back onto pavement and into a lot beside a building marked, "Beacon Grove Community Center."

Once we were stopped, he stepped back out of his car and walked up to my window, staring in at me expectantly. There was something off about him, that much was obvious. But he'd managed to lead me where I was asking to go and didn't appear to want to harm me.

In fact, his oddness stemmed from his unnecessary concern for me. With that thought in the back of my mind, I rolled my window down halfway so we could talk.

His entire demeanor had shifted back to the authoritative figure that approached me from the start. Any fear or concern that he showed before about me or Aunt Ash was washed away during our short drive, and I couldn't help but wonder if I should have taken his warning more seriously. He clearly knew something dark about this place.

"There's one hotel and it's just up the street. It's run by Tabatha Granger and her granddaughter. They'll take good care of you during your stay. Let you know the best places to eat and such." He pointed a finger toward a street that headed north. "You'll find the town's center just down that way. Might have spotty cell service anywhere on the outskirts, but we do our best to keep Wi-Fi connected throughout."

"Okay, thank you, Officer."

"Please, call me Kyle," he insisted, his eyes softening a bit at the sides again as they grazed over my face once more. "You're a spitting image of your father."

That had taken me back. What was wrong with this man to think that was an appropriate thing to say to a complete stranger? I'd expected to find people in this town who knew my parents—that was the whole point of coming here. But not this quickly, and not in such a creepy way.

Maybe they were so far removed from society, they'd forgotten simple customs. Perhaps that's why my parents left in the first place.

"I'm sorry. I don't mean to scare you. I grew up with your mom and dad. I suppose you should get used to people bringing them up. They were pretty popular around here and there's no denying that you've got their blood." He dropped his voice and warned, "Just be careful who you spend your time with."

Part of me wanted to ask more. If he was one of their friends, he must know a lot about them, or at least who they were before they left. Maybe he knew why they left. But another part of me was screaming to get away from him. To take at least one of his warnings seriously and not trust him or anyone else. I decided to go with the latter, at least until I learned more about Beacon Grove and the people in it.

Speaking of which, where were all the people who lived here? We'd been parked for nearly fifteen minutes, and I still hadn't seen a single soul besides Officer Kyle. It was the middle of the day. Surely, someone had to have crossed our path by now.

Almost as if he had read my mind, he explained, "There's a town meeting in progress. They're held in the town's center on nice days. Gives everyone a breath of fresh air while they deal with any issues. They should be finishing up soon."

I nodded my response, eager to be alone and begin exploring. It might be beneficial to see the town before any other nosey townsfolk could bother me again.

"I'll let you get to it."

"Thank you for all your help," I said, offering a tight smile.

"If you have any questions, feel free to holler. I'm always around." He lowered his head, his face a little too close to mine as he whispered, "Don't forget what I said, Storie. Trust no one."

With that, he slapped the top of my car and walked off. I pulled out of my spot and headed in the direction of the hotel, a heavy boulder of doubt now placed firmly in my stomach.

CHAPTER THREE

STORIE

T abitha and her granddaughter came walking down the road shortly after I arrived at their hotel. I had been trying to pull up the map on my phone to figure out exactly where Beacon Grove was when I felt eyes on me.

Assuming it was them, I lifted my head and found the most intense man openly gaping at me. He stared as if he'd never seen another human before and his attention sent chills down my spine. He was tall and muscular, wearing a black t-shirt with the sleeves cut off to expose his toned arms. His golden skin practically glistened in the sun. Just as I'd grown uncomfortable enough to stand and leave, people began walking toward us down the street.

He noticed the incoming visitors at the same time and abruptly abandoned our stare-off. When he turned and left, he passed the old woman I assumed was Tabitha and her granddaughter on the way. They each avoided eye contact with him while he appeared to ignore their existence. The entire exchange was odd, given his curiosity toward me.

They didn't notice me waiting on the bench just beside their porch until they were unlocking the door, too focused on whatever whispered argument they were having.

"Oh, hi. Can we help you?" the young girl finally asked on a gasp as she assisted her grandmother over the threshold.

She had to be close to my age. Her red hair was tied back in a braid that hung below her butt. Light brown freckles littered her entire face.

"I'm looking to rent a room."

The old woman swung her head around, finally offering her attention, and then stopped dead in her tracks. She looked like she'd seen a ghost.

If Officer Kyle hadn't told me they were related, I never would have guessed. Tabitha's hair was completely white, the color drained out from old age, but her weathered skin was a light mocha color and her plump figure stood at least six inches shorter than the young girl. The only resemblance they shared were the odd shade of deep, dark green that their eyes pinned me with.

"You shouldn't be here," her deep voice croaked.

Her granddaughter blanched, eyes widening in disbelief. "Grammy," she warned, but was quickly dismissed by Tabitha. I watched her wilt under the old woman's warning stare.

I had no idea how to respond. Her cold glare chilled my entire body, sending an involuntary shiver through my limbs. She appeared to enjoy inciting that reaction from me, grunting out her disappointment with a smirk before she shook her head once, then turned her back on me and walked inside.

When we were alone, the young girl—who had introduced herself as Blaire—gestured for me to follow her into the office. She was cordial and overly polite to make up for her grandmother's crassness.

"I swear, she's losing her mind. She's been pulling cards like crazy and talking to herself more every day," she rambled, mostly to herself while I awkwardly waited for her to hand over my room key.

"It's not a big deal." I laughed, hoping that speaking the words into existence would make them true.

In reality, Tabitha's greeting scared me a little. She was the second person I'd come into contact with in a matter of hours who told me I shouldn't be here. It fed the doubt growing in the pit of my stomach, screaming at me that this trip was a mistake. I knew Aunt Ash would be upset at me if she were alive, but she was the main reason I was here.

Her death didn't make any sense. None of my family's untimely deaths did. While each one was slightly different, the similarities between them were what sent me on this rogue trip. I needed answers, and this was the one place they all had in common.

I had no choice but to explore it... right?

"Well, hopefully you'll enjoy the rest of your time here. Room seven is just that way, three doors down. Stop by if you need anything else."

My room was small and outdated. A queen size bed took up most of the floor space with two nightstands adorning either side. It narrowed into a little nook in the back with a small round table and single chair tucked beneath. The table butted against a buffet that held a microwave and old tube-style television. The bathroom was equally crowded, and the shower floor was stained with rust from the town's well water. The bedding, curtains, and towels all matched with a horrible pastel floral print.

It wasn't glamorous, but it would do.

I set my suitcase down on the bed and headed into the bathroom for a quick shower, eager to scrub the past two days of travel from my skin.

As I settled in, I swore I could hear distant shouts coming from somewhere within the hotel. They were blood-curling; filled with anguish and desperation. Silence took over the space just as quickly and I told myself I'd imagined it.

CHAPTER FOUR

STORIE

The center of town was not at all what I expected it to be for such a small, secluded place. A white gazebo served as the centerpiece, surrounded by flowers of various species and colors. The roads that curved around it were paved with white cobblestone, and the sidewalks looked to be newer and in pristine condition. Not a single thing was out of place. It was so unlike the polluted cities I grew up in.

The buildings were set against each other in varying sizes and styles, fighting to showcase their own individuality through the layer of matte black paint they were covered in. Copper awnings hung above every door, the color popping out amongst the uniformed black and white.

It was beautiful. The contrast made everything look a little more magical.

There were people mulling all around, too caught up in their own worlds to notice me gazing at the architecture and style of their home like a true out-of-towner. The coffee shop on the corner seemed to be the most popular spot with a constant flow of people going in and out. I decided to try that first, noting the rest of the stores as I passed them.

The whimsical patterns and styles showcased in the display window of the clothing boutique caught my attention. Next to it was an art gallery that wasn't open, and Granger's Pharmacy was the largest, taking up the space of three storefronts. I noticed Tabitha and Blaire's last name on the sign and made a mental note. They seemed to have their hands in everything.

The tavern on the opposite corner was closed, but I was willing to bet based on the worn tables and chairs sitting on their patio that they rivaled the coffee shop's popularity at night.

The library stood alone near the coffee shop. While it didn't take up much of the street the way the pharmacy had, it towered over the others. It had to have been at least five stories high. The sign on the door was flipped to CLOSED and the hours weren't posted anywhere, but I knew that would be my best bet for finding information. Surely, it held some answers about the history of the Graves family and why my parents left. Maybe some birth records or newspaper articles that could point me in the general direction I should be looking in.

When I stepped into The Grind, I was hit with the familiar nutty aroma and instantly felt at home. The walls were painted bright orange with large yellow and red swirls, imitating a flowering rose. My barista was quick, and the coffee was better than I expected it to be.

The guy from yesterday was leaning against a tree in front of the shop with three others as I left. I almost didn't notice him, too focused on where I'd head next, but his eyes were locked on me with a predatory glare this time, as if he had been waiting for me.

The other three shifted their gaze my way, each one looking scarier than the last. Their appearances were almost otherworldly. All of their features were more pronounced, their colors more electric than anyone else around.

Their beauty looked menacing.

Unapproachable.

People avoided looking at them as they passed, opting to look down at the ground or straight ahead, just as Tabitha and Blaire had done the day before.

I felt a few passerby eyes land on me in response to the undivided attention I'd received from the four strange-looking men. I scowled in response, irritated at the spectacle they were drawing toward me. That only seemed to please the first one as a smile crept across his face.

I turned my back to them and walked in the opposite direction, away from town square. I decided I would just have to explore a little later, when my embarrassment faded, and people forgot about the weird exchange that just happened.

Those guys were clearly unhinged and a sick feeling in my gut told me I needed to stay away.

Aunt Ash told me to trust my intuition because it was always right. I never knew what she meant by that. Was I supposed to go with the first initial thought that entered my head about a person or thing? To believe the little seeds of doubt or excitement that planted their way into my thoughts as time went on?

I'd always thought it was another nonsensical piece of advice she'd tried to bestow upon me. That she was crazy.

Now, I knew exactly what she was talking about. Intuition was a strange, unexplainable feeling—almost like a voice in your head or a tug on your heart—where you just *know*. There's no science or logic behind it. It just *is*.

"Oh, hey," Blaire called out as I passed the hotel office.

I turned back and smiled my greeting, hoping she didn't have anything else to say. I wanted to be alone.

There was nothing negative or menacing about her. In fact, I felt calm and secure in her presence. She was safe. But apparently, I could only take Beacon Grove and its odd inhabitants in small doses.

"I just finished up a shift," she explained, closing the distance between us. Disappointment sank into my stomach at her next words. "I thought maybe I could show you around. I've got nothing else to do."

I looked back in the direction of the town, trying to form some sort of excuse to decline. "I actually just came from there. I was going to head inside and grab a snack," I lied.

I still haven't even had time to grab groceries.

"No way. I'll take you to the best diner around. It's kind of a secret amongst us locals, but I think I can trust you not to tell." She winked at me teasingly. "You'll be in a food coma for days."

With that, she turned her back to me and gestured for me to follow. I hesitantly trailed behind her, and to my surprise, we walked the opposite way I'd just come from.

We traveled a few blocks south, into what appeared to be more of a residential area. The houses of Beacon Grove were more approximately matched with the age of the town than the square had been. Decaying, two and three story brick homes littered the streets with varying colors and conditions, telling the stories of those that lived in them. It was obvious that some had been split up into apartments with staircases that led to each level wrapped around them.

That was also the case for the building Blaire stopped at. I looked around for a sign or any other indication that we were heading into a diner and not someone's basement or kitchen, but fell short.

"Maisy Sanford isn't big on tourists," she explained when I gave her a puzzled look. "She tries to keep her place under wraps. Only those who live here know about it."

She opened a rotting side door and waved for me to go ahead. It led to stairs that went down into what appeared to be a basement and for a split second, I questioned Blaire's intentions.

Had I underestimated her? Was I being led into some sort of dangerous trap?

But then a burst of laughter broke out behind the door at the bottom of the stairs and my doubts faded away.

Once we got to the end of the staircase, Blaire reached ahead of me to open the second door and a room full of people appeared. They were chatting and laughing at separate tables as an older waitress ping-ponged between them.

"We caught the end of the lunch hour," Blaire whispered, grabbing the last open table off to the side. "Most of them will be leaving in a few."

I followed her lead and sat down, grabbing one of the menus off the end of the table.

"What did I tell you about visitors, Blaire?" the waitress appeared out of nowhere, stern eyes boring down into my new friend.

"I know, I know. But she isn't just a visitor. Her parents were born here, so that kind of makes her one of us, right?"

I shot Blaire a questionable glare. I never told her who my parents were, let alone where they were born. Surely, there was more than one Graves family in town for her to mix me up with. Why would she think she could make that statement so boldly?

When my eyes flicked back to the waitress, I realized her attention was zeroed in on me, and I swear the entire diner quieted down to hear our conversation.

"What's your name?"

That was met with my irritated scowl. I was tired of being asked that question, as if it meant anything to a group of people I'd never met before. After seeing Officer Kyle and Tabitha's reactions, I was hesitant to offer a real name to the nosey old woman. If she didn't want me to eat at her basement diner, I'd happily leave. There was no reason to cause a scene.

But Blaire piped up before I could offer my snarky response. "Her name is Storie Graves. Grammy says her parents were good people."

The woman's facial expression shifted, as I was learning most people's in this town did when hearing my name. She softened a bit, placing her wrinkled hand on my shoulder.

"I'm sorry about your loss. You just can't be sure who to trust around here anymore."

I nodded hesitantly, realizing that was another common theme in Beacon Grove. No one trusted each other, though as an outsider, the town appeared to be a tight-knit community. I lost myself in thought, wondering who or what happened to have made these people so weary of each other, when Blaire kicked my foot under the table.

"Sorry, what?"

"What can I get you to start with?"

I placed my order and Blaire continued to talk my ear off as people around us slowly filtered out. With the diner less crowded, it was easier to take in each face as they passed. A table of four men stood to leave and I noticed the man from Aunt Ash's house a few years ago.

My heartbeat pounded into my ears, drowning out the clattering of the diner as my focus zeroed in on him.

He was the one who had set her paranoia into full swing. Nothing about our life together was the same after that day, and I'd always wondered what he could have said to send her onto the path that ultimately caused her untimely death.

He was the reason I drove all the way to Beacon Grove to find answers.

We locked eyes and he nodded at me, a smug smirk tugging the left side of his face as if he knew. He knew that I was here to investigate him. He knew he played a part in Aunt Ash's death. And he didn't seem to give a damn.

He was dressed in the same type of clothing as before, all black and professionally pressed. We continued to hold each other's stare as he walked through the small space, silently daring the other to speak.

Blaire noticed and followed my gaze. Her voice dropped to a whisper, and she cupped one side of her mouth with her hand. "That's Rayner. He's a real creep. He's basically the leader of the Movement."

My eyes snapped to her, and she clamped her lips shut, clearly realizing she'd said too much. "The Movement?"

The memory from that day was faded and distant, but I recalled hearing him mention something about a movement to Ash.

The door closed behind Rayner, and it was like my lungs could fill with air again. After years of constantly dreaming of the man who had turned my life upside-down, being so near to him sucked all the breath out of me.

Blaire swatted her hand between us in an attempt to downplay her statement. "It's nothing. More of an idea than anything with substance. I'm not even sure you could call it that. It's kind of just a rumor, really..." she rambled.

"Blaire," I cut in, leveling her with a desperate look. Her liquid green eyes fell to the table. "Please... you can tell me. I need to know."

"I really don't know much about it. No one bothers including us in any of it. We're kind of the outcasts, you know? Being the town's midwives, they blame us a little."

When she noticed my confused expression, she shook her head and paused, glancing around to make sure no one was listening. "We can't talk about it here," she finally whispered.

I couldn't argue with that. I really didn't want anyone knowing that I was digging into Rayner's business, or that I might suspect him of taking part in my parents' or Aunt Ash's deaths. It was probably best if we had this conversation in private.

The thought occurred to me that Blaire might end up feeding me lies. Distrust seemed to spread through this town like a cancer, and I'll admit it had infected me a tiny bit. But once again, my gut told me Blaire was an ally. She was terribly naive about most things and didn't take social cues very well, but I realized I really liked spending time with her. The more she spoke, the more genuine she felt, and it was nice to know there was at least one person who I could somewhat believe in.

CHAPTER FIVE

STORIE

I shouldn't even be talking about this to someone outside of the coven," Blaire groaned, shoving a throw pillow into her face to hide.

"My parents were a part of Watchtower, weren't they? Doesn't that make me an honorary member?"

Blaire's eyes appeared above the pillow and glared. "No."

"Come on, Blaire. This is important. I'm asking as a new friend."

She sighed, and I knew I had her then. Blaire was desperately deprived of friendship. I'm not sure why, but people in this town seemed to walk in the other direction whenever she came near. Sure, she was quirky, but everyone had their tribe who accepted them no matter what. Everyone except her. She mentioned something about being left out because her family were the town's midwives, but that didn't make any sense.

Either way, she needed companionship and I needed answers. I liked being around her and we were basically fast friends at this point. It's not like I was being too dishonest.

"Every coven has a hierarchy, right?" she looked to me for confirmation and I just shrugged cluelessly.

"Sure."

"Well, Watchtower has kind of a unique system. Most covens have to call the four elements into their sacred space for protection and guidance. They address each direction and element and invite them in. It's a ceremony of calling the quarters. Watch-tower is unique in that we're such an ancient coven, we've been given our own set of Quarters by the gods. It's a role that's been passed down through those four families for generations. Do you follow?"

I nodded.

"Okay, the story goes that in order to keep a balance, the universe creates an opposite for each Quarter—a counterpart," she held her hands together into a circle and then separated them in two halves. "Counters are born exactly twelve hours after the Quarter on a new moon and are rumored to be the only people that can take the Quarter's powers away from him. Quarters are trained from the moment they can walk to hunt and kill their Counters, so they can keep their powers and continue to serve the coven."

She took a deep breath and smiled sheepishly. "See, it sounds insane."

She was right. None of that seemed realistic. It was like she was repeating a fairytale she'd heard before being tucked into bed every night. As if she knew the story and hadn't believed in it. But an isolated town full of witches and magic once sounded like a fairytale to me too, yet here I was.

I had so many questions. "How do they know who the Counter is?" was the one I landed on first.

Blaire shrugged her shoulders. "They used to track who was born within the twelve-hour period of a Quarter and kill the babe before it could grow up and become a threat."

I looked at her with my lip curled in pure disgust. "They killed babies just for being born at the wrong time?"

"Yeah," she stated and nodded quickly, stuffing popcorn into her mouth, muffling her words, "until parents began hiding their children's births from the coven. The Quarters are cruel and unpredictable. No one really goes near them if they can help it."

She swallowed a large chunk of her popcorn and went on. "The women in my family have always been the town's midwives, so they're usually the one's relied upon to keep track of births. But women were afraid to admit they were in labor at the same time as a Quarter mother. They'd birth their children without assistance and hide them until the new moon was over. A lot of times, the mothers would die before then due to lack of medical attention."

"That's horrible," I whisper, my thoughts lingering on my own mother.

She died from giving birth to me, or at least that's what I'd always been told. Could she have been hiding me to protect my life?

"It was a rough time, especially for my family. We were accused of helping the Counters and their families escape their fate. Grammy was all but cast out until my mom agreed to take over as the town midwife. Grammy was put on desk duty here at the hotel that her parents owned. Mom was only eighteen at the time."

"Have any of the current Quarters found their Counters?"

Blaire stopped chewing again and looked over at me, her eyes going wide. "No. That's the weird part. They couldn't find any babies born on their new moons. It's the first time this has happened. The town is going a little crazy over it. Like, how did four children go undocumented and manage to slide under the radar?"

My skin broke out into chills. It was starting to make sense: my parents' deaths, Aunt Ash's paranoia, the warnings from Officer Kyle and Tabitha.

Could I be a Counter?

No. *That* was insane. I could entertain the stories and pretend all of this made any sense, but to suggest I had a role in any of it? That I was a part of this crazy town's history? That may have been taking it too far.

But I was here to find the truth about myself, and every possibility had to be explored.

Right?

"All I know is that the mystery over who the Counters are is splitting the town in half. Some believe they're a threat to the coven's existence and need to be hunted quickly. The other half thinks it's time to end the Quarters' reign over us and rely on our own magic." She pointed a salty finger at me. "That's the movement Rayner has been pushing. His brother was suspected of being a Counter to the Forbes when they were younger. They executed his father in front of the whole town to make a point: You can't hide from the Quarters. They took his brother away to be killed in private since he was so young."

My stomach flipped thinking of the poor boy and his father. How many people have lost their lives due to this silly tradition? How many children? Were they even sure that the Counters had the power over the Quarters that they were accused of having?

I wanted to ask what side she was on. To know if I could trust her with my crazy newfound suspicions about myself and my past. But just before the words made their way from my mouth, Tabitha opened the bedroom door and waddled in.

Her eyes lingered on me as she barked, "There's a customer at the desk, Blaire."

Blaire walked out of the room wordlessly, leaving me alone with Tabitha and her withering stare. Once she was out of earshot, Tabitha finally broke our silence.

"She's a smart girl, but she's regurgitating fables that were told to her by people who only speak out of fear. I've warned her to protect herself from them, but does she listen?" She clicked her tongue disappointedly.

A tight smile was all I could offer. She was so intense, and I was afraid to admit my own thoughts on the matter, especially to someone who would be so unforgiving if she believed I was on the wrong side.

"I know what you're thinking, little girl. You cannot tell a soul about it," she whispered. "Your parents died protecting your secret. You are either a threat or a pawn to these people—nothing more. If you want answers, you need to find them on your own. Don't trust anyone here to help you."

"Grammy, no one was there," Blaire's voice called out from the hallway as she approached her bedroom.

"They must have left," Tabitha simply said, offering one last warning glare before she turned and left.

"She's really losing it," Blaire sighed.

I didn't respond. I couldn't stop thinking about her warning—the same words Officer Kyle told me before even entering Beacon Grove.

Did they both know what I am? And who else in this town was privy to my past?

I purposely didn't bring the topic back up with Blaire and she seemed to have forgotten all about it, returning her focus to the movie and stuffing her face with popcorn. But my mind was too chaotic to pay any attention to what was happening on screen.

I had to find a way to get Tabitha alone and make her explain more. She told me I needed to find out on my own—that I couldn't trust anyone here—but did that include her?

Was she guilty of what they accused her of?

Was she part of the reason my father and aunt left Beacon Grove so suddenly?

CHAPTER SIX

REMY

I once read about a study conducted on rats that tested their perseverance with the presence of hope and support. First, a group of rats were placed in a bucket of water and left alone to swim until they drowned. The process hadn't taken long, as they quickly gave up once they realized they weren't going to be rescued. The second time, the rats were brought out of the water just before they drowned, and then immediately placed back into the bucket to swim.

The study found the rats that were rescued lasted significantly longer than the ones that were left to drown. They'd pushed their bodies to swim past their limits because they had been introduced to the concept of being rescued.

They believed that eventually, they'd be saved again.

When I first read about it, I thought the second group of rats was foolish, and that the study hardly represented how far one would go if only they had hope—this elusive concept of waiting for someone else to save you.

Then, I grew up.

I witnessed people drown in their metaphorical buckets because there was nothing left to hold onto. I also witnessed people survive simply because they believed they could. They believed someone would come along and save them, or that they could save themselves.

Now, I sympathize with those rats. No one had ever reached their hands out to keep me from drowning. Yet, I felt this glimmer of hope that one day, someone will come along and pull me out of this hell. All I had to do until then was tread water.

Of course, that was an incredibly stupid mindset to have. No one was coming to save me. They weren't coming for any of us. As the coven's Quarters, *we* were the ones responsible for instilling hope. They trusted us to keep them protected and stop their magic from going too far.

If only they knew how powerless we truly were. How long we'd been treading water; waiting.

There were four of us born every generation. It was a requirement to produce at least one heir and continue the Quarter bloodlines. The gift was always passed on to the firstborn of each Quarter. It didn't matter if they were male or female, though the past four generations have all been male.

Each of us was homeschooled as we didn't need the standard education to fulfill the duties of the roles we were born into. Instead of Math and English being our core curriculum, we were taught how to master our gifts and eliminate the only threat against them: our Counters.

We were considered guardians of the Watchtower coven, each assigned a corner to protect and an elemental gift to use. As the Quarters of the west, my family drew magic from the water element.

It didn't mean much outside of us being able to tap into ancient powers and make sure everything was in order for our coven. We weren't superheroes or anything, saving the world with our imaginary superpowers.

Though, the rest of the town acted that way. In their attempts to offer the respect and honor that our fathers and grandfathers demanded, we've been isolated from the people we shared a home and coven with.

It left us no choice but to lean on each other.

We managed to create a bond between us more akin to brotherhood than anything else. No other generation of Quarters had stuck together the way we have, always too distracted with greed and competition.

We made it clear that we didn't want to be anything like them.

That was our first mistake.

I found that the best time to be in town was when the mayor held their monthly meetings. In the cooler months, they gathered in the community center and spent the hour bickering back and forth about their menial issues. I'd take advantage of the peaceful opportunity to walk the downtown streets without being gawked at or treated like I was diseased.

Unfortunately for me, they held their meetings in the town's center during the warmer months, so walking through town wasn't much of an option. Still, I found myself taking the empty back streets just to get out of the house.

This time, an unfamiliar girl sat across from me, outside the hotel run by the Grangers. She was staring down at the phone in her palm with pinched eyebrows and pursed lips, irritated at whatever was on the tiny screen. Her golden locks were pulled to one side of her shoulder and curtained her face.

Beacon Grove attracted a lot of tourists, especially in the fall months. They were easy to spot and ignore, always too engrossed in soaking up the town's history to bother any of the locals. But something about this one felt off to me. I couldn't put my finger on it.

I stood on the sidewalk and openly gaped at her for a good sixty seconds before she sensed my gaze and lifted her head. We locked eyes for a moment, and it felt as if the air had been stolen from my lungs. The feeling was so intense, I was the first to break eye contact just to recover my breath.

Whoever this girl was, she was trouble.

I didn't have time to investigate it any further, though. Tabitha and her granddaughter, Blaire came walking down the street then, the rest of the town following closely behind. With one last look in the strange girl's direction, I stepped off the curb and walked in the middle of the street to avoid the oncoming crowd.

"There's nothing special about her," Rhyse muttered when Mystery Girl walked away.

I asked them to meet me downtown and see the anomaly for themselves, though they appeared unaffected. Lux and Enzo nodded their agreement, turning back toward the Alden estates to continue discussing our plans for Mabon in private.

Most of the town would be celebrating at the harvest festival held in the town's center each year, but we were never allowed to join in on the fun. As the Quarters and families of the current and former High Priests and Priestesses, it was our responsibility to guard our four corners and keep the coven safe, especially when so much careless magic would be cast.

The problem was that each year, our gifts dimmed. It took too much effort to do what was once an easy task for our ancestors. Our fathers and grandfathers were able to support the coven with little thought, even joining in on the festivities now and again.

Now, it was us four in charge and we could no longer handle the burden. We'd managed to hobble by the past few years, barely making it work with what little magic we had to offer. This time, our fathers planned to step in and help and we were doing all we could to avoid it.

Help from them always came at a cost.

Anyway, it was the Counters. Each year that they lived took power from us and put the entire coven at risk. None of us were any closer to finding them and time seemed to be running out. If we weren't able to eliminate them as a threat, we'd lose everything.

They were wrong about the girl, though. I knew the instant our eyes met that something was different about her. It was like my body was set on fire and my veins ran icy.

The elders warned us there would be a reaction when we came into contact with our Counters. They'd never experienced it themselves since their Counters had always been eliminated before they became a real problem. But I couldn't hunt the girl based on a whim or a guess. We thought that if one Quarter felt it, the others would, too. Apparently, that could not be the case.

I'd have to get closer to her to find out if she needed to be taken care of. That didn't seem like it would be an easy task when she looked at me like a serial killer. And if she were a Counter, I was sure there was someone protecting her. I couldn't be as obvious about my interest in her as I have been.

Quarters don't typically interact with the rest of the coven, let alone the town. They'd know I was on to her before I ever had a chance to eliminate her as a threat.

"We need access to the Quarter Book of Shadows," Enzo complained, his eyes narrowing in on Rhyse.

Rhyse's father was the last known Quarter in possession of the sacred text, and Rhyse was the only one with access to his chambers. As the current High Priest, his father was impossibly hard to get close to.

"I told you, I've looked. It's not there."

"How do we know we can trust you? Forbes men have been known to betray the Quarters in the past," Enzo growled, his ashy blond hair falling over moss eyes as he lunged toward Rhyse.

"This is bullshit. We should've been given the book when they handed over power," Lux intervened, placing a calming hand on Enzo's chest to back him away. "We shouldn't be turning on each other over this. Our fathers are the ones who can't be trusted."

"None of it matters if we don't have access to the book," I added, offering a reassuring nod toward Rhyse. We all knew how much he despised his father, and it was a low blow for Enzo to accuse him of doing anything the same way he did.

"We can't allow them to step in on Mabon. It'll be the beginning of the end for us. They're already gunning to take back their Quarter roles and send us into the flames. I wouldn't doubt if it were them keeping our Counters from us to snuff us out completely." Enzo shook his head in frustration, pacing behind Lux to release some of his built-up tension.

As the Quarter that drew power from the earth, he was the most hard-headed and stuck in his ways. It had always been difficult for the Eastons to release their grudge on the Forbes after Rhyse's grandfather betrayed the Quarters in an attempt to retain his power. They were big on keeping promises and maintaining honor, and once that trust was broken, it was next to impossible to earn back.

But Rhyse didn't deserve to be punished for his family's mistakes. Not when he strived so hard to be nothing like them. His grandfather betrayed him as well in his attempt to hold on to power.

Our fathers weren't any better.

"We can find a way around it until we get our hands on the book," Lux assured.

We walked up the dirt path leading to Lux's sprawling mansion, the summer sun beating down on our necks.

Beacon Grove's Quarter families were treated like royalty. Our properties were carefully placed at each corresponding directional corner of the town, so we could protect and watch from the comfort of our own home. It was a horrendous waste if you asked me.

Though, no one ever did.

After generations of Quarters taking advantage of the coven's monetary resources, we didn't even have to work normal jobs anymore. We'd become lazy and entitled over time with a desperate need to get back to why we started this town and coven in the first place.

Lux's property was on the east end and farthest from mine, which sat exactly six miles away in the west, beside the ocean. Rhyse's sat three miles to the south and Enzo's was three miles to the north, in the mountains. The town was stationed directly in the middle.

At any given point, our families have always held the title of High Priests and Priestesses of the coven. It was usually cycled through the four families every three years when elections were held. They were more of a formality than anything else. Rewarding us with the title was part of their way of repaying us for our services and ensuring the rest of the coven could practice magic without worrying about negative or harmful energies interfering.

Rhyse's parents were our current High Priest and Priestess, which only fed our distrust toward them. No one ever ran against us. At least, not yet.

Our fathers have become reckless, taking advantage of their status and acting as if they're invincible because of it. When the four of us aged into our roles as Quarters, they tried to fight it, gripping onto the last shreds of power they had as if their lives depended on it. They managed to piss a lot of the coven off and isolated us from the rest of the town.

With no need to work or interact with our community, Quarters have become detached outcasts, completely out of touch with the needs of the people we're supposed to be helping. Lux was the only one out of the four of us willing to step into the High Priest role, and that wouldn't happen until all of our fathers died off.

He led us through his home and into his library to share whatever new information he found about us in the past week. Since our gifts began weakening, he has dedicated all his time to pouring over random texts and town records to find some shred of a clue about what was happening. So far, none of it has been of any use but we had no other option at this point.

Rhyse and Enzo sat on opposite ends of the room, and we listened to Lux drone on in tense silence. My mind kept wandering back to Mystery Girl, slowly forming a plan to stop whatever threat she posed.

CHAPTER SEVEN

REMY

I t had been a week since my first encounter with the mystery girl and I hadn't been able to get her out of my head since. I had to get near her to find out how big of a threat she was to me and my brothers. My curiosity had only festered into an unhealthy obsession in that time. I knew she got her coffee from The Grind every day because I overheard our maid, Marta pestering her daughter about befriending the girl before she was ostracized with the rest of the Grangers she kept getting seen around town with.

That only made me more suspicious of her. The Grangers were the biggest suspects for hiding Counters. It would be no surprise to me if they were protecting her once again.

I generally avoided being in town when it was busy. It was nothing but a reminder of how these people—my coven—treated me like royalty when my power barely matched their own. They didn't know that, though, and it only made me feel even more deceptive. I was a fraud walking among them, taking praise and garnering respect for things I couldn't even do. And if they weren't worshipping us, they were avoiding us out of fear based on the reputation our fathers built. But I swallowed my distaste and found myself standing in The Grind after spending an embarrassing amount of time waiting for her to show up.

"It could be argued that you're stalking me at this point," she called over her shoulder, not bothering to fully look back at me.

Her tone suggested she was irritated, but the paranoid way her eyes kept shifting in my direction gave her away. She was afraid that her words might be spot on, and I truly was stalking her.

Which wasn't exactly wrong.

"Don't flatter yourself. You aren't *that* interesting," I lied with a sarcastic laugh that burned as it left my throat.

I hadn't laughed playfully like that in years. At least since I took over as Quarter at eighteen. The sound was almost too foreign.

I glanced around us. No one in our immediate vicinity seemed to notice the conversation that was happening, which made me grateful she refused to look at me.

"I'm here for the coffee."

"Okay," she sarcastically sing-songed before stepping up to the counter to place her order.

Once I'd done the same, I walked over to the pick-up counter and stood a safe distance away from her. Again, I did a sweep to see if anyone was watching us before I began talking again.

"Are you busy right now?"

It was nearly impossible to speak through the pain of being so near to her. She appeared to be unaffected by this strange sensation. If she wasn't my Counter, she was some other kind of threat placed in my way—there was no doubt about it. I just needed to get her alone.

"No thanks. I've seen enough murder documentaries to know better than to spend time alone with my stalker."

The barista had heard the last part and sent a confusing glance my way as she handed out the drink. No one spoke to Quarters that way—even visitors. Mystery girl took the cup and walked right out the door. Once mine was ready, I followed her, carefully keeping my distance so we didn't draw any more attention.

"You're well aware that I'm not stalking you. It's practically my duty to show a newcomer around. Especially a legacy of the coven," I bluffed.

I was one of the last people who would ever be found responsible for showing a tourist around, but she wouldn't know that. If she were as ignorant to her past as I've heard, she shouldn't know anything about how Watchtower is run.

She abruptly stopped walking and faced me as I nearly stumbled into her. From this close, I could see that her owlish eyes were the oddest shade I'd ever seen. Endless dark purple seas with black specks floating inside them—I say floating because it's almost as if the longer I stared, the more they seemed to be slowly circling around her irises.

"I don't need to be shown around by the welcoming committee. In fact, I'd like it if everyone just ignored that my family was born here and treated me like a regular old tourist instead. You don't seem to bother them at all."

"You're incredibly stubborn."

I didn't mean to say it out loud. I'd grown too used to keeping my distance from people, and I was far removed from proper etiquette. But I didn't regret saying it as her cheeks reddened, and her eyes flashed with anger.

"And you don't seem to take a hint."

Once again, she gave me her back and walked in the opposite direction I'd come from. I couldn't let her get away, though. I'd come here to find out more about her, and I couldn't give up. Not when mine and my brother's lives were at risk.

"You want to know more about your family, right? About Watchtower?"

I was grasping at straws, blindly casting my reel and hoping to catch her attention in any way. I didn't even know who her family was. As far as I was aware, no one with the name Graves had lived here for years. The original bloodline was severed long before I came into the picture. But I knew enough about Beacon Grove's history to fake it.

Her feet stopped on the pavement. *Finally.*

"You have questions, I have answers."

"Fine. But you have to agree to answer any question I have."

CHAPTER EIGHT

STORIE

I was out of my mind.

Taking a complete stranger, who had clearly followed me into that coffee shop as a ruse, up on an offer to show me around town? Just to learn more about my background?

It was insane.

But I was growing impatient waiting for the people of Beacon Grove to give me answers. It seemed as if everyone knew who I was and where I came from, yet no one wanted to share what any of that meant. I never expected the information to come to me easily, but I hadn't expected it to be nearly impossible to find.

My original plan was for this trip to last a few weeks—maybe a month at most. That's what I budgeted for from my newly padded savings thanks to Aunt Asher's "accidental" death. I'd already been here a whole week and hadn't gotten anywhere. It was infuriating. So, I took advantage of the ruse and accepted the stalker-boy's offer.

I learned his name was Remy.

He spoke about Beacon Grove and Watchtower with confidence and pride and kept a respectful distance between us as we strolled around the town's center. Eventually, my anxiety and suspicions about him faded away, and I focused instead on pulling whatever details I could get out of him. He shared small, random facts that didn't quite interest me, but the way he spoke was so captivating, I didn't have the heart to stop him.

On the plus side, I managed to get the wonky library hours out of him. Even if he offered nothing else, I'd call that a win. Blaire had looked at me like she had no idea there even was a library in Beacon Grove when I asked her, so she was useless in that regard.

Eventually, we quit circling the same buildings and headed on a dirt path that fed off the side of the art gallery. I'd finally gotten the nerve to ask him about the Watchtower coven and after a bit of probing, he gave in to answering.

"Not everyone in Beacon Grove is a part of Watchtower," he explained patiently. "The initiation process is brutal, even for legacies. Not many are willing to endure it."

"Then how is the coven still in existence?"

"What do you mean?"

"What's the point of making the process of joining so impossible if it deters people from wanting to be a part of it."

He pondered that for a moment, his gaze directed ahead at the shaded path we were on. So much time passed, I thought he was going to ignore the question altogether. Then, his eyes swung over to mine and the passion that burned in them almost made me stumble back a bit.

"Watchtower is an ancient coven. The original thirteen members came to these woods for protection from those who couldn't understand our ways. They built Beacon Grove from sticks and mud and turned it into the beautiful place that it is today. We want to honor them by making sure every member is here because they want to be, not simply because their parents are members or because it sounds interesting."

He sent me a pointed glare. He was accusing me of the former.

"I have no interest in joining," I defended, my tone a little more harsh than I'd intended. "I told you, I just want to get to know where I came from."

"Being a Graves, those are one in the same. Your family was one of the originals. You can easily trace them back to the town's conception."

Then why did they all leave when I came along? Like everything else, it didn't make sense.

It was clear that Remy knew a lot about the town, and he took pride in his coven. Maybe Tabitha wasn't the only person I had to turn to.

"So, you went through the grueling initiation?" I asked conversationally. He obviously had, since he was an active member. I wanted more details on what the process was like.

A shadow cast over his features. I watched them darken within an instant and almost convinced myself I'd imagined it—that they were that dark all along, I was just finally noticing it. Except, the haunted look on his face didn't falter, especially when he spoke.

"I didn't have to."

"Why?"

"Those are the rules."

"I thought the rules were to go through initiation," I teased, but he didn't seem to catch my humor.

"Yeah, well I'm a Quarter. We don't get a choice."

If he noticed my shocked expression, he didn't make it obvious. We had stopped in the middle of the path a few moments ago. The trees swayed and leaves danced around us, but I was completely still.

I knew something was off about him.

Different.

He'd captivated me the moment our eyes met across the street at Tabitha's hotel on my first day, and I haven't been able to stop thinking about him ever since. He wasn't like anyone else who lived here. A darkness followed him—it haunted his entire being.

I'd been warned about the Quarters from Tabitha and Blaire. They were completely off-limits to the townspeople. No one ever spoke to them, and they liked it that way. But they hadn't ever told me *who* the Quarters were. Never pointed them out on the street so that I knew which faces to avoid. I'd assumed they stayed away from town if they didn't want to be bothered.

Yet, Remy had practically thrown himself at me. He had insisted on taking me on this silly tour and showing me around. *Why?*

Was he confirming what I suspected from the beginning? That I was a Counter, and he only wanted me dead? Even if I weren't *his* Counter, surely he'd take the opportunity to help one of his own and eliminate their threat. Because that's all the Quarters saw their Counters as: a threat.

A cool chill ran down my spine. I hadn't realized how far we walked into the woods before. I couldn't see anything but thick trees and dense foliage all around. We were surrounded by nothing but nature without any other living being around to help. I could hear ocean waves somewhere in the distance and tried to picture the map I'd used to get here. I couldn't remember seeing water anywhere near Beacon Grove—just woods and mountains.

"Where are we?" I failed at my attempt to keep the fear out of my voice. It shook just like the rest of my body.

If he noticed, he didn't make it obvious. "The west end of town. Technically, we're on my family's property."

My mind spiraled.

Why would he want to take me to his family's secluded woods if he didn't want to hurt me?

"I thought you were supposed to show me around Beacon Grove," I accused weakly.

He shrugged. "I guess I got carried away with all the Watchtower talk. I wasn't really thinking about where we were going."

A stick snapped a few feet away from us and both our heads whipped around to see what it was. Nothing appeared out of the ordinary, but I was officially spooked. When I glanced at him from the corner of my eye, he was wearing the same dark scowl as before, his eyes still surveying the forest. I didn't want to be alone with him for another second longer.

"I think we should go back."

When he turned toward me, his brows pinned farther together in suspicion. I instinctively took a small step away from him and the sound of my feet shuffling in the dirt was practically deafening.

His shoulders tensed.

"I just really want to go back," I insisted breathlessly, turning back in what I thought was the direction we came from.

Or was it? I was completely turned around. Why did the waves sound closer now?

"Okay, okay," he soothed. His hands lifted in front of his chest in a calming manner, as if he were approaching a wild animal and couldn't predict its next movement. "It's this way."

A long finger stretched in the opposite direction I would have guessed.

I'd been wrong. Hopelessness weighed deep in my stomach. What was I thinking, coming out into the woods with a complete stranger? I had better instincts than that, didn't I? But for some reason, all logic flew out the window when I was near him. I couldn't even run to safety if I had to—my sense of direction was nonexistent.

I kept a large gap between us as we trekked back to town in complete silence. Remy appeared to be battling his own conflicting thoughts about the last twenty minutes. His pushy and upbeat mood had shifted into the morose, thoughtful disposition that more closely matched the way Quarters had been described. He also didn't seem to care about the change in my mood and he wasn't surprised when I bid him a rushed goodbye and practically ran to the hotel.

Blaire was occupied with someone in the office, so I took the opportunity to rush past her window and shut myself into my room to recover from the odd feelings Remy had just stirred up.

I knew I should have stayed away.

CHAPTER NINE

STORIE

E ach of my mornings were spent at the library since learning of their odd hours. The librarian's name was Esther. She was a small, mousy woman who wore her silver hair tied back into a tight bun and the same brown cardigan each day.

Outside of me asking her to point me in the general direction of what I needed on my first day there, we never spoke. After about a week of showing up as soon as she unlocked the large front doors, she started waiting and holding them open for me. She never bothered with a greeting, and I found comfort in her cold nature. I hadn't felt it since leaving the city.

Every morning, I'd march up the stairs to the third floor where all the town records were held and she'd shuffle behind the desk that sat in the center of the first floor, never speaking a word.

I made a point to get up and out of bed before the sun and didn't return to my hotel room until Blaire was just getting done with her morning shifts at the front desk. We'd walk to the secret locals-only diner and have lunch before she went back to work, and I went back to my hotel room to mull over whatever I found. The days easily blended together, and each one was more infuriating than the last, leading me down nothing but dead ends.

The Graves played a huge part in Beacon Grove's history, but their personal history wasn't documented very reliably. Every

news article and book raved about James Graves' acts of kind-
ness and charity as the town was being built. They all felt off to
me, though.

He felt off to me.

A few early issues of The Beacon were missing from the stack
and when I asked Esther about them, she'd just shrugged and
claimed they had every single issue documented and preserved.

I followed my family's journey through time, taking note of
each menial piece of news they were involved in to reference
later. There was a trend of only positive stories published where
the Graves name was concerned, which was odd considering
it seemed as if the editors of The Beacon were always after
exposing a juicy story. No other family had been given the same
respect, including the Quarter families, which were mentioned
regularly.

It wasn't until I got to the more recent issues that things took
a turn for the worst. Two years before my father was born, my
grandfather was involved in an affair with Betty Castle, one of
the women who worked at the tavern downtown. Betty fell
pregnant and he refused to acknowledge the baby as his own,
claiming her to be a loose woman whom he'd never had contact
with outside serving his drinks. He accused her of making false
claims to get her hands on his family's estate. In response, she
agreed to do a tell-all with The Beacon on the entire Graves
family.

I could tell by the tone of the article that the reporter, Marvin
Winkle, was excited for the story and wanted to take full advantage of the opportunity to expose my family's secrets. There was
a particularly curious line where he wrote: "Despite the Graves
gag order that The Beacon has been under since its inception
over one hundred years ago, we've been offered a unique opportunity to dive into the dark, sordid history of the founding
family and expose these twisted minds for the bullies that they
are."

The front page of the following issue read: BETTY LIED in large, black lettering. About a month later, buried deep into the third page of the paper, was a story written by a different reporter glumly stating that Marvin Winkle had been found dead in his home after an apparent suicide. A separate search on Betty revealed that three months later, she was involved in a fatal car crash on the road leading outside of town. There were no surviving witnesses.

The Graves facade continued after that. Not a single negative thing was published in The Beacon or anywhere else. When my father was fifteen and Aunt Ash was thirteen, my grandfather suffered a heart attack and passed away. He left behind his wife and two children, all of whom denied any interviews with the paper.

Upon review of the town's death records, I found that my grandfather had three brothers who passed away within five years of his death. Only one of them had been married and none of them left behind any kids. My dad and Aunt Ash were the last known descendants of the Graves line. Their dates of death were scribbled in the town's history with no true explanation documented.

There was a trend of indisputable accidental deaths in the Graves bloodline. Like a genetic disease that was passed down, members were plucked off one by one until there was no one left but me. By the time I ran out of public records to search, exhausting every option the library had to offer, I was able to conclude one thing: someone had been targeting the Graves family line.

The only question was, who?

We're just days away from Beacon Grove's annual Mabon festival, and locals can't wait to see what this year has in store for them.

For those who have been living under a rock, Mabon is the hallmark Autumnal Equinox harvest festival where Beacon

Grove residents take the time to reflect on the past year and give thanks for the abundance of blessings they've been granted by Mother Earth.

Local shops set up tents in the town's center, a carnival is held in the community center parking lot, and guests come from all over the country to kick off the eight-day celebration.

This year is rumored to be the biggest one yet as the mayor has allegedly allotted nearly twice the usual budget toward outside marketing. This means more tourists, more business, and more fun.

There's a little bit of everything for the whole family to enjoy.

Mayor Douglas says his favorite part of the festival is the opening and closing ceremonies, where the town gathers together as one to revel in their hard work.

"Everyone deserves some sunshine and fun. This year will be our best one yet."

Check out the Mabon Festival guide below for more information about the lineup of events.

THE ❋ BEACON

17 SEPTEMBER 2021

ANNUAL MABON FESTIVAL TO ATTRACT MORE VISITORS AND NEW BUSINESS

We're just days away from Beacon Grove's annual Mabon festival, and locals can't wait to see what this year has in store for them.

For those who have been living under a rock, Mabon is the hallmark Autumnal Equinox harvest festival where Beacon Grove residents take the time to reflect on the past year and give thanks for the abundance of blessings they've been granted by Mother Earth.

Local shops set up tents in the town's center, a carnival is held in the community center parking lot, and guests come from all over the country to kick off the eight-day celebration.

This year is rumored to be the biggest one yet as the mayor has allegedly allotted nearly twice the usual budget toward outside marketing. This means more tourists, more business, and more fun.

There's a little bit of everything for the whole family to enjoy.

Mayor Douglas says his favorite part of the festival is the opening and closing ceremonies, where the town gathers together as one to revel in their hard work.

"Everyone deserves some sunshine and fun. This year will be our best one yet."

Check out the Mabon Festival guide below for more information about the lineup of events.

CHAPTER TEN

STORIE

I n the few weeks since I drove into Beacon Grove, the entire town had been transformed into an Autumn-themed wonderland. Tree vines with leaves of yellow, red, and orange were strung along the white gazebo and dried, pale corn stalks were tied to every pillar. The blackened storefronts provided a contrasting background to the varying sizes and colors of pumpkins and haystacks that sat against them.***

I'd seen Fall depicted in movies this way—with Mother Nature's seasonal color palette tastefully splashed across every surface. Though, I'd never seen it replicated in real life. Where I came from, Fall always fell short with its muddy grounds, cold transitional weather, and overly spiced palette.

According to the banners hung all around town, the festival responsible for the town's face-lift started tomorrow.

"Mabon is a big deal around here," Blaire explained as we weaved our way around tents that were littered across the grass to get to The Grind.

"The town holds a big festival every year to kick off the week. Mom makes me man the pharmacy's booth."

"Your mom runs the pharmacy?"

I still haven't met her mom. Her absence seemed to be a normal thing in Blaire's life. I spent most nights this week eating dinner with her and Tabitha—too spooked by the moaning and screaming I often heard from my hotel room to stand being alone for too long. It never bothered them that her chair was always empty.

"Oh, yeah. Well, she's the town's herbalist. Mr. Bradbury is the pharmacist. They run the shop together." She opened the door and gestured for me to go first. "Ooh, they've finally got the pumpkin spiced cappuccino back!"

As always, anyone within earshot glared at Blaire and her outburst. I pulled her attention back to me while we waited in line before she caught their eyes. For some reason, I was growing protective over her.

"What even is Mabon?"

"How are you a Graves and you know nothing about your own history?" she asked, dumbfounded.

I shrugged my response.

She grabbed a newspaper off the stand that sat against the wall beside us, pointing to the headlining story.

"It's a celebration of the Autumn equinox and the abundance of harvest Mother Earth Goddess has given us this year. I guess it's like Thanksgiving, but better."

The barista called us to the counter to place our orders, and then we moved to the other side to join a small crowd of people also waiting for their drinks.

"Beacon Grove always has a huge festival with carnival rides and tents set up for each business. We get a ton of visitors from out of town, too. It's one of our busiest times of year." She nudged her elbow into my side. "Lucky you showed up when you did, otherwise we might not have had a room for you."

"I'm not sure I'd call that lucky," a female voice snarked from behind. We both turned to see who it belonged to, and Blaire rolled her eyes, her body visibly tensing.

The girl sneered at my friend before offering her hand to me. "Julia Rist."

I shook it hesitantly, irritated with the smug look she wore from insulting Blaire. She was a few inches shorter than me, though the confidence that shined out of her made her seem much taller. Her straight golden locks hung lifelessly against her pale face as dark brown eyes considered me. She was painfully average looking, and I was confused about what made her special enough to regard anyone the way she was Blaire.

"Storie Graves."

"Oh, I know who you are. The whole town's talking about you. We should have lunch sometime."

She gave Blaire a once-over and her tone suggested she'd be doing me a favor. A saccharine smile spread across her face then, and I immediately disliked her even more.

"You can get a real feel for Watchtower from someone who's actually on the inside."

Our names were called for our drinks, so we turned away from Julia without another word. Blaire hadn't taken a breath until we exited the shop.

"Goddess, I hate her," she hissed.

Her hands aggressively worked to roll up the thick newspaper, the ink turning her fingers black. We rounded a corner to take the back streets to the hotel.

"Who is she?"

"Her family works for the Winters family."

When I didn't have a reaction, she released an exasperated breath.

"The Winters are the Quarters of the west. Their abilities are powered by the sea, and they're rumored to have a pull over the underworld. Julia's family has been their housekeepers for centuries."

That sparked some recognition for me. I thought back to my scary walk with Remy and recalled that he mentioned his family's property was on the west side of town.

So, his last name was Winters. And Julia worked for him.

"*Housekeepers*? Her mom is a maid, and she thinks that makes her something special?"

Blaire nodded. "It does. The Winters especially treat their staff very well. I'm surprised she even bothered talking to you. No offense."

"What did she mean about Watchtower? I thought it was your coven, too."

Blaire's shoulders tensed back up. "That's just her group. They've always acted like Grangers aren't a part of Watchtower after everything that went down. It's their parents' fault for feeding into the lies."

We took another turn and the hotel appeared within view. I had no idea the streets wove together like this. I tried to keep track of each turn, hoping to use this new shortcut as a way to avoid the town altogether on my daily coffee runs but I kept getting lost. It was like the streets had shifted themselves to get us here.

Blaire was still seething as she walked through the hotel's office door, past Tabitha at the desk with a line of customers, and back into her room. I kept my mouth shut and hung back, allowing her the time she needed to work through this uncharacteristic rage. I'd yet to see her in such a foul mood. It was almost scary to watch.

Tabitha's hostile, questioning eyes swung to me through the open office window. I quickly looked away and ducked my head, returning back to my room before she had a chance to stop me.

Blaire had convinced me to help her with the pharmacy's booth. Most people walked past us without a second glance, ignoring the free samples of elderberry syrup we offered and the small emergency stand with various first-aid materials in case anyone got hurt.

I spent the first hour of the festival meandering around aimlessly by myself, stopping at a few booths that caught my attention. The clothing boutique had a mini shop set up under their tent and I couldn't help myself from looking around at the unique, colorful styles. I chatted with the woman who was running it for a bit.

Based on the rainbow tunic and headband she was wearing, I assumed she was the owner. As with everyone in Beacon Grove, she'd known who I was the moment I entered her tent and excitedly introduced herself as Hazel.

"Your mother was one of my closest friends," she explained as she rang me up for the purse I couldn't seem to walk away from.

She grabbed a few handfuls of things from the displays around her and shoved them into the bag with a wink.

"I'd love to hear more about her."

"Of course! We'll grab a coffee sometime. Oh, I have so many crazy stories I could tell you, though I probably shouldn't."

When I was finally able to get away, the small purse I'd picked had been completely filled with different colored crystals I had no idea how to use and accessories I'd never usually wear. We parted with the promise of getting together in the next week and I couldn't help but feel a little closer to my mother after hearing such kind words about her.

The next booth that caught my attention was set back from the others at the end of the row. Tapestries with different zodiac signs and spiritual symbols blocked all four sides off, with one small opening in the front. An ancient-looking woman stood in the gap, her eyes directed toward the sky, far away in thought. As I passed by, she grabbed onto my shoulder and pulled me back to her.

"It's you," she breathed next to my ear. Her fingers tightened their grip on me, holding me firmly in place as I struggled to get her off of me.

She was at least six inches shorter than I was and much older, but her grip was surprisingly strong. From this close, I could see her eyes were covered in a cloudy white film. While they peered directly into mine, I assumed she couldn't actually see anything through it. She must have had me mixed up with someone else.

"Storie Graves, you've been given an enormous task from the fates. We're all relying on you. You must not avoid it any longer," her raspy voice whispered.

Someone ripped us apart from behind and shoved me into the main walkway, nearly sending me tumbling into a group of people passing by. I caught my balance and turned to find Tabitha face-to-face with the woman, their noses practically touching. They appeared to be in a heated argument, though both were speaking extremely low. Tabitha was the first to step away and when she did, her eyes found me. She looked pissed.

I was irritated that she'd practically thrown me to the ground, but that couldn't compete with the fear that ignited in my chest as her thick legs quickly carried her over to where I stood and she grabbed me by the wrist, leading me in the opposite direction.

"What did she say to you?" her stern voice demanded.

"N-nothing that made any sense. You're hurting me," I whined, and then tugged my arm out of her grip. I rubbed the sore spot, noting the red fingerprints that were sure to leave a mark later.

"She's just an old woman spouting out nonsense. She's got nothing better to do with her time."

I nodded my response—biting back my own retort about *her* being an old woman with nothing better to do—and she jutted her chin out defiantly, her eyes falling to the aching spot on my wrist. When she was satisfied with whatever she saw, she turned her back to me and her plump body limped away.

"That woman is something else." Julia approached me from behind. Her mouth *tsk*ed dramatically, and then she smiled.

"Yeah."

"A few of us are going to grab some dinner if you want to join."

Her thumb hooked behind her at a group of people who circled around one another in the open field. They were all looking our way, each one more fashionably dressed than the last. My black jeans and t-shirt felt severely casual compared to their getups, and the same insecurities I'd always fought in high school came creeping up in my mind.

"No, thank you. Maybe another time."

I didn't think I could handle being blindsided any more tonight, and I was sure Julia and her friends had something else planned besides dinner. I could see the mischievous gleam in their eyes. It was the same one I wore when Aunt Ash became a helicopter parent and all I wanted to do was get away from her.

Julia didn't bother hiding her disappointment, but didn't try to push. "Okay, I'm going to hold you to that," she promised, then left to join her group.

I made my way back to the pharmacy tent and was relieved to find Blaire sitting alone. It didn't take much convincing on her end to get me to stay.

Blaire's mother finally came to check on us around eight. It was hard to believe that the stunning woman before me was related to Blaire or Tabitha, and her bubbly personality only added to her allure. She wore a long maxi dress with a psychedelic pattern that she must have bought from Hazel's boutique.

"I'm Callista," she introduced with a warm smile. "And you must be Storie. Mom and Blaire have told me a lot about you."

Her auburn hair fell in waves along her back without a single strand out of place. She and Blaire stood at the same height, though her body was long and slender where Blaire's was thicker in some places. Her skin was a shade darker, more closely matching the beautiful tone of her mothers. The only resemblance they truly shared was that odd shade of green eye color that her mother and daughter also possessed.

"It's almost time to begin," Callista shrieked excitedly at Blaire. She waved her hands and walked toward the gazebo, encouraging us to follow.

"Begin what?" I whispered quietly while we hurried behind Callista.

"Our Mabon opening ritual," Blaire threw over her shoulder.

I didn't know what a ritual for a group of people who openly identified as witches entailed. Aunt Ash had her own small rites and rituals she practiced around the house on certain holidays, but I mostly ignored them.

I couldn't even remember if there was one that she'd practice specifically around this time of year, and that realization had my mood taking a dive as we weaved through the crowd. Maybe she held on close to her family's traditions despite being forced away from them by me. Did she suffer from loneliness without her chosen community surrounding her, instead stuck with some moody teenager she was burdened with?

Why didn't I ever bother paying more attention to her?

Those were the guilty thoughts that carried me to the open field I just left Julia and her friends in. My eyes searched the growing crowd for Remy's haunted glare and fell short. I wasn't sure why I'd expected him to be here, knowing how isolated the Quarters preferred to be from everyone else, though I had spotted them sitting together in town earlier.

They were dangerous. I knew that. And they were especially dangerous to me if my suspicions were correct and I was a Counter. But there was something inside of them that called to me. Something completely impossible to ignore—a feeling deep in my bones.

It could have been the connection we shared. That abstract thing I might have possessed inside of me that posed a threat to their very being. Whatever it was, it had me ignoring every warning I'd received from the people of this town—including the one in the pit of my stomach—and drew me closer to them. It had me searching crowds for their ethereal faces and hoping they were doing the same for me.

Or at least hoping Remy was.

But he wasn't. None of them were. They probably weren't even bothering with the silly festival, instead focusing on whatever it was Quarters spent their time doing. I still wasn't sure. The only thing anyone told me about them is that they were off-limits, and they protected Watchtower from harm.

What did that entail? I had no idea.

Callista stopped in the back of a gathered crowd where a larger bonfire pit sat before us with flames that reached so high, I swore they licked the sky. She and Blaire joined hands as a man I hadn't seen before began talking from the opposite side of the fire on a small wooden platform. Others joined us from behind, but everyone stayed quiet. Whoever this man was, I could tell they valued and respected him.

"I'll keep this short, so we can all get back to our ales and celebration." He smiled at his audience teasingly, but it didn't reach his eyes.

"Mabon is a very special time for us. We get to reflect on the season's blessings and enjoy the fruits of our labor. Of *your* labor. None of it would be possible without the hard work and sweat that was poured into this season by the wonderful people of this town and coven. So, without further ado, let's begin our prayer for blessings of love and abundance."

Friends and neighbors joined hands and bowed their heads as the more rumble of their collective voices repeated the same prayer as the man on the platform. I took in the scene before me, overcome by their sense of harmony and togetherness. The comforting feeling I got when I first drove down the winding road leading into Beacon Grove had returned, filling my heart with a sense that I could only describe as being *home*. I never imagined witches could be so peaceful and connected with one another.

The praying went on for a few more minutes before I realized the sky darkened overhead as gray clouds chased away the sun rays and snuffed them out. I looked over at Blaire and Callista, who had both stopped their chanting and stared ahead at the chaos that was forming above us in complete terror.

"Something is wrong," Callista muttered quietly.

She tugged at Blaire's wrist and waved her hand at me to follow. No one seemed to notice when we headed toward an alley between the pharmacy and art gallery, taking a quick right when we made it behind the buildings. Once again, the streets I'd grown familiar with in the past few weeks now looked completely foreign to me, though Blaire and Callista had no issues finding their way.

The rest of the people at the festival had finally caught on and stopped talking. In the distance, I could hear chaos starting to ensue as fear took over.

"She warned us," Blaire breathed out just as the hotel came into view. I could've sworn we were still too near to town to see it.

Tabitha's head popped out of the office entrance. She looked completely calm, her body relaxed as she watched the three of us sprint toward her.

"We have to stop them," she called out to Callista, who only nodded her response.

Once we reached the porch, she didn't bother waiting for Tabitha to lead her through the door. She brushed past her mother in a huff with me and Blaire on her heels. A loud bang echoed through the streets and more screaming followed behind it.

Tabitha slammed the door shut and locked it, ushering us into her living room. I jumped at the noise as my breath caught in my throat.

This was too much. The chanting, the spells, the magic. None of this seemed real. The witchcraft Aunt Asher practiced was always just a silly hobby I thought she'd wasted her time on. I never believed it to be real.

But it was.

It was *too* real.

This was what she was trying to prepare me for, and I was too dense to listen.

"What happened, Grammy? Where are the Quarters?" Blaire's shaking voice gave me a strange sense of comfort. It let me know I wasn't alone in my downward spiral. At least she was a little panicked, too.

Tabitha and Callista's calmness was unsettling.

"They're trying, but The Movement is too strong."

"Why would The Movement want to do this?"

"Hush, girl," Tabitha spit.

She turned her attention to her daughter, and they began to have a silent conversation. I watched their faces change as questions were asked and answered without words, until a final decision was made.

It was bizarre and chilling to watch. There was clearly information they were keeping from Blaire and I, though I had no idea if that bothered me anymore. It seemed like the more I knew about this place, the farther I wanted to run.

"Hold my hand," Callista's soft voice whispered to her daughter, who took her outstretched hand without hesitation. "You too," she said to me.

Just as my fingers brushed hers, Tabitha swatted me away.

"We don't know what kind of effects she'll have on this. It's best to keep her out of it."

"Worst case, she strengthens us. Come on, Mom. We need all the help we can get."

Tabitha huffed out her frustration and shook her head but when Callista grabbed my hand again, she allowed it. The moment our fingers touched, I felt a jolt of electricity course through my body. I recoiled, trying to pull my hand away, but Callista only held on tighter.

"It's okay," she assured. "That's a good sign."

The three of them started speaking out in a language that I recognized but couldn't place where I'd heard it before. Their eyes remained focused on the table we circled around, each of them staring into the dancing flame of the black candle that Tabitha had already lit before we got there.

I couldn't focus on anything. It was like a part of me was somewhere else and my mind kept trying to take me there, but the words they were mumbling were grounding me back to my physical body. It was a feeling unlike anything I'd ever experienced before. I was ripped in half, my feet stuck in two places at once and it only got stronger as the women around me chanted louder. I tried to ask them to stop, but my mouth wouldn't say the words.

My vision finally flashed between Tabitha's living room and a view of the ocean, its waters angry and black with white caps spraying all around. Waves crashed against dark gray rocks in fury, and the longer I allowed myself to sink into the vision, the heavier my chest felt.

My head was pounding. I wanted to scream, but nothing in my body was working. My arms and legs were no longer under my control, and I could feel my energy being drained from inside me, like someone had somehow tapped into the source and was sucking me dry. I was stuck in the prison my mind built with the chanting that was floating in the space around me.

Then, just as fast as it began, everything stopped, and I was surrounded by blackness.

CHAPTER ELEVEN

REMY

B eacon Grove was buzzing with excited anticipation as the final countdown to Mabon had officially begun. Out of towners were rolling in, taking up vacancy in Tabitha's hotel and any spare room that our residents rented out for the occasion. The town's square was filled with tents for every business and hobby we had and the parking lot to the city buildings was taken over by carnival rides. This was one of our most profitable times of year, and the coven often poured that money into the Quarters' pockets as a thank you for making it all possible.***

I'd strolled into town to reprieve from my father's constant nagging. He and the other elders made their expectations of us for Mabon very clear. If we screwed this up, they were going to step in and take over as Quarters.

Their constant pestering was only making us lose confidence even more and fed the insecurities we were already fighting to keep at bay. Rhyse, Lux, and Enzo were somewhere around here, waiting for me to join them so we could come up with a plan for the next twenty-four hours. We still haven't gotten access to the Book of Shadows and the library provided us with no new information.

We were stuck.

We needed a sudden shift in power to happen if we wanted this to be successful, though it seemed the gods weren't willing to budge. Our Counters needed to be found and eliminated if we were going to reach the next level of our gifts.

Just as the thought crossed my mind, the new girl walked by with Blaire Granger at her side. They appeared to be inseparable since the moment she walked into town. I'd overheard Marta digging into Julia again just this morning about befriending her. I'm not sure why the old maid had such an interest in Storie, but it always made me more suspicious to hear her name mentioned between the two. Since she entered Beacon Grove, I realized I was losing trust in everyone around me.

Our time alone only fed my confused, jumbled thoughts. While she appeared to have no intention of coming after me or the others, her dramatic reaction to my telling her I was a Quarter was peculiar. And the way my blood practically boiled anytime she was near didn't help the uncertainty and mystery that surrounded her.

We were supposed to have been prepared to meet our Counters, yet I felt far too incompetent to take her on.

I took three steps in her direction to follow them before Lux called my name from behind. Ignoring the pull I felt toward the strange girl, I turned and jogged over to the cafe table the three of them were sitting at.

"Our best bet is to draw power from the spirit world," Enzo was saying as I pulled out the chair beside him and fell into it. They all nodded in agreement, then looked at me expectantly.

"What?"

"You're going to have to open the realm to us," Lux explained calmly.

I knew this was coming. It was the only solution we'd been able to devise that didn't involve anyone else helping. The problem was, the spirit realm was next to impossible to master.

The Winters were the only Quarter family with access to the underworld and were notoriously bad at keeping records, so there wasn't much information regarding how to go about it.

My own father had given up on the task years ago, and he was more desperate for the extra boost in power than anyone.

For some reason, gaining access to the underworld hadn't ever been difficult for me. I often visited while on my post, using the energies from our ancestors to make up for any areas the others may have been lacking in—a problem that came up more often lately. It was the only reason we hadn't already lost our roles to our fathers.

But opening the realm to the other Quarters wasn't going to be easy. I didn't have the training or abilities to keep them safe while they drew power from their ancestors yet, and allowing them in without proper protection could result in one of them getting stuck between worlds or dying.

"We know what we're signing up for, Winters. Just get us in," Rhyse muttered quietly. I looked to Enzo and Lux for confirmation and they each nodded once.

"Fine."

The clock struck six and the four of us settled into our individual altars—a designated spot built into our homes that kept us safe from interruptions and threats—as the coven began the ritual spell. I took our sacred family knife that was said to have been carved out by Hecate herself and passed down through Quarter families for generations to draw blood and offer it to the gods in exchange for their protection and guidance, then fell into a deep meditative state. The coven called onto the four quarters, and we opened ourselves up to them.

The tourists usually didn't realize the ritual was happening. Too distracted with the sounds of the carnival and festivities, they never noticed the quiet spellcasting that came from mem-

bers of Watchtower. Their excited presence also brought an
additional buffer energy to the ceremony.

Once I was sure it was safe, I opened the underworld to the
others to draw the connection with our elder spirits and use
them as a power source. When the shield was lifted into place,
we allowed ourselves to reenter the physical realm with our
minds still halfway connected to spirit. This was always an easier
task for me. I tried to keep my nerves about them entering the
spirit realm at bay. I didn't want the negative vibrations to affect
them, though it was difficult to ignore the risks when I could
feel the stronger energy buzzing off them now, even from miles
away.

The night started off smoother than usual, and each minute
that passed without issue allowed me to relax a little more. I
could hear the sounds of the Mabon festival through the window, though they were muffled by the ocean's soft chorus beside
me.

It wasn't until after about three hours, just before the sun
set around nine o'clock, that I felt the shift. The waters below
darkened, morphing from their usual aqua hue to completely
black. I could hear distant chanting coming from the town's
center, but the sounds of the waves were fighting it. The energy
within the spirit realm frenzied and I could feel the others panic
as they sensed the shift, too.

Our shield was falling away with each passing second and our
energy was depleting. Whatever magic they were practicing at
the festival felt as if it was targeted at syphoning every ounce of
power from us.

Weakening us.

Somehow, I'd gathered enough strength within me to shove
the others out of the underworld and close off the opening
before anyone got hurt.

When I was sure everyone else was safe, I focused on the energies surrounding me, stopping when I recognized the presence
of black magic. It was almost a tangible, living thing—impos-

sible to ignore. Everyone in Watchtower knew better than to practice anything dark, especially when our shield was lifted and we were vulnerable. It was the coven's most rigid and indisputable law.

Yet, someone had clearly disrespected the bylaws to put us into harm's way.

With our connection broken, I could no longer feel the magic coming from the other Quarters. It was just me, the raging ocean, and whatever magic that was set on draining me.

I wanted to give up. My body felt as if someone had slashed it open and sucked all the blood out. Whatever this was, it was clearly stronger than anything I could handle.

Just as my eyes began to close, I felt someone's presence beside me. I could no longer see the waters thrashing their anger against the rocks below, or the white candle that once flickered before me, fighting to stay upright against the wind that now whipped across my face. The stone floors beneath me felt cold and dry, though I was positive they were covered in blood.

But the entity—whatever it was—stayed still by my side as the scene unfolded. I felt it shift, and then I became lighter. My energy was being restored and my powers were slowly being regifted to me.

It was a few moments before I could open my eyes again, but I knew the storm was ending. Instead of succumbing, I would be able to fight the darkness that had tried taking me down. When I felt strong enough to sit up, I glanced to my right to see who had saved me but found the spot to be empty.

I was alone.

CHAPTER TWELVE

REMY

B eacon Grove was a disaster. Festival debris circled around us in a painful reminder of how the evening unfolded. The elements had raged down here just as harshly as they had for us in our towers.

Once we were sure the four of us were okay, our fathers summoned us to the town's community center to discuss the night's events. Only members of Watchtower were present, though it was the largest turnout I'd seen since our Quarter initiation ceremony.

I have no idea where they corralled the tourists and carnival workers. The town looked completely abandoned, so I'm sure it was far enough out of ear shot for us to hold our meeting.

We were sat down into folding metal chairs on the small auditorium stage beside Mayor Douglas and our High Priest, Silas Forbes. When we tried to decline, we were told it couldn't wait.

Mayor Douglas slammed his gavel three times to silence the frenzied crowd before us. Nearly one hundred pairs of eyes turned our way, each one looking more frightened than the next.

"We've called this emergency meeting to order to discuss the night's events," the mayor called out to the crowd of people, his voice maintaining its usual official tone, although he looked just as ragged and worn as the rest of us.

A few people shouted out insults at the Quarters, insisting it was our fault a darkness was able to get through and poison the town. The mayor fought to keep them quiet, but his shouts and the slamming of his gavel only riled them up more. We were forced to sit and absorb the slew of verbal abuse that was flung our way until Silas lifted his hand to quiet them, and everyone stopped talking at once.

"Thank you, High Priest," Mayor Douglas sighed. His face was covered in a shiny layer of sweat and had taken on the brightest shade of red I'd ever seen in a human's skin tone.

"We need answers, Silas," Rayner shouted across the sea of faces. The crowd parted as he worked his way to the front until he was nearly standing on the stage with us.

"That's what we're here for," Silas' bored tone responded.

"Yet, none of these boys have offered their explanations." Rayner lifted his arm in our direction incredulously.

Still, the Quarters stayed quiet.

"Sit down, Rayner," Mayor Douglas demanded, his usual cloak of calmness slowly coming undone.

"I'm sorry, Mayor, but I think I and everyone else agree that it's time for change," Rayner's deep voice bellowed over the crowd when he turned to speak directly at them. "Our town and our coven deserve better."

A few grunts of agreement encouraged him to continue. I attempted finding who they came from and fell short. At this point, after what just happened, any one of these people could have been working against us.

No one was to be trusted.

"We've allowed these families to capitalize on our fear. They've been given the highest ranks in our coven since its conception, received praise and gifts for doing a job that any one of us could do..."

A few audible gasps give him pause. He turned his shoulders to address his peers, his back facing us and Mayor Douglas.

"Am I wrong? Have we been convinced that our own abilities are that much less than those of young boys?"

"The Quarters were given their gifts from the gods themselves. You have no right to suggest you're their equal," Mayor Douglas argued.

"Then what happened tonight? Why were their powers so weak, they couldn't handle a simple Mabon celebration? How long are we going to risk our lives by putting all of our trust into these families when they've shown us time and time again that they can no longer handle it?"

Rhyse shifted in his chair beside me, and Lux placed his hand on his arm to try to settle him. We were exhausted beyond belief, hardly able to keep our heads up. There was no way we'd be able to handle a brawl if Rhyse said the wrong thing while tensions were already high. Our coven was scared, and it was our fault. We just needed to hear them out and get some rest so we could figure out what the hell went wrong today.

"This isn't constructive. We're here to find out what happened," my father piped in. I was surprised he'd allowed Rayner to go on as long as he had. He was usually the most protective over the Quarter name.

"What happened was we trusted your sons to keep us safe and they've failed us. A darkness was able to get through what should have been an impenetrable shield. At least, that's what you Quarters have always claimed." Rayner's disdain was obvious in his tone. He never respected the Quarters—not since what he witnessed our grandfathers do to his family.

He had never been an issue until now. There were rumors floating around of an uprising for a few years. We brought it to our fathers' attention in fear of the coven finding out that our powers were fading, and they blew it off, refusing to believe anyone would go against us. Now, it was clear what was happening, and Rayner appeared to be at the head of it. We couldn't make it obvious that we felt threatened by them, though. That would only fuel their fire.

"The Quarter shield is stronger than any sort of protection spell you could attempt to cast. You have no right speaking against us when it is our protection that has ensured your safety and comfort while practicing whatever magic it is you've taken up to these days. You'd be smart to remember your place." My father's patience was wearing thin.

"I'm speaking as a concerned member of this coven. What ever happened to this being a democracy? Or are we not allowed to speak against our leaders when they've wronged us?"

"We never wronged you," Rhyse answered. His cheeks were now the same dark shade of red as the blood vessels that were glowing in the whites of his eyes.

"Then what would you call your little blunder?" Rayner taunted, a cocky smile turning up on his lips.

He'd finally gotten what he wanted all along: a reaction from one of us.

Lux attempted to calm Rhyse once again, but it was no use. This whole meeting was going nowhere.

"I'd call it sabotage. Someone broke the bylaws and was practicing dark magic within our shield. If anyone should be up here answering to the coven, it should be those who are actively working against us."

A few people gasped and Rayner rolled his eyes with a condescending chuckle. "I don't know what you're alluding to."

"Okay, that's enough," Mayor Douglas cut in before Rhyse could retort. A sigh of relief was heard across the entire crowd. "This meeting was organized to find answers, though that doesn't appear to be happening anymore. I think our High Priest would agree that we could use some rest before we continue this conversation any further." He looked to Silas for confirmation and received a stiff nod.

Typically, Mayor Douglas didn't take the lead on coven business, but the damage to the town and the danger it posed to the tourists gave him some authority over the situation. Still, Silas' silence throughout the whole conversation was suspicious.

We didn't have time to dwell on it. As the coven filtered out of the balmy room from the back, we were ushered off the stage and guided through a side entrance.

"It's just not worth the risk," Mayor Douglas explained, gesturing toward the crowd he had failed to control.

CHAPTER THIRTEEN

REMY

Our fathers silence at the Watchtower meeting was a false indication of their true feelings toward how the night went. While the nightmare was over for the rest of the coven and they were free to head back to their homes to rest and recover, they had a different agenda planned for us.

Rhyse, Enzo, Lux, and I were immediately taken from the community center to a black Suburban and driven to the Forbes estate.

"What the hell just happened?" Rhyse hissed once the back door was closed on us, his voice breaking the thick tension that coated the darkness surrounding us.

"They're going to come for us," Enzo's suspicious voice added.

"We don't know that," Lux defended, ever the optimist.

"Wake up, Lux. If these bastards aren't successful ripping our power away from us, The Movement will finish the job. We're fucked. Did you see my dad's face?" Rhyse's panic was growing with each mile that took us closer to his home.

"Who do we think is responsible for what happened?" I asked in an attempt to redirect the conversation.

"Who knows? It could be anyone." Enzo breathed, glancing at the driver in distrust. He was right. This conversation couldn't happen until we were sure we couldn't be heard.

"We almost got trapped in the underworld. Do you think they knew we were there?" Lux whispered.

"I don't know anything anymore," I answered honestly.

Three grunts of agreement sounded in the dark, then the conversation was cut off by the car shifting to park and the doors whipping open, revealing my father's disappointed face.

"Come with me, boys."

Boys. I hated how smug he looked saying that. As if we weren't all fully grown men who'd taken over our Quarter roles years ago and managed to get along just fine.

I despised how much our fathers loved to see us fail. How they salivated at the possibility of us having less power than they did. At the thought that they were still needed as Quarters for the coven.

We followed him in silence, each of us refusing to give in to the fatigue we were feeling from the past twelve hours and show any weakness. I already knew we would be meeting in Silas' study. It was where all private Quarter business was handled. We'd walked these halls hundreds of times, but never with such looming dread.

Silas was the first to speak once the door was tightly closed. He was perched behind his large, black marble desk, looking completely relaxed. The rest of the elders took their seats in the plush, red leather chairs pushed against the wall behind the uncomfortable wood ones we were guided into.

"You know why we've called you here."

"Someone is obviously trying to make us look incapable to the rest of the–" Rhyse began. He was cut off by Silas' raised finger.

"You were warned. If you couldn't handle the magic of Mabon, you should have come to us."

"It's not that we couldn't handle it. Someone was practicing black magic within the shield," Rhyse defended.

"That's beside the point," my father dismissed, waving his hand in the air.

"How? Even the most skilled Quarter would struggle with being blindsided by their own coven." This time, it was Lux's soft voice that piped in.

"Your sole purpose as a Quarter is to provide protection to the members of your coven. To offer your own element as a magic source for them to strengthen their spellcasting."

"And that's what we did. Until the darkness took over and pushed us out," Enzo finally spoke. His usual deep tone was heightened with emotion.

"Mind your manners, Lorenzo," his father reprimanded from the side of the room, and Enzo shriveled into his seat.

"You should have admitted that we needed to step in. We're not even sure how you managed to keep the shield intact as long as you did," Silas admitted.

Good. That meant they had no idea that I was able to draw power from the underworld and share it with the others.

"Are you saying you think you'd be more equipped to ward off the darkness? Do you have some sort of special powers we aren't aware of?" Rhyse's hands went up into the air incredulously. He was now sitting at the edge of his seat, nearly nose to nose with his father.

He shouldn't have accused them of such a crime. Keeping powers from future Quarters was a grave offense in our bylaws. They were required to share every ounce of information they had with us when they passed on the gift.

We knew they were keeping the Book of Shadows and any content that might help them reverse the shift in power hidden, but we didn't want them to know we were on to them. Not until we had concrete proof.

An accusation like that without the evidence to back it up would have us all burned immediately. I shot Rhyse a warning glare, internally screaming for him to stand down.

"Of course not. I'm saying it was irresponsible to put the rest of your coven in such danger when you knew you needed help.

You're lucky enough to have us available to you as resources. Use. Us."

When no one bothered responding, Silas cleared his throat. He folded his pale hands on the desk and leaned forward.

"We're not allowing another mishap like this. We'll discuss Samhain when it gets closer, but any Quarter business that involves magic will be handled by us until then. And we will begin training with you again as soon as possible. Clearly, you've still got much to learn."

The atmosphere in the room changed immediately. They expected a strong reaction to his condescending words—that much was clear by the way the three behind us stood abruptly from their chairs, legs spread and arms widened in a defensive stance. Silas remained seated at his desk, his dark eyes boring into his son's in a challenge. I turned and found the same look in my father's eyes.

They hadn't just expected a reaction, they *wanted* one. They were desperate for any excuse to fully strip us of our magic and had resorted to setting us up.

But when I looked at Rhyse, he was locked in with Lux, who was silently pleading with him to stay quiet the same way I had before. Enzo was equally confused, waiting for someone else to make a move. After what felt like an eternity, Rhyse nodded once at Lux, and the anxiety swarming around the room dropped to the floor.

"Fine," he said to his father, who couldn't seem to hide his bewilderment behind the usual passive stare that masked his face.

"Okay, then. You're free to go." Silas stumbled over his words a bit. He finally stood from his chair to bid us goodbye. "Rest up. We'll be starting work on you boys first thing tomorrow."

On the way out, Enzo tried whispering his concerns to us, but we quickly shut him down. We couldn't have this conversation yet.

THE ✳ BEACON

22 SEPTEMBER 2021

MABON CHAOS ENSUES, INJURING MANY: ARE WE STILL SAFE?

Disaster ensues just one day into the coveted festival ceremony, leaving locals and tourists wondering: what the heck happened?

An eerie feeling. A loud boom. Screams of horror. Panic in the streets. These are just a few things festival patrons experienced as we kicked-off our eight-day celebration of the Autumnal Equinox.

The Beacon Grove community has now come together to clean up the aftermath of what appears to have been a breach in the Quarter shield. Locals are left in the dark as Mayor Douglas and Watchtower coven High Priest, Silas Forbes, refuse to offer any insight to our staff here at The Beacon for how they plan to proceed with the rest of the event.

In last night's emergency town meeting, Rayner Whittle insisted the Quarter families were responsible for the disruption and has maintained his political stance against them. Mayor Douglas ended the meeting abruptly with no concrete plans.

"Whatever happened, it was a horrifying way to begin what was supposed to be one of our best years yet," Watchtower Tavern owner, Lisa Golden, commented. Golden says Mabon and Samhain are her most profitable times of the year, making up about twenty-five percent of her income.

But the Watchtower Tavern isn't the only local business suffering. Tabitha Granger at the Compass Hotel has confirmed that nearly fifty percent of her guests have checked out early.

Without the foot traffic from tourists, business owners are left wondering if the celebration will be cancelled altogether, and if so, how they'll manage to make ends meet.

The Beacon will continue to provide the most accurate and up to date news regarding this tragic event.

CHAPTER FOURTEEN

STORIE

W hen I awoke, I was alone in Blaire's room. The morning sun shone through the window beside her bed, brushing the walls in a tangerine-peach tint. I must have been out for at least a few hours, though it felt as if I'd only blinked and the sky had transitioned from the dead of night into morning.

Pots and pans clanged in the kitchen across the hallway. I heard hushed, irritated conversation in between the violent bangs. Whoever was making such a ruckus clearly wasn't happy.

"Oh, you're up!" Blaire entered the room with a smile and a glass of water. "I figured you could use this."

"What time is it?" my morning voice croaked, and I realized how dry my throat had been. I took the glass from her hands gratefully.

"Eight o'clock. You've been out for a while."

"What happened last night?"

When I think back on it, none of it seemed realistic. The spooky chanting, the loud bangs, the panicked crowd. Whatever ritual Tabitha, Calista, and Blaire did afterward. I was almost convinced I'd imagined it all. At least, until Blaire's cheery expression faltered and her eyes fell to wringing hands.

"We're not really sure. What did you see before you went out?"

I tried to recall the last few moments prior to everything going black but could only remember the furious ocean waves being so close, I could practically feel them spraying me. I wasn't ready to share that part with anyone until I figured it out myself.

"I can't remember," I admitted, only half lying.

"Well, you looked terrified."

"Blaire! I still need your help!" Tabitha called out, annoyance lacing her tone. She must have been the one making all the noise.

Blaire rolled her eyes. "We made breakfast. You should come eat when you feel up to it," she said, then turned and walked out of her room.

I chugged my water and peeled myself from the bed. The idea of facing Tabitha's ornery attitude didn't sound very appealing, but I felt odd sitting in Blaire's bed while they moved around the kitchen. Heavy, sluggish legs dragged me toward where all the noise was coming from, and my nose filled with the aroma of cinnamon and butter. Someone had made French toast. My stomach gurgled at the sight of them, begging to be fed.

"Sit. Eat," Tabitha demanded. I didn't bother arguing.

She didn't bring up last night or try to ask me what happened the way Blaire had. She just plopped herself down in the chair across from me and read the morning paper while I shoveled food into my mouth and Blaire stood at the sink, quietly humming while she washed the dishes.

The headline of her newspaper was printed in thick, black ink.

Mabon Chaos Ensues, Injuring Many: Are We Still Safe?

So many questions bounced on my tongue, begging to be asked. It felt like every day I spent in Beacon Grove only created more mystery around my family, their departure from the town, and their deaths.

Tabitha knew more than she was willing to share with me. She had even gone as far as preventing someone else from spilling too much. The old woman from the festival was obviously out of her mind, but Tabitha felt threatened enough by her to physically assault me and prevent me from hearing what she had to say.

And how did she know something would happen to me during the incantation they practiced? Why hadn't she wanted me a part of it?

Nothing made sense anymore, but she was the one person always standing at the center of my confusion.

Blaire excused herself when someone rang the bell impatiently in the office. Tabitha still hadn't bothered looking up at me, so I spent the rest of my meal taking in every detail of their outdated kitchen. It felt so similar to the one I grew up in with drying herbs strung up across the cabinets and cinnamon sticks hanging in each window. It wasn't the first time since I drove into Beacon Grove that I was overtaken with a sense of being home again.

When my plate was empty and rinsed, I quietly exited the kitchen without a word. I passed Blaire on the way, listening to her apologize profusely to the furious tourists who were demanding a refund for their room. With a simple wave, I left her alone and headed to my room.

I wanted to take a hot shower and try to process the past twenty-four hours. Possibly attempt to recall whatever events transpired before I was knocked out. I was worn down from the constant mental stimulation of interacting with the exhausting people of Beacon Grove, and it felt as if I hadn't been alone with my own thoughts in days. I needed to decompress and refocus on the reason I was here before I got too caught up in the town's drama.

By the time I was stripping down for a shower, I was convinced that's all this was. My passing out was simply mental exhaustion and the sooner I got out of Beacon Grove and back into the real world, the sooner things could return to normal.

It wasn't long after my shower that the moaning and screaming through the walls began again. The sounds were so distant, I could have blocked them out with the TV or popping my headphones in if I'd wanted to. But for some reason, I felt like I needed to hear it. To listen to whatever it was these women were calling out in anguish, so I could figure out if I could help them.

I sprawled out on the bed and relaxed into my pillow, slowing my breathing so I could really focus on the muffled sounds. This time, it was only one woman. Maybe it always has been. But her guttural moans and roars came in waves, with long stretches of silence in between. It was in those pockets of silence that I found myself lost in deep thought, accessing a part of my brain that felt unfamiliar and foreign to me. It wasn't long before I fell into a deep meditative state, and with it, I was brought back to the place I'd left when I passed out the night before.

The waves were calmer this time, gently kissing the shore instead of the harsh pummeling they'd given it hours before. Perhaps the tides were a psychological metaphor, and they represented my subconscious thoughts. I was calmer now than I had been last night. The waters clearly symbolized that shift. I kept my mind focused on the soft swaying, too afraid to turn and look at any of my other surroundings for fear of losing this once again.

It wasn't until I heard a voice behind me a few moments later that I was willing to tear my gaze away from the vast ocean. Remy's tall figure filled my vision, his black hair lazily draped over tired, dark eyes. He was talking to someone, and though I couldn't sense the other person or hear their words, the conversation felt intense. I could see it in his rigid back and the defensive tautness of his muscles.

"I told you, I don't need your help," his deep voice insisted.

Small details of my surroundings slowly fizzled into view as I spent more time looking at him. I took three steps in his direction, through the open French doors that appeared between us, and watched his expression shift while the other person spoke. I noted how hard he was trying to keep his composure. Whoever he was speaking with, he didn't want them to see how badly they were affecting him.

The conversation ended abruptly, before Remy had a chance to retort whatever it was the other person had said. He was visibly upset and while I never heard a door close or saw them walk away, I could tell when his nuisance left by the obvious change in his demeanor.

Even if this were a dream or some twisted figment of my imagination, seeing him in such a vulnerable state felt like an invasion of his privacy, so I turned my back to his frustrated form and took in the new details of the room we were standing in.

The walls and ceiling were both covered in a deep, dark blue paint that made them feel like an endless pit. The furniture was sparse. A simple hand carved, maple-brown dresser was pushed against one wall with a bed set and matching nightstand directly across from it. The bed was neatly made, and nothing sat on the nightstand but a simple digital alarm clock. There wasn't a speck of dust anywhere to be found and the shining floors hardly looked walked on.

If this was Remy's room, there was no evidence of him anywhere inside of it. My imagination was clearly lacking creativity.

He walked out the French doors and onto the balcony I'd come from, stopping to lean against the iron railing and stare off at the waters. I slowly followed, testing my footsteps to make sure he couldn't hear me approaching him. When he didn't react, I walked more confidently, stopping right at his side so I could get a good look at this mysterious, dangerous man.

From this close, I could see that his nearly black eyes had leaves of gold hiding deep inside their irises. I knew he was close to my age, but the shallow frown lines that adorned his pale forehead—deeper now that he was full-on pouting—aged him a few more years. His round, scarlet red lips were pulled down and every few minutes, whenever a troubling thought seemed to cross his mind, he tugged the bottom one into his mouth with his teeth.

I was supposed to be afraid of this man. If my intuition was correct, then we were natural born enemies. My family gave their lives to save me from him. Yet, everything about him pulled me in. His soul screamed to mine to come closer—to get to know him on our own terms, without our families' history or influence.

When he released his lip from its assault once again, I couldn't stop myself. I reached out and gently touched it, rubbing my fingers across its soft, pillowy texture, positive now that this must have been a dream.

But he flinched at the contact.

No. He didn't just flinch, he recoiled and stumbled backward. Then, his own hand flew to his mouth to trace the exact spot my fingers had just left.

I froze, terrified that he might suddenly see me. What would he do to me if he knew I was here?

Was I really even here? I had no idea how this worked.

His frown deepened as his eyes found the spot I was standing in and lingered there. So much time had passed, I was sure he saw my terrified expression and was simply deciding what to do next.

Would he kill me? Hold me prisoner until he spoke to the other Quarters, and they could figure out who's Counter I was? What then?

My mind ran wild with every possible scenario.

But then, his shoulders turned back to face the water and he shook his head in disbelief. I backed into his room as quietly as possible and tried to bring myself out of whatever vision I was trapped in. Surely, if I could get here through deep meditation, all I had to do was break that concentration and snap myself out of it.

I tried focusing on the hotel room. I envisioned myself sprawled across the bed in a deep sleep and imagined shaking myself awake. When that didn't work, I screamed and pinched and punched, but nothing happened. I was stuck alone in Remy's bedroom and making a complete fool of myself.

Just as I was about to give up, Remy walked back through the doors and stopped dead in his tracks. I was standing in the center of the room, breathless from my ridiculous attempts to escape his space.

But he saw me.

Our eyes locked in on each other, and right when he opened his mouth to speak, my lids flickered open, and his terrified face was replaced with the water-stained ceiling in the hotel room.

CHAPTER FIFTEEN

REMY

S he had been here.

I'd seen Storie plain as day, standing in the middle of my bedroom, looking completely distraught and nearly translucent. I knew I'd felt something touch me on the balcony but chalked it up to nerves or paranoia.

I was going out of my mind trying to figure out how to tap into the power source that appeared beside me on the night of Mabon and refused to show me their true face. I knew that source was the key to helping the Quarters, if I could just figure out how to master it.

Then suddenly, she appeared in my bedroom.

Could it have been her that night?

How else was she able to project herself into my space?

The Winters estates had enough protection spells surrounding it inside and out. No entity should have been able to penetrate those barriers and make it all the way up into my room. She had to have been using some sort of ancient magic that was stronger than ours. Unless I was truly losing it.

But no, I was positive she was here.

What did she want, anyway?

She looked equally horrified, disappearing before I could even get a word out. How long was she watching me? Had she heard the conversation with my father?

I needed answers, and the only person who could give them to me was the one who posed the biggest threat. If anything, this encounter only brought me closer to believing she was my Counter. If that were the case, then being alone with her was incredibly risky. Especially with our fathers breathing down our necks and the Movement desperately trying to push us out.

Though Storie didn't fit into anything that had been drilled into our heads about Counters over the years. If she really were the entity I felt from before, why would she have saved me if she wanted me dead? Why would she have saved all of us? We were perfect targets at that moment.

Scattered thoughts bounced around my head, presenting themselves faster than I was able to comprehend. I was torn between following my gut or listening to a lifetime of warnings aimed against Counters from sources who have proven themselves untrustworthy. Our fathers want the same thing the Movement wants—for us to be burned so they could continue their reign as Quarters.

I decided I had to get out of my house and think. The energy here was constantly buzzing with chaos and aggression, just how my father liked it to keep everyone on their toes.

"The moment they get comfortable, you've lost all credibility," he always said.

The close proximity to him didn't help.

I always found myself at the ocean when my head got like this. My feet carried me there when my mind was in too much of a flurry to focus. The waves calmed me in a way nothing else could, even when they were overwhelmed themselves.

No one else typically bothered coming to the black sandy shore, especially when the weather shifted and the breeze had a bite to it, scaring away the faint of heart. The only access to it was technically on private Winter property. Sometimes, in the summer, the staff and their children would take advantage of the ocean's beauty and spend their time off swimming and playing on the beach. Outside of that, only the brave dared coming up here to swim in our waters, but we never punished them for it. After all, none of it would exist without their contributions to our wealth. Plus, I don't think I've witnessed my parents bother a glance at the ocean in years.

So, it was a surprise for me to find a single, petite black figure standing at the water's edge. Their focus was on the horizon, unaware that they now had an audience.

When a few moments passed and the figure hadn't moved, I closed the distance between us, pushing away the doubtful, cowardly thoughts that were trying to infiltrate my headspace. I could feel that it was her, and that terrified me more than I wanted to admit.

I was a Quarter. Nothing scared me. It was my job to protect people from the things that scared *them*. But this small girl had more power to destroy me than anything else in the world, and I had no idea if she was even aware of it.

When I took her into the woods, though I'd been on my best behavior, she had the nerve to act petrified of being alone with me. Didn't she realize how big of a threat she was to the future of the entire coven she was so greedily asking about? She had no business being on my property—then or now.

My nerves stopped me a couple of steps behind her, but I watched her shoulders tense as soon as she sensed my presence.

"It's real," she muttered to the sea.

I swallowed my fear and loathing and walked up beside her. "Why are you here?"

"I thought I was hallucinating. Or maybe it could have been a weirdly vivid dream, I don't know. But it's not. It's real." Storie had yet to turn in my direction. I was standing inches away at her side, completely facing her. But she continued to stare out into the distance.

"You were in my room."

She shoved her hands into the pockets of her hoodie as her hooded head bobbed slowly.

Disbelievingly.

"Nothing about this place seems plausible. It goes against everything I've been taught in the real world. Every moment I spend here, I feel like I'm losing my mind even further."

"Would that be so bad?"

She finally turned her face toward me and revealed the shimmer of tears running down her cheeks. "What?"

"It's only when you lose your mind that you can discover who you're truly meant to be."

My mother had said that to me once, back before I'd taken in my gifts and we were closer. That felt like a lifetime ago. She was practically a stranger to me now.

"That... is exactly the kind of confusing thing I'd expect someone from Beacon Grove to say."

I laughed, forgetting my reservations about her for a moment. She had a point. The waves sluggishly crept onto the shore, bringing me back down to Earth. "Why did you come here? To Beacon Grove?"

Storie's eyes roamed my features, bouncing back and forth as her scowl deepened. They looked pale and mauve against the blue and green landscape around us, and her reddened, raw lids only contributed to the ethereal effect of them.

"I thought I wanted answers. Now, I'm not so sure."

Why would someone go through such great lengths to find answers about who they were? Did her family truly keep her in the dark? That seemed odd, given their reputation, which I'd shamelessly looked into after our time together in the woods.

The Graves were apparently a prideful and dangerous bunch. They'd never let their heroic tales remain hidden away and conveniently ensured all their faults were forgotten.

Unless there was a reason for it. Unless the information she was seeking couldn't be found in a simple online record search, or even at the local library.

I knew what it was like to feel like a visitor in your own body. Or to feel like life had a set path decided for you long before you were even born.

I could relate to her.

But was that enough of a reason to help her?

A potential Counter?

My nemesis?

It would be easier to kill her.

I could do it right here, on the beach and no one would know. I doubted she told Tabitha or Blaire where she'd gone—they would have discouraged it.

The others would help dispose of her body. They'd understand why I did it. She wouldn't even realize it was happening. The foolish girl kept her back to me the majority of our conversation, offering ample opportunity to quickly take her life. Perhaps, that was what she wanted to begin with. That was why she was truly here.

If I was anything like my father, I wouldn't even regret it. Wouldn't think twice about it. That was the price of offering your trust to a desperate Quarter. That's what the Movement wanted the rest of the town to believe, so they could isolate us.

But I wasn't my father. I couldn't take a life if there was a chance it wasn't mine to take—and a Counter's life *was* mine to take. I wasn't the dangerous vigilante that the Movement attempted to paint me as, eliminating anyone in my path who slightly resembled my enemies.

I was desperate for my full gift, but not desperate enough to senselessly kill for it.

No, I'd let her live through her pity party another day and continue to toy with her. I doubted that was much better than the alternative, anyway.

"I'm not even sure why I bothered coming here. All I've done is create more confusion."

Her small hands wrung together nervously at her waist. When I didn't offer any comforting response, she turned to walk away.

I hesitated until she was nearly off the beach, her soft sighs of pain somehow overpowering the sound of the waves beside me as her bare feet met the rocky road that blended into the sand.

"Why does it matter?"

She stopped and turned. Her mouth was now pulled down into a frown. "Because it's my family. They'd want me to find answers."

I could tell she didn't fully believe those words. Doubt and unease danced in her already sulking expression.

"Have you always done whatever your family wants you to do?" I goaded.

Who was I to even say that? My whole existence was centered around meeting my family's expectations. It felt good to project that frustration onto someone else—to see the rage that it ignited inside of her and know exactly how hot it burned.

"Excuse me?"

"I mean, have you ever considered that with them out of the picture, you should move on and live your own life?"

Her feet carried her back to me effortlessly through the dark sand and a thin finger shot into the air at me, stabbing my chest when she was close enough to reach.

The sensation it sent through my entire body was impossible to mask. I'd grown used to the constant ache that hummed inside my chest any time she was near, but we'd never touched before. This was a thousand times worse.

It felt as if I'd been struck by lightning, poisoning my blood and spreading through my veins from the spot her finger jabbed into the rest of my body. It didn't cease until it reached my fingers and toes, and I could swear I felt it beyond that as well.

It was the most alive I've felt in ages.

That was such a strange thing to admit. That this insignificant girl, who I was sure was my sworn enemy intent on killing me, was the one thing that had come along and brought me back to life.

I desperately wanted our contact to end. Yet, I wanted her to keep her finger on me forever. To spread her palm across my chest and see how far and hot we could burn together.

She appeared to feel it as well. Her large eyes widened even further, the strange color of her irises shrinking into the blackness of her growing, inky pupils. Her arm jerked back, and the pain stopped as soon as her skin left mine. She cradled her elbow and glared at me accusingly, as if I'd somehow managed to intentionally inflict the pain she was feeling.

"What did you just do to me?"

My fingers flexed at my sides, itching for more contact. To reach out and touch her cheek. To feel that sweet agony again and know for a fact that someone else was feeling it, too.

"You're more dangerous than you know."

"And you're more trouble than you're worth," she quickly countered, her chest puffed out defensively.

She had no idea how much trouble I could be for her.

We held each other's eyes for a few lingering moments. I felt her stare deep inside my marrow, as if she were seeing right through to my core. I'd never felt so exposed, completely at the mercy of someone else.

She could destroy me.

I don't doubt that she will. But something told me that being destroyed by her would be the most exhilarating thing to ever happen to a person like me.

A pawn. A tool for others to use and abuse and place blame onto when nothing seems to go right.

She'd been holding her breath. I watched as her lungs filled and her chest rose, my eyes falling to the skin that her low-cut shirt left exposed. When she released the breath, it was slow and shaky. Somewhere along the way, she'd taken a step toward me, closing the short distance between us so we were now standing nose-to-nose.

Not a single part of our bodies was touching, but I felt the vibrations of her skin bouncing off mine as if we were. She was buzzing, and I was completely wasted on her.

I drowned in her pools of violet. They pulled me in and refused to release me from their depths. She was a siren, and I was a mere mortal trying to resist her deadly call. But I'd failed.

My mind went completely blank, as if she somehow managed to turn off all thought processes and render me defenseless. I leaned into the vastness of the space between us, and my lips were met with fireworks.

The pain from before had returned, but it was no longer an unbearable ache that left me with conflicting urges. No, the longer we kissed, the deeper she leaned into me, and the more places our bare skin met, the duller the ache became, turning instead into something completely different.

Something addictive.

Like a fiend with their vice, I couldn't stop. The moment I gave into the urge to use, I became her slave. She owned me now, and there was nothing I could do about it.

Her mouth opened the slightest bit, granting me permission to explore with my tongue. And gods, she tasted so sweet.

But then, without any warning, she pulled away and ran, never once looking back at the wreckage she'd left behind.

CHAPTER SIXTEEN

STORIE

M y body took me to him faster than my mind was able to comprehend what was truly happening. I awoke from my deep meditation tangled in floral sheets and covered in sweat and bruises. Those were my first indication that any of it was real. Then, before I could grab shoes or my purse, I was in my car driving in the general direction I knew his property was in—the same way we walked in the woods together. I recalled an old map of Beacon Grove I'd found in the library and hoped it was still accurate enough to get me there.

It wasn't until halfway through the drive that I realized what a dangerous thing I was doing, but I couldn't back out. Something about him called to me and the sound was impossible to ignore. By the time I reached the familiar beach from my visions, I lost all momentum.

His home was larger than I pictured it to be, surrounded by the same unique black sand and stone I'd just seen from the balcony.

My courage grew wings and flew away as soon as I stopped my car and shifted into park. Fear took its place, as if finally, my brain had kicked into gear and realized how dangerous it was for me to be there. In the mouth of my predator's den.

I walked to the beach instead of going to the front door like I originally planned, my eyes avoiding the beautiful sprawling mansion that overlooked it in fear of finding those coal black eyes gazing out at me. The ocean waves lazily nipped at my feet, somehow feeding the frenzy that was my mind.

I wanted to scream every frustration I had built up inside of me at it. To see the water split and shift with the sound waves as they vibrated off me, releasing every negative feeling into her depths.

A monster had grown inside of me, green with envy and red with fury. He fed off me for so long—my fears, my weaknesses, my complacency—that he managed to become a being all on his own.

I'd grown tired of other people making decisions for me. Of being at the mercy of everyone else for information about myself and where I came from.

There was a mystery surrounding my identity and why I was in Beacon Grove. I could feel the weight of curiosity in every stare as I passed by the town's locals.

Could they tell that I was just as clueless as they were? Was it obvious that while I'd spent a lifetime as a girl named Storie Graves, I had no real idea who that person was?

A piece of me was always missing, even as a child. A hole of ignorance about my purpose in this world that no one wanted to fill in.

So, he filled it.

This fiery, jealous, raging monster.

At first, I was afraid to acknowledge him. I thought if I ignored him, he'd shrink away to nothing and disappear into the darkness inside my mind with the rest of the parts of me I was taught shouldn't see the light of day.

It wasn't until I befriended my monster that I gained clarity.

I saw my oppression for exactly what it was, and I would become a threat to everyone who wanted to keep me under their thumbs.

They had no idea how dangerous I'd become when I had nothing left to lose. If anything, what happened between me and Remy on the beach solidified that. Because we were very clearly connected in a way that no one wanted to admit—myself included. I was realizing that maybe that connection was more significant than I could have ever imagined.

He kissed me and I was drowned in the sensation of it—painful at first, then blissfully perfect. I felt like I'd been injected with the sun's bright and beautiful rays, full of heat and energy and power.

It was all I could do not to hand myself over to him right there on the beach. To succumb to whatever pain or pleasure he intended to offer me. I had a feeling he'd have me begging for mercy either way.

But something had me step back and put distance between us. A nagging feeling in my gut screamed that it was too soon. I didn't have the full picture yet, and without it, Remy was nothing but a threat to me.

Once again, my feet took me back to my car without a single word and I was driving in the opposite direction down the same winding dirt road that took me to him.

No one could know about this. On the drive back to the hotel, I promised myself that I would take what happened between us and every emotion it conjured up to my grave.

Hazel stopped me the next day to have lunch. I'd nearly skipped going back into town altogether, opting instead to hole up in my room and process what has happened over these past few weeks. It felt like the world spun a little differently on its axis since the first time I drove down these sleepy streets, and I needed time to plan my next move.

I was feeling paranoid from my exhausting interaction with Remy and the tension that was radiating off Blaire and Tabitha from losing so many guests over Mabon being canceled. The chance of running into any of them made my stomach turn. But once I poured myself a thick cup of muddied coffee from the stash Tabitha supplied in all the guest rooms, I couldn't resist. I needed sustenance and caffeine.

When Hazel stopped and offered lunch, the need to know more about my mother outweighed any other fears and frustrations I had about everything else.

"It's really too bad that this was your first Mabon here. It's usually a great time. You'll see next year, though."

We sat down at one of the tall tables beside the front window of The Grind. It was unusually empty for the time of day, but I was grateful for the privacy their lack of business afforded us.

The entire town seemed to be stuck in a glum mood since the Mabon ceremony, though Hazel's spirits remained high.

"I'm not sure I'll be here next year," I confessed sheepishly. I don't know why I felt so embarrassed by that admission, but her surprised expression didn't help me feel any better.

I felt even worse when her hand reached across the table to cover mine. "Beacon Grove will always be your hometown, Storie. Even when your living relatives have all died away. You're always welcome."

I offered a small, awkward smile. It sure didn't feel that way to me, but I chose to focus on something else she said instead of dwelling on my insecurities. "I thought all the Graves have passed on."

"Oh, they have. Your maternal grandmother is still alive, though. Gods, Lunet has got to be pushing ninety now," she mused, unaware that her words sent my heart crashing into my ribcage and blood rushing into my cheeks.

I *did* have family here.

How had I gotten so distracted with my father's side that I'd forgotten my mother was from Beacon Grove as well?

"I would love to meet her," I rushed out, cutting off her rambling thoughts.

"Of course! I'm surprised you haven't yet. I'll write down her information. She's a little out of it these days, so it's probably best to call and talk to her nurse before dropping in."

She rifled through her colorful, patchwork purse until she found a pen, then flipped over one of her business cards and scribbled an address and phone number on the back.

"I also brought some pictures of your mom. I couldn't resist looking through my old albums after I saw you at the festival. You remind me so much of Bonnie when we were your age."

Her hands disappeared into the endless bag again and pulled out a black envelope that she slipped a stack of polaroids from. One by one, she set them on the table before me and pointed to the same freckle-faced, pale woman with white hair and glowing, purple eyes.

It was the first time I'd ever seen my mother's face. Until now, I could only rely on the image I made up of her in my head. Aunt Ash said she and my dad left town with the clothes on their backs after I was born, so there weren't any photos of family lying around that weren't taken after we all made it to the city. Like most things, she and Dad never explained the situation surrounding their departure. I only knew that it was desperate and rushed.

We almost looked nothing alike, but I knew what Hazel meant almost immediately. She held the same wanderlust gaze that I'd noticed in my own reflection since arriving here. A hope that hadn't been stomped out yet, though I was right on the edge of losing it. Seeing her with the same expression seemed to breathe life back into that part of me, encouraging me to keep going.

"She loved that sweater. She made it herself in our high school sewing class. I designed a whole line of them to honor her. It's still my best-selling product." Hazel's watery eyes rolled to the ceiling. "That's what I get for teasing her about it every day."

She moved onto the next few photos of them doing random things together, like lying on the beach that I assumed was on Remy's property, and standing in front of a Tudor-style home in formal dresses. My father stood beside her in that one, his arm draped protectively around her shoulders. They looked at each other with goofy, lopsided grins while Hazel glared at her date on the other side. The guy in the photo looked familiar, though I couldn't figure out why until Hazel's finger tapped on his suited chest.

"Ugh, your dad's best friend, Kyle. They tried every trick to force us together, but we hated each other. He always held a torch for Asher, anyway. To this day, I can't stand him. He's the town's sheriff, though he had no business going into the police academy after all the stuff they pulled as kids." Her voice dropped and the smile fell from her lips. "After your dad left, I guess he was just lost. Trying to right a wrong that wasn't his to right."

I had no idea what that meant, but I sensed I wouldn't get an answer from her. Instead of prying, I gave her a private moment to collect herself while I stared down at the picture again. That was the officer from the day I first got to town. His shiny black hair had been cropped and his chest and shoulders filled out, but there was no denying it was him. In all the time I've spent in town, I'd yet to see him again. I wondered why that was.

"We were sorry to hear about him and Asher. Such a shame that both were gone too soon." She shifted in her chair just slightly, enough to glance around her back, as if she were checking to see if anyone was listening.

The only other people in the shop were the workers behind the counter and each of them was leaning on the counters, staring into their phones. "I'm surprised Asher didn't return sooner after Mason's accident. She was always such a firecracker. We were sure she'd be coming into town with guns blazing to avenge his and Bonnie's deaths. They were thick as thieves. I guess I didn't consider that she was a new parent in a way."

And there it was: the suspicious look on her face and matching shifty behavior of every single person who mentioned my family's deaths. It was the exact reason I'd come to Beacon Grove in the first place. This town held secrets about my family that none of its inhabitants wanted to spill. They may have been infected with distrust toward one another, but their jaws remained fused shut when it came to talking about their business with an outsider.

Unfortunately for me, I was still considered to be on the outside despite the deep ties that rooted me here.

Hazel's face told me more than her mouth ever would. In those few sentences, she confirmed that my parents' deaths were somehow tied to the people of this town. That my father's "accident" wasn't much of an accident at all. And that Aunt Asher would go to great lengths to ensure his and my mother's passings weren't in vain. She was just held back from her plans by me, and by the time I was old enough to be on my own, they came for her, too.

"I'm sure it's a hard subject for you to talk about," Hazel awkwardly went on when I didn't have much to say aside from a stiff nod.

She leaned back into her chair and waved away the emotions that were taking over her face again. "Anyway, I hope that I was able to provide you with some comfort. I miss your mom every day, but it's nice to have a piece of her back in Beacon Grove."

"It has. Thank you for bringing these." I motioned to the pictures still sprawled out on the table between us.

The rest of our meal went on without incident. I found her to be an extremely easy person to get along with and our conversation flowed once we got past the topic of my family. She reminded me so much of Blaire with her odd views on things and uncaring attitude toward the people around her. When it was time to leave so she could reopen her shop, I wasn't ready to say goodbye and she made me promise we'd meet again soon. Not soon after the bell above the door rang with her departure, Julia and her friends surrounded my table.

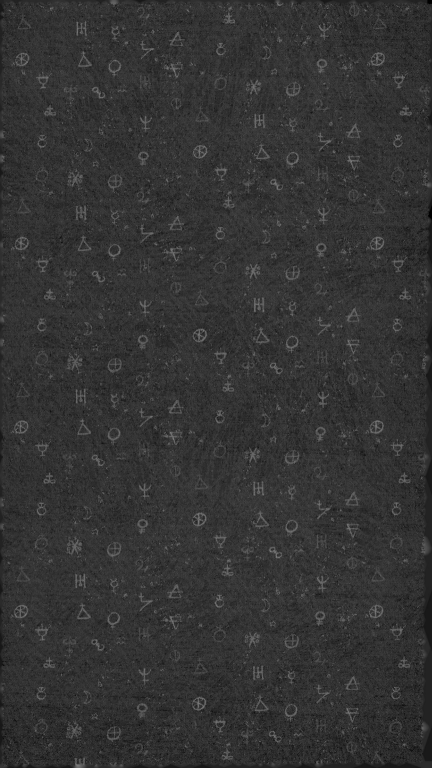

THE ✴ BEACON

2 5 S E P T E M B E R 2 0 2 1

MABON CANCELED

After days of refusing to offer comment, Mayor Douglas has officially confirmed that the town has no plans to continue with this year's Mabon festival.

"I'm confident that Beacon Grove can recover from the damage we've sustained from this horrific event and come out the other end even stronger," Douglas states at the most recent impromptu meeting.

Business owners are still reeling from their loss of income and wondering what the city plans to do in order to help them recoup their losses.

"I don't see how they can make this decision without consulting with the townspeople first. Now, we're left floundering and figuring how to make ends meet," Lisa Golden, owner of the Watchtower Tavern comments after the mayor's official statement.

Many are still wondering what happened at the Mabon kick-off and why the Quarters were unable to protect the town from this horrific attack.

When asked about how the Quarter families are handling this colossal disappointment, Rowan Wildes insisted, "You can rest assured that we're handling this issue internally and working day in and day out to ensure our sons are well-equipped with the necessary tools to avoid this from happening in the future."

Wildes went on to add that while they sort the matter out amongst themselves, he and the other three elder Quarters have stepped in and taken over the Quarter tasks until further notice.

CHAPTER SEVENTEEN

REMY

The woods behind the Easton property were the safest place for us to talk without interruption. Enzo made us wait until he could draw up a soundproofing spell. It finally lifted with some help from us to ensure no one overheard in the case that we were followed. He should have been able to handle the magic himself, especially being in his own element, but all he could manage were a few wisps of wind that stirred up the fallen leaves surrounding us and then died away.

It was proof that we were weakening by the second while our fathers capitalized off us. None of us shamed him when he admitted how difficult it was for him and with the protection spell in place, we released our grim thoughts.

"We're fucked," Rhyse began, taking a seat on a fallen log. His large body made the rotted wood creak and crack a little.

"We don't know that," Lux soothed. "Something is definitely syphoning our magic from us, though." He stood with his arms crossed against his chest. His usually bright cerulean eyes drooped with fatigue.

All of us looked like worn-down and tired versions of ourselves, aging beyond our years when we should have been enjoying what our fathers promised would be the prime of our lives.

"I'm not doing any more of these training sessions with my dad," Enzo started, his feet pacing the forest floor. Leaves and sticks crunched beneath his shoes, practically turning to dust against them. "They're obviously gunning to take their roles back. It has to be them syphoning."

"We don't know that. Rayner has been picking up momentum with the Movement. People are pissed about Mabon. It could have been them practicing with dark magic that night to weaken us. Our fathers are just opportunists," Lux reasoned.

"I'm not even sure how we got out of that. I was next to dead." Rhyse shook his head.

Enzo and Lux silently nodded their agreements.

"Something showed up at my altar that night and fed me power," I admitted, and three pairs of eyes shot over at me in irritated bewilderment. I avoided their glares and took a seat on the other half of Rhyse's log.

"Why the fuck didn't you tell us this before?"

My shoulders lifted in a pathetic, noncommittal shrug. The truth was, I had no idea why I didn't tell them right away. We'd barely had a chance to talk much since that night, but I could have found a way.

I wasn't going to expose Storie as the entity and put a bigger target on her back, though. Not until I could figure out the truth about what has been happening between us.

"Never really had a chance. But it was the only reason I was able to get you guys out of there."

"So, now we've got secret entities feeding us power while someone else tries to steal our magic away?" Lux wondered aloud. He followed Enzo's lead and began pacing, his hand scratching at his overgrown beard.

"We're fucked," Rhyse repeated.

This time, no one disagreed.

"We need to make a plan. Starting with playing nice with our fathers." Lux sent a look at Enzo, who rolled his eyes. "We don't know their true agenda and we can't trust a word they say. We just need to lay low while we gather any information we can about what happened. If they find out that we're sniffing them out, they'll only act faster."

"So, we're just supposed to roll over while those assholes take everything out from under us?" Rhyse scoffed. "It's like you said; they're opportunists. They're not smart enough to pull off something like this alone."

"As of right now, now one is going to take our side against theirs. They're playing politics with the coven and the town, and we've got bigger things to worry about."

"Yeah, like what is feeding Remy power while the rest of us wither away?" Enzo's feet finally stopped moving in front of me. His tone was harsh; accusatory.

"I think there's more to this than we're being told."

Storie's face popped back into my mind. I was nearly positive she was my Counter, yet I had no urge to kill her. In fact, I wanted to do the opposite. I'd wanted to grab her up from the sand and carry her back to my bedroom to see how far we could push ourselves past the pain of being near each other and discover what was on the other side of it.

"That's why we need to be smart and not turn on each other," Lux pushed.

"Then he shouldn't be keeping things from us." Rhyse flexed his enormous bicep and pointed a finger at me.

"I'm not keeping anything. I just told you what happened and if it weren't for me, you'd be dead."

"Let's just lay low and keep looking for our Counters. Any information we can find on them will lead us to ending this." Lux looked to the three of us for agreement.

"How do we know that everything we've been told about our Counters isn't a lie?" I voiced the thoughts that have been swimming around my brain since Storie drove into town, regretting it immediately when they each looked at me like I'd lost my mind.

"Why would you say that? If there's one thing we know as Quarters, it's that our Counters are our biggest threat." Rhyse held his palm up and a small orange flame burned bright against his skin. After a few seconds, the flame flickered out and his eyes slid over to mine to prove his point. "Ours are the first that haven't been found, and we're the first to have our magic wane."

"Yeah, but who told us that? Have any of you ever read the words for yourselves in any of our studies? Maybe this is all related."

Lux shook his head. "That's true. I've only ever heard about it from our fathers and grandfathers, and they've proven that they can't be trusted. This could be their failed attempt at weakening us."

"Are you seriously entertaining this?" Enzo interjected. He regarded Lux the same way they had all just done to me. Silence lingered between us, and he remained still in front of me while the gears in his brain worked overtime until he shook the thought from his head. "It's not just Quarter knowledge that Counters are our one true weakness. The entire coven knows. That seems like too elaborate of a lie for those assholes to come up with."

"Maybe, but it's not completely impossible." Lux's fingers worked through his beard again.

If I were truly loyal to them, I would have spilled everything about Storie right then and there. I would have explained how I felt since we first made eye contact and how I've been working behind their backs to get closer to her and evaluate the threat she posed.

It started off as a noble cause. I wanted to make sure she couldn't hurt any of us, and they hadn't taken me seriously the first time I brought her up. But it morphed into something completely different when she projected into my space and saved us all from being turned to dust. When I felt her skin against mine and it burned hotter than any fire Rhyse could conjure up, somehow leaving me wanting more.

If I told them about her now, they'd hunt and torture her. Just as they've been trained to do with a Counter. But I couldn't allow that. Not yet. So, like a spineless coward, I remained silent and let them think I was just as clueless as they were.

Our meeting ended with us agreeing to stay under the radar for now, just as Lux suggested. We'd be our coven's punching bags as they got over Mabon being canceled and allow our fathers to believe we were dutifully obeying them and unaware of their agenda. But each of us was tasked with finding out more.

More about the Book of Shadows.

More about our history as Quarters.

More about The Movement's agenda.

And more about our Counters.

We'd blindly believed the words of our fathers and grandfathers, never once questioning their sources or reasoning. Never once wondering why we weren't shown the history books or given concrete proof to study. We never had a reason to, until now. And none of it was readily available to us.

CHAPTER EIGHTEEN

REMY

Rowan Winters was not known for his patient demeanor or soft tone. He was one of the most closed-off, intimidating men I'd ever known, aside from my grandfather. No one ever crossed him, and most were afraid to even speak to him unless completely necessary.

I had been blessed by the gods to have this stony man as my father. He taught me everything I knew about being a Quarter, fighting technique, and serving my coven, and left the rest of my upbringing to my mother. If we weren't discussing Quarter business, we likely weren't speaking at all.

Since stepping into my role as a Quarter and claiming the gift that was once his, our relationship was more strained than ever before. He hardly acknowledged me when we passed in the halls of our home, and he made a point to avoid me in public. In fact, his sudden interest in my life had only just peaked when the Movement grew stronger, and he recognized the opportunity to regain his magic and relive his glory days—all while robbing me of mine.

Which was why I had such a hard time following his lead as his aging body slowly dodged and ambled away from my strikes. We were working on fighting technique and reaction time, though he appeared to be the one receiving the lesson while I was practicing a simple warm-up. I'm not even sure why this was a part of our "training refresher," as he referred to it.

If he were truly concerned with my lack of magic, we wouldn't be standing in our backyard pretending that he was teaching me anything I didn't already know. Instead, he would be scouring our history books to find the missing piece or coming up with ways to stop Rayner from poisoning the minds of our coven and turning them against us.

I already knew the missing piece, though. She haunted my brain every chance she could get.

The power I felt when I was around her was the most addictive thing I've ever tasted, and I planned to use her for every ounce of it that I could squeeze from her curvy little body. I wished I could seek her out the way she had done to me. Appear in her space and watch her every move without her knowledge, taking notes on every strength and weakness she possessed.

But I was stuck here, playing the game like I agreed to do.

"Where is your head? You should have stopped that," my father chastised through labored breaths.

I let him believe he was leading this thing and allowed a strike to pass through. His hand wrapped around my wrist, and he pulled me into a choke hold.

Now that I knew how weak and defenseless my Counter was, all the physical training felt quite useless. Before, she had been some faceless enemy, highly trained and ready to defend her life just as I had been. Instead, she was a sad little girl with next to zero knowledge of her role in the world and beautiful eyes that perfectly matched the lavender fields out on the Forbes property.

It was Lux's voice in my mind that had me swallowing down the snarky responses that were burning in my throat. Even if Storie was my Counter and the missing piece to regaining my gift, she could only serve in that role to me. The others still hadn't found their Counters, and their lives were in danger because of it. I couldn't risk them losing everything simply because I no longer had to worry about it. They were the closest thing I had to a family, including the sweaty man standing before me.

So, I took the low blows and stroked my father's ego long enough to pacify him until his aging body could no longer handle it.

Once we finished up, he took one last jab at me, then swaggered over to one of the patio chairs and fell into it, swiping sweat away from his forehead with his arm.

"Mayor Douglas had canceled the rest of the scheduled Mabon celebrations." His gravelly voice delivered the news without emotion, his eyes focused on the whiskey he was swirling around in his glass.

"Oh, yeah?"

His brows furrowed together. He stilled and the black pits that I'd inherited from him slowly drifted up to pin me. "This is your fault, Remington. You should show a little more remorse."

A flame of fury burned through my chest, encouraging me to counter with some sort of defense. To point out that we wouldn't be in this situation if he and the others hadn't failed at finding our Counters. But the words fell flat on my tongue when I once again reminded myself of the end game and what was at stake.

"I'm sorry," I mumbled in a non-committal tone. That only seemed to piss him off even more.

"We can't help you fix this if you're unwilling to show some respect to the coven who is relying on you," he chastised, finishing off the amber liquid. "You're lucky we're so willing to step in and help you boys. I can't say my father would have done the same for me."

He didn't wait for me to respond. He knew he'd made his point and effectively pissed me off in the process. He just stood from his chair and swaggered off without looking back. I hadn't seen such confidence in him since I was too young to understand how cruel of a man he was. How it stemmed from igniting fear in others instead of the respect I had once thought.

He assumed he was going to end up on top—all our fathers did. While it killed a piece of me to allow them to make a mockery of us, it only proved that we were doing exactly what we set out to do. For now, they were too blinded by their own egos to even see us coming.

I walked to the opposite end of the house, up the two flights of stairs to my room and straight out to the patio.

This wasn't the bedroom I grew up in. That one had long since been converted into a craft room for my mother's hobbies. This was the room I took over when I stepped into my Quarter role and claimed my gifts. It was tradition for the current Quarter to move closer to their altar. I was just happy to be farther from my father.

If I ever decided to have a family, my parents would move into the guest house or one of the rooms on this side of the main house and I would take over their room. It seemed like an awkward exchange that I didn't see myself doing anytime soon.

So, for now, I settled here. My favorite part was the balcony I was currently standing on that overlooked the ocean. It was the only place I felt like I could catch my breath anymore.

That unmistakable sensation moved through me in waves. It was no longer a painful ache, just a buzzing that reached my core, letting me know that my counterpart was near.

She had to be here. Somewhere around my home. What would possess her to stumble into the most dangerous place this town had to offer her again?

When I was just about to turn my back to the beach and go searching for her inside, I spotted the housekeeper's daughter, Julia, rounding the corner of a large boulder that sat on the edge of the sand and the woods with my weakness in tow. The rest of her friends trailed behind, their arms full of towels, coolers and a small keg.

Her family worked for mine for longer than anyone could remember. We always made sure to pay them a generous wage while providing more than suitable living arrangements, and they made sure to protect our privacy from the rest of the town.

Both sides trusted each other to take care of the other, and over the years, they'd become closer to family than anything else.

Julia grated on my nerves, though. She was cocky and entitled and flat-out annoying. Her friends weren't any better. We were the same age, but they've always acted much younger. Never held responsible for anything in their lives. Never forced to work toward a single thing outside of who was paying for the next keg that night.

Julia was training to take over for her mom, and the rest of them worked in the various retail shops downtown, never taking advantage of the freedom they had to leave Beacon Grove and find a life in the outside world. They were Watchtower's most recent recruits, solidifying their futures here.

Storie looked out of place with the motley crew. In fact, she seemed downright miserable. I wondered how they managed to pry her away from the Granger girl and her obsessive digging into her family's business long enough to drag her down here.

It was none of my business. Being around her only confused and infuriated me, especially after she ran off the last time we were together, leaving me with a horde of unfamiliar emotions I had no idea how to deal with and the worst case of blue balls.

I could hear them laughing and joking once they settled into a spot, uncaring of how far their voices carried, or that technically, they weren't allowed to be out here. Julia knew the rules and never bothered with following them, but my father didn't care, so no one else did either.

It felt wrong to watch them any longer, though I could have kept my eyes on Storie for hours, studying her every move. Disgusted with myself, I turned and walked back into my room before a loud thud followed by a grunt sounded from below.

"What the hell did you do, Beau?" Julia hissed, her shrill voice floating straight through my balcony doors. I stepped back into the ocean air and saw Storie standing before me, translucent once again.

She wasn't looking at me. Her back was turned my way as she watched the beach in horror. The group of people she'd traveled with circled her physical body with their mouths open in panic.

"What happened?" I asked, startling her. The group was talking below us in hushed whispers, arguing about what to do.

"I-I don't know. They forced me out here with them. They were acting really weird, but I figured it was harmless. Then, that big one attacked me from behind, and now I'm here." Her arm lifted over the balcony to point at the hulking man that was now bending over to grab her by the armpits and drag her to the side of the beach.

I can't replay a single thought that passed through my mind in the span of time it took for me to make it from my room on the third floor, all the way down to the beach. It was as if I blinked and was there, standing before the guilty group of six individuals who looked terrified to see me.

Storie's body wasn't anywhere to be seen, so there was obviously some amount of time that slipped away from me. But not much. Hopefully, not enough for them to do any damage.

"Where is she?" I heard my voice demand from somewhere far away. Perhaps my own spirit was still standing on the balcony with hers.

"Who?" Beau tried to ask, failing at acting casual. His voice shook and sweat was pouring down from his prematurely balding head in thick drops.

The others were stunned sober, their buzzes and good moods completely wiped away. They stood still behind Beau, as if his bulky body could protect them from any harm. And if they didn't tell me where Storie's body was, there *would* be harm.

My eyes shifted behind Beau and found Julia's. I lifted my brow at her in a challenge, offering one last chance for her to come clean. She knew how dangerous the Winters men were when they were tested. She'd witnessed some of my father's wrath firsthand, but was always sworn to secrecy about the horrors that happened behind closed doors. I wouldn't doubt if she told her friends all about it, though. That would explain their terror.

A few beats passed and I was officially prepared to reach into each of their chests with my bare hands and rip their hearts out. When I stepped forward toward them, Julia's hand popped out from behind Beau's enormous arm and pointed to the west.

To the water.

I can't explain why the idea that something was wrong with Storie had affected me so much. Sure, she was likely my Counter, but that only meant I should have killed her myself. Before any of those braindead nonachievers ever had the chance. But it wasn't anger over the missed opportunity that had my feet propelling me through the sand.

No, there was that strange, nagging feeling deep inside my bones—embedded into the marrow—that pulled me into the opposite direction. It told me that killing her would be a mistake and fed this angry side of me that would rip them limb from limb if I found out they had harmed her beyond return.

"She's going to be okay. We didn't mean to hurt her. We were just having fun. It was an accident..." Julia was mumbling to my back. Her voice faded away into the sound of the waves as the dark sand kicked up behind me, tickling my legs.

They had dragged her body into the thick beach grass and propped her head onto one of their towels. It was rolled into a ball and soaked in blood that had also seeped into the golden locks fanned out around her face. Her pale skin was nearly translucent, leaving little difference between the version of her lying before me and the ghost-girl who met me on my balcony minutes before.

Raindrops sprinkled on my head when I kneeled beside her body, my hands hesitating just above it. I had no idea what the extent of her injury was or if moving her might only make it worse, especially after they had been so careless with her before. But I had to somehow pick her up and get inside before the downpour began and the tide lifted. After considering every possible outcome while the pace of the drops quickened against my skin, I just said fuck it and slid my arms beneath her neck and her knees, hoping the contact wouldn't disrupt the cut on her head too much.

The instant our skin touched, her lungs filled with air and I stilled. She coughed a few times, her eyes rolling to the back of her head with each attempt she made at opening them. I watched her stubbornly try over and over again to focus on the scene above her and fail until finally, her hand blindly reached behind her head and brushed against the arm that was balancing her in the air by her neck. Heavy lids pried open one last time and those odd-colored irises focused on mine. A relieved breath swept through her body.

"You came," she rasped, then sputtered out a cough.

The rainfall was getting heavier. I knew it would be a difficult walk back to the house while carrying her through the wet sand, so I didn't waste any more time. My legs stood us both from the ground and I began the trek back to shelter, silently praying to the gods that Julia and her friends had cleared out. I wasn't sure I'd be able to stop myself from killing them all if they braved waiting.

When the thick drops of water began pelting her face, she turned in my arms and buried it into my neck. Soft, hot breaths met my skin and encouraged me to make it through the last hundred feet to our covered patio.

I wasn't thinking about her being my Counter, or what harm would befall me from not simply letting her die out on the beach and allowing nature to do the job I was too weak to execute. For the first time ever, I wasn't considering the other Quarters and what it would mean for them that I was saving the one and only soul I'd been tasked with separating from its body.

None of that mattered.

The most important thing to me was getting her safely up to my room without any witnesses and stripping the soaked clothes from her body so she would stop shivering. I wanted to assess and care for her injury before infection took over. Then, when I was sure she was safe and resting, I was going to hunt down that waste of oxygen, Beau, and show him exactly how it felt to be attacked by someone more powerful than he was.

"I'm fine," she croaked when I sat her up on the bed to look at the back of her head.

Her hair was knotted, half soaked, and caked in thick blood, but I couldn't find the source of the bleeding. There didn't appear to be a single scratch, even in the area that the blood seemed most concentrated. It was as if the injury completely healed itself.

Her torso began swaying as her eyes fought to stay open. I didn't waste any more time on the puzzling injury, figuring I could recheck it when she was finally resting.

I peeled her shirt off her, trying my best to respect her privacy but finding it increasingly difficult when I wanted to inspect her for any more wounds that could have produced that amount of blood. I lifted her arms and checked her ribs, noting that her milky skin was in perfect condition and slowly gaining its color back. She interrupted my inspection by bracing her hands on my shoulders and lifting her bottom so I could do the same with her pants.

Once I was sure she wouldn't bleed out, I dragged her up to my pillow and rested her head, then covered her shaking body with my comforter.

"Th-thank you," she whispered through chattering teeth, her eyes already falling shut.

I didn't bother responding. Instead, I gathered up her clothes so they could be thrown into the wash and offered one last glance to make sure she was okay. Then, I headed out to find Julia.

CHAPTER NINETEEN

STORIE

J ulia and her group of friends surrounded the table I was just sharing with Hazel. Each of their eyes trained on me and I took turns observing each of their ruffled appearances before finally settling on Julia. She appeared to be leading this infiltration.

"We're going to the beach, and we'd love for you to come," her falsely sweet voice rang out. The smile her lips spread into never reached her eyes.

"Oookay," I drawled, scowling at her. Someone walked into The Grind and the Autumn air bit at my arms where my sweater sleeves had been pulled up. None of them seemed affected. "I'm actually pretty busy, so I'll have to pass."

Every other time she offered to hang out, she was alone and took my rejection with ease. The presence of her posse apparently gave her the courage to insist I come, ignoring every polite excuse I came up with until she gave up trying to convince me and her arm shot out to grab me by the wrist. She dragged me toward a van that was parked just outside the coffee shop.

Her friends were prepared for the quick attack, surrounding us so no one could see that I was being taken against my will. The big one shoved me into the open sliding door and quickly slammed it shut while the others piled in on the opposite side.

There weren't any seats in the back of the van, so we all sat facing each other on narrow benches that were built along the sides. They crowded together on the driver's side, leaving me to sit along across from them.

"What is wrong with you?" I screamed into the small space. My hand rubbed at the sore spot on my arm where Julia's nails dug so deep, they left tiny slits in my skin that were beaded with blood.

"I'm over this cat and mouse game you're playing. You're going to come to the beach with us and have a good time."

Her pupils were dilated, nearly erasing the color of her irises. I glanced around at the others, noting that theirs looked the same.

The big guy who shoved me in was driving. I heard Julia refer to him earlier as Beau. In addition to Julia and Beau, there were three other girls and one guy. I tried to remember their names from when Julia introduced me at Mabon, but I honestly hadn't planned on ever spending any more time around them, so I didn't really pay attention.

The girl with black hair was staring at me with wide, panicked eyes. "Remind me why we're doing this again," she turned and hissed to the side of Julia's face.

"Because my mom seems to hold special interest in her, and she's driving me up the wall about it. Miss Perfect can't be bothered with a simple cup of coffee, so we're doing it the hard way."

Why would her mother even have me on her radar? As far as I knew, I've never met the woman before.

The van turned onto the dirt road that I knew led to Remy's property and rocked us back and forth as Beau carelessly navigated it over the potholes.

"Listen, Julia. I'm not sure what you think you're going to accomplish with this, but I can assure you, I'm not worth the trouble." Beau hit a bump and the back of my head banged against the metal behind me.

"It's no trouble, really. You see, it was supposed to be me. The Rists and the Winters have always been intertwined. We figured it was just a matter of time before he needed me. Then you came along, and it's like you're all he can see. Inquiring minds want to know why."

She was rambling on in code, clearly out of her mind. The others watched her with confused expressions that likely matched my own, but she didn't pay them any attention.

No, her focus was solely on me.

Her lips curled into a sinister grin when she noticed my frown at the mention of Remy. She looked me up and down and the grin turned into a snarl.

If I didn't know better, I'd guess that she was jealous. Of what, I couldn't say because whatever was happening between me and Remy wasn't glamorous or worth flaunting. It was raw and carnal and terrifying.

Beau suddenly pulled over to the side of the road and slammed the van into park. The others gathered their gear and filed out the same door they came in. Julia hesitated behind them, shoving my shoulder when I didn't move out before her. I stumbled forward and nearly fell onto the gravel but caught myself at the last second.

They let Julia lead the way and I was told to walk behind her while the rest hung back a few paces to make sure I didn't try to run away. She walked us into the woods beside the road, probably trying to avoid being seen by anyone who might drive down the private street.

It was such a surreal experience. I'd never considered what I would do if I were kidnapped, and now I knew I was absolutely useless in a crisis situation. I'm sure Aunt Ash would've had something planned out. She'd already have escaped somehow, always able to think quickly on her feet. I wished I had paid more attention to her. If only I listened to what I assumed were the ramblings of a paranoid woman, I'd be better prepared for every curveball Beacon Grove had thrown me thus far.

Julia's steps progressively became sloppier as whatever drug-induced cloud she was floating on fully kicked in. We took one last turn from the woods and were spit out onto the unique black sand. When the Wintes' house came into view, I couldn't stop my eyes from scaling it for his balcony. Of course, he was there, witnessing my attack but completely unaware that it was happening.

I wished I could scream or signal to him that I needed help. I knew there was no guarantee he would rescue me. It would be worth a try, though, wouldn't it?

The group made it seem as if I'd chosen to be here with them. They spread out and walked as one unit now, keeping me directly in the middle. Julia stopped abruptly and spread her towel onto the sand, claiming a random spot off to the side. Everyone else followed suit and the conversation flowed easily between them while they set up camp and passed around plastic cups that Beau was filling with beer from the small keg he had carried in.

The weather was colder this close to the water and wasn't ideal for a day at the beach, making the scene before me feel even more off. The sky was overcast in gray and heavy clouds hung low, threatening to open themselves up to us. I watched my captors motionlessly, unsure what my next move should be.

I wouldn't doubt that based on how difficult it had become for all of them to walk, I had a good chance of escaping if I made a quick break for it. The only problem would be navigating the woods. I think if I found the road again, I'd be able to get back into town quickly and find someone to help me. Maybe Remy would witness my escape and realize something was off.

But would he care?

It was a silly, desperate thought. If he knew what I was to him, he'd hunt me down himself. I'm sure he was far more dangerous for me than any of these people combined. Yet somehow, he was the only witness to this horrible twist of fate.

My only hope.

"So, New Girl. Tell us what makes you so special. Everyone seems to be in an uproar over you being here," Julia slurred, interrupting my trailing thoughts.

Everyone besides Beau had formed a circle around me on their towels while I stood in the middle of them. The beer she was holding sloshed around in her hand as she swayed, spilling onto her legs and towel without her even realizing it.

"I don't know," I answered honestly, afraid to say something that might get her even more riled up. She was too unpredictable to argue with right now.

One of the nameless girls let out a sardonic laugh, lifting her beer to her lips as she peered at me over the cup. Her nude bikini left little to the imagination and when she leaned back onto her elbows, Beau and the other guy openly stared.

"Come on now, that can't be true," Julia purred. "You've clearly got a huge ego, thinking you're too good to make time for us. I'm sure you love talking about yourself. Tell us where you're from."

"Just leave her alone, Julia. Don't you think you've taken this far enough?" the girl with black hair braved.

I wished I remembered her name. I wished I remembered all their names, so I could try to appeal to at least one of them. To beg for them to let me go before this went any farther.

Julia glared at the girl, and they locked into a stare-off. The others shifted uncomfortably for a moment before attempting to make conversation with each other to avoid the tension between the two girls. The exchange seemed familiar to them, and they handled the quiet argument that erupted between their friends with ease, not bothering to get involved.

Each of them was so distracted with the drama that they'd left the perfect opening for me to run. In a split second, I made the choice.

My feet carried me over their towels and through the sand easily, until Beau took one step toward me, reached out and swung something at the back of my head.

With a crack and a grunt, I fell to the ground and the gray skies filled my vision until they slowly faded into black.

CHAPTER TWENTY

STORIE

I woke up to his familiar scent filling my nose. A mix of warm, fresh air with a salty sting from the sea. My lids felt like they were weighed down by mounds of sand. It took a moment for me to pry them open and survey my surroundings. I tried to sit up and was met with a jackhammer pounding into the back of my head.

Leaning back into the pillow, my hands fell to my sides and grasped the soft comforter that my body was tightly tucked into, melting into it like warm butter. I noted the dark blue and white plaid pattern and immediately recognized where I'd seen it before.

I was in Remy's room.

"There's a glass of water on the night table beside you and some ibuprofen in case you've got a headache," his voice softly cooed from somewhere near the end of the bed.

I looked over at the table, and sure enough, a tall glass of ice water was there with a metal straw sticking out and condensation dripping down the sides. My tongue slowly ran over my lips as I fantasized about gulping the entire thing down at once, but I knew my body wouldn't allow me to sit up to drink the glass myself, and I was too embarrassed to ask him for any more help.

Based on my lack of clothes beneath the blanket, he had already helped me enough.

Remy must have taken notice of my desperate fantasy though, because without a word, he stood from wherever he was sitting and walked to the side of the bed to grab the glass. He held it over the bed for me and our eyes locked in on each other. After a few seconds of me entertaining my stubborn pride, I leaned over and took a long drink from the straw.

"You've been out for a solid twenty-four hours," he explained as he set down the glass. "I was going to call Tabitha if you didn't come to in the next hour. I probably should have called her hours ago, but I needed to ask you what happened without an audience."

He peered down at me expectantly, waiting for an explanation that I wasn't sure I had.

"They were on something," I found myself saying through a thick, raw throat. I don't know why my first instinct was to defend the people who attacked me. It just seemed like something he should know before jumping into anything. Not that I thought he'd care enough to punish them, but I was sure someone did.

"And why did you end up out here alone with them? Were you going to take whatever they were on?"

"What? No." I shook my head and the jackhammer started up again. Tightly closing my eyes to stop the pain, I continued, "They threw me in their van and drove us out here. Julia said something about her mom wanting to know more about me and it always being the Rists and the Winters. I don't know. She wasn't making a ton of sense."

I felt the bed sink down beside me under his weight and when I could open my eyes again, he was watching me with a confused scowl. He was trying to make sense out of a nonsensical situation, and it was driving him crazy.

"Where are my clothes?" I asked, tugging the blanket farther up my exposed chest. Even my underwear was missing.

If Remy noticed my discomfort, he didn't bother doing anything to make me feel better. He just absent-mindedly pointed to the dresser across the room where my clothes had been neatly folded and stacked.

"I couldn't get the blood out. I'm sure if I asked one of the housekeepers for help, they could have done it, but I didn't want to risk anyone knowing you're here," he rambled, then stood from the bed to grab the pile and set it on the nightstand. He took a seat beside me again.

I reached my hand behind my head and felt around for the cut that was surely there after Beau clogged me.

"There's nothing there," Remy said in bewilderment. "I've looked multiple times."

"Then where did the blood come from?" I asked, raking my fingers through my hardened, matted hair.

Remy shrugged his shoulders and shook his head in confusion. "I was going to treat the wound when I brought you in here. It's like it healed itself."

"It... healed itself?"

That wasn't possible. I knew it.

Maybe I just wasn't injured that bad.

But why else would my head be pounding and covered in dried blood?

He rapped against his leg. "Storie, I'm going to make this right. They shouldn't have come anywhere near you, especially over something that's between my family and Julia's."

His fingers brushed my arm, sending that familiar shock into my core in the way only his touch could do. The aching in my head ceased immediately and I stared down at his hand in complete surprise.

He didn't pull away at my reaction, though. As if the contact gave him a sense of courage he'd been missing before, he watched my face change as the soft pads of his fingers slowly trailed up my arm, leaving goosebumps in their wake. I sighed, hating the way he made me feel with the smallest amount of effort.

He reached my shoulders and then turned around, moving his hand farther inside my arm to also brush against the blanket and my torso underneath. It was the most sensual, torturous thing I'd ever experienced in my life. Even worse than when he kissed me, because this was so innocent yet sinful at the same time.

I wanted to swat his hand away and pull it under the blankets with me so he could explore every other part of me.

I wanted him to quicken his pace and stop at the same time.

He left my mind in such a jumbled mess, I couldn't control my own actions.

I felt like putty in his large, capable hands. All I wanted him to do was gently caress me. To sculpt me into whatever he wanted so long as his skin never left mine and the buzzing between us never ended.

A soft, mortifying moan escaped my lips and he paused, glaring down at me. I wanted to scream. I hated myself for allowing my body to react in such an embarrassing way. That I craved the touch of my enemy so deeply, even my bones ached for it.

"I've never done this," I admitted through a bated breath.

After a few weighted seconds where I contemplated throwing every ounce of pride I had out the window and begging him to torture me just a little while longer, his hands moved to the top of the blanket and pulled it down, exposing my naked body to the cool, ocean air.

I resisted the urge to fold my arms over my chest and cover myself up. I'm not sure what possessed me to sit still under his gaze and allow those deep, deadly eyes to slowly drink my imperfect body in.

My admission still hung in the air between us as he slowly considered me. A soft nagging in my mind told me I should still be embarrassed, but I refused to give it life.

It was almost as if the knowledge that he was so dangerous brought out this side of me that wanted to test him. To see how far we could take this before someone got hurt.

My arm slid across the velvet sheets until my nails scraped against his jeans. I tugged at the material, bravely asking him to expose himself to me the same way. To make this horrible mistake into a mutual decision.

With a low rumble in his throat, he leaned into me and cupped his hand on my jaw, his face hovering just above mine. I could feel his breath on my lips and couldn't stand the teasing anymore. When he didn't make a move, I opened my mouth the slightest bit and leaned forward into the space left between us. Then, throwing all caution to the wind, I sucked his bottom lip between mine and bit down.

That was all the permission he needed. In a frenzy of rushed movements, he managed to hop into the bed and place his body between my naked thighs, rubbing himself against my damp center with the rough denim material of his jeans. I could feel every hard part of him as it pressed into me.

I watched him through my lashes and was somehow met with an even deeper, darker black than usual. His gaze burned into me like molten lava pouring onto my skin, and I welcomed the pain it incited. Featherlight kisses trailed my cheek and neck as he slowly tortured me—playing with my patience as if it were something to be tested.

When he journeyed back to my mouth, he nibbled at my swollen lip the way I had done to his before, then he replaced the playful nipping with a slow, tentative kiss. We took our time finding the perfect fit while he allowed my hands to explore the taut, toned muscles of his torso beneath his thin cotton shirt.

His arms were braced above my head, holding the top half of his body up so that he didn't crush me. When he shifted a little to reach his tongue deeper into my mouth, his stiffened erection pressed harder against me, and another moan left my lips. I could feel his smile against my mouth just before he thrust himself against me once more, nearly sending my head spinning into the next galaxy with the simplest movement.

Without warning, he shifted onto one arm and snaked the other between us. I felt his fingers against my slick slit and jumped, sending them just a little farther into me. He chuckled against my mouth, then pressed one finger into the perfect spot. That was all it took. I couldn't stop myself from unraveling beneath him as he rubbed and caressed me in ways no man had ever attempted before. All the while his warm mouth stayed connected with mine, intensifying the stimulation.

It was embarrassingly quick, but shame had no place in our tiny bubble. I waited for the negative feelings to come crashing into my chest, reminding me what a mistake this was.

They never did.

Once I was thoroughly satiated, Remy rolled over and settled into the spot beside me. We simply stared into each other's eyes—me completely naked and him fully clothed and soaked in my juices—exchanging the secrets we knew our mouths could never share.

"They're going to pay for what they've done," he promised.

I didn't have it in me to discourage him. The earnest expression he wore told me there was no way I'd be able to stop him anyway.

CHAPTER TWENTY-ONE

STORIE

When I arrived back at the hotel, I stopped by the office to tell Blaire and Tabitha that I was still alive and to check in with them. As soon as she saw me, Blaire jumped out of the office chair and wrapped her arms around my neck in a tight hug. My hands awkwardly patted her back until she pulled away with her hands still gripping my shoulders. Her expression turned horrified when she scanned my bloodstained clothes and matted hair.

"Where have you been?"

"It's a long story."

"Well, I've got time. Have a seat." She pulled one of the chairs lined against the wall up to the desk and took a seat on the opposite side.

After what happened to me in the past two days, I wasn't sure if I could trust anyone in Beacon Grove anymore. Not that Julia had ever proved to be a person I was interested in befriending, but she and her friends appeared to be harmless and my miscalculation about them nearly cost me my life. I wanted to trust Blaire, though. I wanted to share what happened with someone who wasn't involved in any way. Eventually, that won out over every hesitation I had.

"Julia and her friends," I said on a sigh when I fell into the chair.

"What did they do? You look like you've crawled out of a grave." I shot her a sarcastic scowl and she laughed, shrugging her shoulders unapologetically.

I peered out of the windows of the office and dropped my voice in case we were overheard. "It was really weird. They threw me into a van and took me to the Wilde's beach. All of them seemed to be on some kind of drug. They were acting pretty out of it, especially Julia. She was saying things about the Winters and the Rists always being connected and that it was supposed to be her." Blaire scrunched her nose and tilted her head, equally confused by that as I was. "Then, I saw an opportunity to run and the big one hit me over the head."

Her gasp filled the quiet room, the same look of horror returning. "Beau? He's like a teddy bear."

I shook my head. "Well, he was more like a grizzly bear."

"What happened then?" Glowing green eyes widened in interest.

I paused, considering her for a moment. Telling Blaire about what happened with Remy might lead her onto the path of realizing I was his Counter.

Why else would he have cared if I washed away with the tide that day?

Then again, if my instincts were correct and we were somehow connected in that way, why wouldn't he have just let me die out there? Wouldn't that make his life a lot easier?

"Well, I'm not super clear on what happened after that," I admitted. My eyes fell to my wringing hands as I went back and forth over telling her. Finally, my lips began moving. "I woke up in Remy Winters room with no injuries. Just some blood-soaked clothes and a rat's nest on the top of my head."

A noise in the kitchen stopped her from responding. I wondered if Tabitha heard any part of our conversation. If she had, I wouldn't doubt that she'd be in here chastising me over being so stupid.

Still, I didn't want to risk the rest of our conversation being overheard. Blaire seemed to catch on to that because she raised her finger to her lips and signaled that we'd continue talking later. I nodded my agreement and dragged my chair back to its home along the wall, then waved goodbye and headed to my room.

CHAPTER TWENTY-TWO

STORIE

I t only took a few days of recovery from my attack in private before I was pacing the perimeter of my hotel room. The caged feeling reminded me of all the times I felt this way with Aunt Ash during our time in hiding and how she always seemed to have a solution for it. Back then, I had no idea that there were real threats lingering just outside of every door of the places we stayed in. That we were being hunted and it was only a matter of time before we'd be found.

Now, I knew exactly how she felt. I only wished I could go back in time and apologize for making everything so difficult for her. To thank her for every minute of her life that she spent sacrificing her safety and mental health for an ungrateful me.

While that wasn't a plausible answer, gaining more information surrounding her death was. I decided to use the number Hazel gave me and make an appointment with my maternal grandmother. She may not know much about Aunt Ash, but there was a possibility she could open up a new door to look behind.

L unet's home was buried inside the maze of residential streets in Beacon Grove. I'd nearly gotten lost multiple times. My GPS refused to work this far away from the town's square, so I was stuck relying on her nurse's vague instructions that I scribbled on a piece of paper as she rattled them off over the phone.

When I pulled into the driveway, I recognized the house right away. It was the same one in the photos Hazel showed me. Time had sunk its claws into it, wearing it down quite a bit since the photo was taken, but it stood proudly amongst the rest of the homes surrounding it that had been taken better care of.

I wanted to take my time admiring it but was hardly out of my car when a tall woman opened the front door and greeted me from the large, wrap-around porch. "She's been practically bouncing off the walls all morning waiting for you," she called out through a smile.

She introduced herself as Mary, Lunet's live-in nurse who I'd spoken to over the phone, as she led me through the foyer and into a sitting room off to the left. The interior of the house was as outdated as the exterior and held that dusky, stale scent that always seemed to linger in the homes of the elderly. Mary offered me a seat on one of the sitting chairs covered in red lighthouses and left me alone to grab Lunet from her bedroom.

I glanced around the small room and felt an overwhelming amount of emotions wash through me. I'd never been as close to my mother as I'd gotten since entering Beacon Grove. My plan was to get answers about my father and Aunt Ash's deaths, but I hadn't even considered the possibility of learning more about the woman who gave her life to bring me into this world. It was such an unexpected gift.

My eyes swung from the red brick fireplace to the opposite side of the room, through the glass French doors leading back into the foyer. My mother had walked these narrow halls once, passing by the old photos littering the walls in various frames. Her feet padded on these hardwood floors each time she entered or left her home. If my suspicions were correct and the furnishings in the home haven't been updated, she could have sat in this very chair, once upon a time.

It was almost like I could feel the ghost of her beside me. See the past versions of her casually strutting through her home as if she had all the time in the world.

"There you go, nice and slow," Mary's voice released me from my thoughts as she helped the old woman into the room. She guided her over to the maroon loveseat across from me and helped her lower herself into it.

As soon as my eyes met with hers, my lungs tightened in my chest. I recognized her immediately as the woman from the festival. The same one Tabitha practically beat me away from. The cloudiness of her eyes had somehow disappeared, but I was certain it was her.

"I'm so glad you've come," Lunet's strong voice greeted.

I knew from Hazel that she was elderly, and based on the way she had to be helped in, I expected her to be much more frail. But as soon as Mary got her settled in and left us alone to talk, Lunet straightened up and spoke as if she was full of energy.

"I wasn't expecting to see you again after the way Tabitha pushed you away," she went on, leaning over to the coffee table between us to pour herself a cup of tea from the kettle Mary had just carried in.

With no true reference aside from the few photos Hazel shared with me, it was difficult to draw a connection between the woman before me and my mother. They shared the same dramatic cupid's bow on their lips and her aging eyes appeared to be in the same almond shape as the ones I saw on my mother. I wondered if she'd been able to age beyond her twenties, would she look more similar to the lady before me?

"I'm so sorry about that. I had no idea-" I began, but Lunet lifted a finger in the air to stop me.

"It's not your fault. Tabitha has her own secrets to protect."

Wasn't that the truth?

"I assume you're here to find out more about the gift."

I cleared my throat. "The gift? No, I'm just curious about my mother. I had no idea she still had any living relatives." I reached out to grab the teacup from her hands when she lifted it into the air toward me, whispering my thanks.

"Yes, isn't that something? Those Graves always had a way of poisoning everything they touched." Thin, weathered lips stuck out in a pout. She set her cup down onto its saucer and leaned back into the couch.

"What do you mean?"

"I warned my daughter not to get caught up with those kids. She didn't listen. Now, look where she is."

"With all due respect, it wasn't my father or aunt who killed my mother; it was me."

"Oh, is that what they've got you believing?" She huffed out a sarcastic laugh, her eyes rolling toward the cracked ceiling as the laugh lines tightened around them. "Convenient excuse."

"I don't understand. Are you saying she didn't die during childbirth?"

"No, my love. Bonnie was a true warrior through your birth. Barely made a peep, even when it was obvious the pain was taking over her. She spent five days with you before they came. It was the happiest I'd ever seen her. I even thought that perhaps the Graves boy wasn't so bad after all."

Ignoring the constant digs at my father, I asked, "Before who came?"

"Well, that all depends on who you're asking." She crossed thin, frail arms over her chest and gazed at me with an amused expression. She was enjoying this special form of torture.

I'd only come here for some anecdotal stories about my mother. Maybe to see more photos of her and hear how she was as a child from her mother's point of view. I never expected for my family name to be disgraced and everything I knew about my mother's death to be turned upside-down.

Though, I was quickly learning that was what happened in Beacon Grove.

Its entire foundation was built solely on secrets piled onto more secrets. Did anyone really know the truth?

"I'm not sure what that means," I admitted, shifting in my seat. Her staring had quickly grown uncomfortable.

"Do you remember what I said to you before? At the Mabon festival?"

"Vaguely." Everything from that day had become a blur.

"I told you that you were given an enormous task from the fates. I might not agree with the choices my daughter made or the outcomes they've created, but that doesn't change anything. It's done. You've been chosen for this. Avoiding it is only delaying the inevitable."

I blinked at her.

"Why don't we see what the other side has to say about it? Usually, I'd channel them myself, but this damn town is littered with low entities."

She reached into the tote bag she'd been carrying when Mary brought her in and pulled out a familiar-looking box of tarot cards, her movements slow and labored. I recognized the design from living with Aunt Ash, though I'd never learned how to use them.

It was another thing she tried to show me, but my stubborn mind was already made up; I wasn't going to be a weird witch like her.

She expertly shuffled the deck between her hands, never once fumbling or losing a single card. I could barely handle a regular deck without them flying all over the place, and these were twice as long.

When she noticed me watching, she asked, "I trust the Graves girl at least taught you how to use these? They're a staple in any witch's practice." I shook my head, earning another exasperated eyeroll. "Did they do anything to prepare you?"

"I'm still not sure what they were supposed to be preparing me for."

She lifted a brow and began wordlessly pulling cards from the deck.

The first card she pulled showed a tall building breaking apart. "Ah, the tower. Your life has been upended. You've experienced a great loss and it's left you questioning everything you thought you knew. But change is necessary."

Next, she held up a card with a woman holding two swords. "You've been presented with choices, and you need to weigh all your options before moving forward with a plan. I can see you're trying to avoid the inevitable, just as you've been trained to do, but there is no more time for that. Just be sure your decision aligns with your own path and not someone else's."

The last card she held up looked to be a jester standing on the edge of a cliff. "The fool: a promising card. You've lost a lot, but you're standing on the threshold of something amazing. It's your fate, my love. Don't be afraid to take the leap. You'll be rewarded tremendously."

She set all three cards back down onto the coffee table and gazed at them, tears forming in the edges of her eyes. "My daughter may have made mistakes that led to her leaving us on this plane far too early, but her sacrifice has been rewarded with you. You're going to save us all."

There were those words again. I had no idea what they meant and the tarot reading only confused me even further, though Lunet acted as if the message was clear as day.

"I know this isn't what you came to hear today. There are so many people jumbling your mind with their own lies and agendas; you must feel as if your world has been turned around. You need to trust your own intuition and ignore everything else. It's all background noise." She placed a spotted, ring-clad hand across her heart and tilted her head to the side.

"Come back when you've settled your deal with the fates, and we'll talk about everything you want. You're going to be the key to erasing the darkness looming overhead. For now, you need to focus on that."

She called Mary into the room and asked to retire back upstairs, claiming she was exhausted. I didn't argue and eagerly took the opportunity to leave before she started spouting more nonsense. Mary walked me out and apologized for the abrupt end to what she believed must have been a very pleasant afternoon. I just smiled politely and bid her goodbye, hoping that everything I'd just been told were fabricated tales spun by an old woman losing her mind.

Deep down, I knew I was only fooling myself.

CHAPTER TWENTY-THREE

REMY

When he wasn't downtown, intimidating our coven members, my father spent most of his time in his study. It's where all my lessons took place growing up. He liked to keep it dark and gloomy, always one to use discomfort and intimidation against people as a power move. If you found yourself within those dimly lit, mahogany wood paneled walls, you weren't walking away unscathed.

That was where I found him today. After days of hunting Julia and her friends and failing miserably, I decided to do some digging on what Storie said Julia told her during her attack.

That it had always been the Rists and the Winters.

I knew what it sounded like. It seemed as if Julia was suggesting that her family was somehow intertwined with our Quarter blood. But that didn't follow the narrative our fathers have been spewing at us our entire lives, because if Julia was meant to be my Counter, she wouldn't have lived past a few hours. Right?

"Remington. To what do I owe this unexpected pleasure," my father cooed sarcastically. His hands shifted slightly on the desk as he inconspicuously pushed a piece of paper beneath his desk calendar.

"May I?" I asked, gesturing toward the chair sitting across from him.

He slowly nodded with a tight smile on his lips, and I took a seat on the edge, bracing my arms on the front of his desk.

"I was hoping to get an update on how things are being handled after Mabon."

"An update? There isn't one. You four have proven to be incapable of handling your roles and continue to do so through each training. We're keeping our temporary order in place until we find the improvement we seek."

I bit back my defensive retort, reminding myself that I was here for a reason. "Have you found any more information about our Counters?"

His coal black eyes considered me suspiciously. "If we had, you would be the first to know."

I nodded, leaning back into my chair. "They're the key to ending this, right?"

"I suppose so. There's a lot that goes into being a Quarter, Remington. Frankly, you boys have been simply coasting for a while. It was only a matter of time before it blew up in your faces." He took a drink from the glass of whiskey sitting before him. "As I said before, you should consider yourself lucky to have such supportive elders who are willing to clean up your messes."

He was trying to get under my skin to deflect my questions. I knew that. I just hated that it was working.

I worked my jaw as we locked onto each other's stares, challenging one another. He wanted me to react so that he could claim I attacked him, the same way they all tried to do the night of Mabon. I couldn't give in to him, though. Not when there were so many questions left unanswered and the others were suffering more and more by the day.

"I guess we'll just have to agree to disagree." I raised my brow at him, waiting for his snarky response.

He surprised me by showing the same restraint I had. "What is it you truly want from me? I'm busy."

"The others and I have been digging into the town's blood-lines to scout out any information we can about our Counters," I fibbed. I think Lux and Rhyse may have spent a day in the library on that but couldn't find anything of substance.

His hands tightened into fists before he dropped them to his lap. "And?"

"There appeared to be a correlation between births in the Rist family and ours." I paused and watched him carefully for a reaction before continuing. "Each time a firstborn Quarter was birthed into the family, the Rists had a child of their own."

"What are you suggesting? That the housekeeper is your Counter?" he mocked. He was trying his best to appear unaf-fected, but I saw the anger flash across his eyes for a split second. I noted the way his brows pinned together and the left side of his mouth twitched.

That reaction was worth far more than anything else he could possibly offer me on the subject. It told me that I was onto something, and that scared him.

Frankly, it scared me as well.

Could I be wrong about Storie, then?

I chuckled, waving my hand in the air dismissively. "You're right. That sounds ridiculous."

He relaxed into his chair, then attempted to take control of the conversation once again. "Maybe you boys should be focus-ing on how to make the disaster you've created right with your coven, instead of going on wild goose chases."

"That's probably true." My sarcastic tone clearly flew over his head when his lips lifted in a smug smirk as I stood up and walked to the door.

I didn't bother saying goodbye or waiting for him to dismiss me before walking out of his office. The hallway was bright and airy, reminding me that it was still mid-morning. I immediately reached into my pocket for my phone and called the others, telling them to meet me at the library as soon as possible.

I took a detour through the kitchen in an attempt to find Julia, but Marta stood at the sink alone. There had to be consequences for Julia and her friends. The members of Watchtower have grown far too comfortable, acting out in the absence of order that was usually kept in place by our High Priest and Priestess. Yet, the Forbes have taken a back seat on all coven matters and allowed our clown mayor and Rayner to send the town running rampant.

I wanted to know why.

And I wanted to know why Julia targeted Storie. How did the Rists tie in with my family, and what did it mean that where Storie lit my bones on fire every time she was near, Julia had barely made an impression on me before any of this?

"What are we supposed to be looking for?" Enzo asked as I rifled through the town's old birth records.

"I don't know, exactly. The Rists have practically been our housekeepers since the beginning of time. Maybe try to find the records for anyone your family keeps under their employ. We can sort through them from there."

"This seems like a lot of work for a hunch," Rhyse whined.

"It's not a hunch. I'm telling you, my dad tensed up the minute I brought them up."

"What even made you think to mention them?" Lux asked. He was the only one kneeled on the ground beside me pulling out files.

I paused, unsure of how much I wanted to share. It wasn't possible to tell them what Julia had done without admitting what happened after with Storie and that I thought she might be my Counter. That we'd spent more time together in the past few days than I was able to tolerate spending with anyone else in years.

"Julia said some weird stuff about our families. I figured anything was worth exploring, especially after my dad acted so cagey when I mentioned finding our Counters."

It was only half a lie.

"That was a lucky shot." Lux eyed me doubtfully, but still continued with his task.

Enzo and Rhyse finally began sifting through the files on the top shelves, and within an hour, we had every birth record of every person our families employed spread out across three tables.

"This is insane," Rhyse muttered in disbelief as we compared their records with our own.

The Bishops, Foleys, Whittles, and Rists were all employed with our families since they came to Beacon Grove. Coincidentally, each family produced a child at the same time the Quarters produced their heirs.

I somehow stumbled into the truth without even realizing it.

"The correlations end with our fathers, though," Lux pointed out. He had written down each Quarter's name and their corresponding employee's birth as we discovered them.

"Yeah, something changed with their generation," Enzo agreed. "But what? These bloodlines must stretch back at least two hundred years. What could cause such a huge shift?"

I was worried that our new discovery would prove me wrong about Storie. It wasn't that I wanted her to be my Counter, but if she wasn't, then that would mean there was some other reason we were so drawn to each other.

Instead, these files only pushed me further in the direction of proving my theory to be correct. That would also explain why Julia was so hostile toward her. She wanted to know why her family role was stripped away.

"These are useful, but they only lead to more questions," Rhyse said in a defeated sigh.

"It's more than we had three hours ago," Lux pointed out.

"It's more than we've had in a while," I added just as the sour-faced librarian approached us.

"The library's closed. You should have had these cleaned up and put away already," she barked, scowling as her withered eyes scanned the stack of files. When she noted the names on the labels, she squinted at us accusingly. Without another word, she slowly turned her back to us and hobbled down the stairs.

"That was weird," Enzo voiced the rest of our thoughts aloud.

We made fast work of getting the files reorganized and replacing them to their homes in the large filing cabinets. Esther glared at us over the tall counter she sat behind in contempt when we made it to the bottom of the stairs twenty minutes later, and her beady eyes followed us unblinkingly until we were out the doors.

It wasn't until we parted ways and Rhyse and Enzo were nearly to their cars when Lux grabbed my shoulder and stopped me.

"Why do I have a feeling this is about the Graves girl?"

"I don't know." There was no use lying to Lux. He had a gift of discerning the truth and insulting him with a lie would only betray his trust.

It seemed our trust in each other was all we could be sure of anymore.

"Remy, we're in the middle of a war. The four of us are all we've got, and if we don't have honesty between us, then we've already lost." His icy blue eyes considered me for a moment, daring me to lie again.

I wouldn't. But I also couldn't share the full truth.

"She's a huge piece of the puzzle," I vaguely admitted.

My eyes did a sweep of our surroundings to make sure no one was trying to listen to our conversation. Beacon Grove was becoming one of the worst places to have conversations like this anymore, especially with so many joining the movement against us.

Lux shook his head slowly, taking his time to consider my words. "I trust you. But they won't be so forgiving if she ends up being our downfall and we learn that you allowed it to happen."

His arm raised in the direction that Rhyse and Enzo left in. Their cars were long gone, but I got the point.

"Nothing I do will ever intentionally put you guys in harm's way. I'm just trying to find a way to end this," I assured earnestly.

I truly believed Storie was the key to freeing us from whatever was holding us down. We've trodden water for so long, we weren't prepared for the storm when it came and washed us up. I knew the others would struggle with placing their confidence in a complete stranger, especially one that could potentially be a Counter. But that was why I was keeping them out of it.

THE ✳ BEACON

15 OCTOBER 2021

DISAPPEARANCES OF YOUNG LOCAL WOMEN SPARKS OUTCRY OVER BEACON GROVE'S SAFETY

Police are now searching for the newest victim in the Beacon Grove disappearances. Charlotte Jones, 21, has been reported missing by her family after she didn't return home, following her closing shift at A Cut Above hair salon last night.

"It's not like her to just not show up after work without telling us first. She knows how much we worry," Jones' mother, Caroline, says in an exclusive Beacon interview.

Jones is the fifth young female to disappear into thin air in recent weeks. Locals are now speculating about who might be hunting these women. They believe that anyone between the ages of 21 and 27 is specifically being targeted.

Officer Kyle Abbot claims the Beacon Grove police department has got the situation under control but did warn that anyone who matches the criteria of the five victims, "might want to travel in groups and avoid being alone at night," until they can gain more information about the kidnappers.

Some are accusing the recently ostracized Quarters of hunting women in a desperate attempt to find their Counters. It's rumored that the Quarter elders have temporarily taken over their son's roles after the failed Mabon celebration. Locals speculate that once the Quarters find and eliminate their Counters, they'll be allowed to resume their positions.

"I wouldn't put it past them. I caught the four of them huddled together over the town's birth records," says Esther Newberry, Beacon Grove's beloved librarian.

The Jones family is pleading with neighbors to come forward with any information that might lead to finding their youngest daughter. "We just want our little girl back home."

CHAPTER TWENTY-FOUR

STORIE

There was a darkness settling over Beacon Grove. It was thick and unforgiving, bleeding into every aspect of the lives of the people inside. Gray clouds seem to have taken residency over the densely wooded area and the sky behind them was dull and colorless. The rain maintained a steady flow for days straight, only offering short reprieves before starting up again. The ocean had darkened, wide waves slowly rolling into shore with a silent warning.

And everyone seemed to be in a foul, miserable mood.

Even as an outsider, I could feel the effects.

"Another girl is missing. This time, it's the Jones' youngest." Tabitha folded The Beacon and set it down on the table to take a bite of her oatmeal.

"How many does that make now?" Blaire poured coffee into two glasses and walked them over to the table, sliding one over to me.

Once again, I just missed Callista. Blaire said she was busy at the pharmacy lately, curing more illness than usual for this time of year.

"Five. They're trying to instill fear."

"Who?" I wondered absently, pouring a spoonful of sugar into my cup. Blaire was terrible at making coffee, but it was still preferable to what was offered in my room.

Tabitha didn't bother looking up from her meal when she answered, "The Movement."

"Grammy thinks they're trying to frame the Quarters." Blaire shook her head at the old woman, a smile teasing her lips.

"One day, you're going to learn to listen to me, girl." Tabitha's tone didn't sound like she was offended or hurt, just annoyed. Always annoyed when it came to Blaire.

"Sorry, Grammy. It just doesn't seem likely. Why would they kidnap local young girls when they're trying to appeal to the townspeople? It seems counterproductive. The Quarters are more believable suspects."

Tabitha's fist slammed onto the table, spilling coffee over the edges of our cups. Blaire and I jumped, and she mumbled something under her breath, then turned her glowing grenades toward Blaire, finally giving her full attention to the conversation.

"You need to smarten up. That's exactly what they want you to think and you're falling prey like a brainless sheep being led to slaughter."

"It's just common sense," Blaire mumbled into her lap. "The Quarters need to find their Counters if they want to keep their gift. Even The Beacon says that all the girls who have gone missing fit the criteria."

Tabitha stood from her chair and threw the empty oatmeal bowl into the sink, nearly shattering the white ceramic. "We're not discussing this anymore."

Blaire didn't argue. We both watched her walk out of the kitchen with wide eyes and held our breaths until we heard the wooden door to the hotel office slam shut.

"She's losing it," Blaire declared once again, repeating the same words I've heard her utter multiple times now.

I didn't think Tabitha was as far out of her mind as Blaire always insisted. But I couldn't defend the Quarters without explaining that I'd been regularly spending most of my time with one of them, and I wasn't ready to admit that to Blaire just yet. Whatever Remy and I shared felt too sacred to gossip about with my friend like a giggling schoolgirl.

Instead, I went another route. "I think the Movement has proven to be pretty desperate in their attempts to get people on their side. Is it really that much of a stretch to think they're just trying to turn more people against the Quarters and their families?"

Blaire scoffed. "Come on. Not you, too."

"I'm just saying. From the outside looking in, you're all being played from both sides."

"Can you really say you're on the outside anymore? You've been here for almost two months with no plans to leave."

Of course, she had me there.

"Are you getting sick of me, Red?" I joked, ignoring the urge to cringe.

My intention was never to stay this long. Even without anticipating the constant secrecy and roadblocks that stood in my way, I should have been out of here a long time ago. Ideally, getting my career started and finding my footing in a new life without Aunt Ash. I'd barely allowed myself time to mourn her loss before taking all my savings and diving deep into the world of Beacon Grove.

Still, something told me it wasn't time for me to leave. I've only scratched the surface when it came to my mother's past, and it felt wrong leaving things with Remy open ended the way that they were. After what Julia and her friends pulled and the intimacy we shared following it, we were spending nearly every free moment we had together. It had only been about a week, but it felt like our souls have known each other for a lifetime.

I supposed I needed to sit down and think about how long I'd realistically be stuck here and make a plan based on that.

"Never. You're the only person here who doesn't treat me like the dirt on the bottom of their shoe."

She busied her hands with cleaning up our spilled coffee cups to hide the emotion in her face. I could sense it, though. Even the way she carried herself across the kitchen was heavy and slow. Depressed.

"If there's one thing I've learned about this place, it's that the people here don't know how to value a good thing when they see it. You shine too bright for them, Blaire. They don't know what to do with that."

Her and Remy were sorely taken advantage of. I'd only known each of them for a handful of weeks and they'd both added more value to my life than anyone else, filling the void that was left by my aunt and father. People like Julia and her odd friends may have seemed like the obvious choice to befriend, but they had no substance. They were empty shells, reaching their peak in a town that most of the rest of the world had no idea even existed.

I remembered something Remy had said to me the last time we were together. We were sitting together on his balcony and he was explaining how his gifts worked with the underworld to me as if it were simply the next town over.

"So, you can see people who have passed?" I asked in disbelief. I'd give so much to be able to speak to my parents or Aunt Ash, and he was talking about it so casually.

"Kind of. I can visit their souls once they've reached the other side."

"Then, you can see my parents?"

"Probably. If I wanted to."

An idea rolled around in my head then. I considered whether or not I should even voice it to him. I still hadn't revealed much to Remy about myself or what I'd found while researching my family. It wasn't that I didn't trust him, per se. I just didn't know what he would do if he knew I was a Counter. Eventually, I just threw it out there. "And you can ask them how they really died?"

He shook his head, his face holding that serious mask it always had as he thought of how to explain it to me. "It's not really like that. Souls that have passed into the spirit world don't dwell on their time here in the physical world. To them, we're just the meat suits that they use to evolve into the next level of vibrations."

Meat suits. *That was a disturbing thought.*

"Oh," I said dejectedly. "So, they aren't really around me like everyone always says?" I felt like a child being told Santa Clause isn't real. Of course, they didn't watch over me.

"No, it's not like that. They know what they signed up for when they came into our world—even their untimely deaths. Each lifetime that a soul chooses to take on is meant to teach them a valuable lesson and help them grow."

When that didn't appear to make me feel any better, he went on.

"For example, if a soul needs to work on their ability to forgive, then they'll spend a physical lifetime being wronged over and over. But when they get back into the spirit world, they let go of all that negativity because they know it served a purpose and brought them closer to the gods. The spirit world is filled with love and light. They know that your journey is different from theirs and they still miss you. They just know you'll return soon enough."

"How do you know all this?"

"I don't know. I've spent a lot of time there."

I'd originally taken offense to the term he used to describe us—meat suits. But now, I could see what he meant. Some of the people in Beacon Grove truly lived up to the disgusting concept of being a meat suit. Those were the ones that didn't appreciate the amazing souls they were sharing their existence with.

The sheep.

"Thank you," Blaire's voice pulled me from the memory, thick with emotion. "I know you don't really like it here, but I'm so grateful you stumbled into our little town."

My arms pulled her into a hug, squeezing tight so she knew exactly how much her words meant to me. I never imagined that on the path to finding out more about my family, I'd find a true friend.

CHAPTER TWENTY-FIVE

STORIE

B eacon Grove was having yet another town meeting. I was under the impression when I first arrived that these meetings were only held once a month, but it appeared the townspeople couldn't seem to get enough of each other. That, and everyone wanted to get their opinions voiced about the incidents that occurred over the past few weeks.

As a business owner, Tabitha was obligated to attend. She griped and grumbled the whole way there, making no effort to keep down her insults about the people she shared a home with in Beacon Grove.

Blaire had been more than willing to attend, and I had nothing better to do since I'd hit a dead end on finding any more information about my family. Besides, any opportunity to learn more about Rayner and his agenda with the Movement was more than enough of an excuse for me.

"Young women don't just disappear without a trace. Someone is hunting them, and I think we all know who."

A few people rolled their eyes at Rayner's dramatics, while others looked terrified at his words.

"Rayner," the mayor warned in an exasperated sigh.

His forehead now rested on one chubby hand, the other holding the gavel that had proven to be useless in silencing the crowd. It took all of ten minutes for him to lose control of the meeting.

Officer Kyle stood to his right with his hand firmly planted on his gun. I assumed he was there to discourage the crowd from getting too aggressive, but they ignored him just as easily as they had the mayor.

"Mayor Douglas, don't you think the families of these young women deserve to have every possibility explored?"

"Of course, I do. That doesn't mean we can accuse those boys of a crime when there's no evidence pointing to them."

"Come on, Mayor. Mabon proved that their powers are weakening, and their families are searching for the Counters responsible."

The room boomed with conflicting thoughts, half agreeing with Rayner and the other half defending the Quarters.

"We should find the Counters ourselves and eliminate the problem at the source," I heard one man grumble. His words gave me pause and stopped my heart from skipping a beat, especially when the few around him mumbled their agreements.

I knew the Quarters were a danger to Counters—trained in eliminating the threat that they believed Counters were to them. But I hadn't considered the possibility of their followers being willing to do the work for them.

Mayor Douglas slammed his gavel and demanded the room's silence. Tabitha and Blaire stayed quiet, observing the chaos with pure amusement. Slowly, the noise died down as friends and neighbors quieted their individual arguments.

"This is insane," Blaire commented beside me.

"Now, that's enough!" Mayor Douglas shouted at the buzzing crowd before him. "We've gathered here to work to-gether as a community and help bring these girls home. They are our neighbors. Their families are our friends. This isn't the time to point fingers and place blame. We have a full staff of police who are doing their jobs and investigating. Rayner, you cannot keep using these town meetings to push your political agenda on everyone. One more outburst, and you'll be banned from attending town meetings for the foreseeable future."

Rayner blanched, placing his hand on his chest in a clearly theatrical attempt to look offended. "Do you see this? Now, we're being silenced for speaking against the almighty Quarters."

The room went crazy again, and this time, Mayor Douglas didn't even attempt to calm it. He simply rolled his eyes and walked off the stage, leaving his constituents to fight it out. Officer Kyle followed closely behind, returning his eyes to the crowd every few seconds. Blaire grabbed my wrist and jerked her head toward the door, where Tabitha was already walking out.

"They can't seriously think the Quarters are behind all of those disappearances, can they?" I wondered aloud. But I realized that I had my own doubts about them, too.

I knew Remy was a Quarter and my first instinct upon finding out was that he wanted to kill me for possibly being a Counter. I still wasn't sure what his intentions were, or why he chose to open himself up to me, but I didn't think he was capable of kidnapping innocent girls.

"They'll grasp onto any theory that makes enough sense in their minds," Tabitha said, still walking at least two steps ahead of us.

I glanced over at Blaire beside me, realizing she hadn't said anything yet. Sometime between our breakfast the other day and now, she'd completely changed her opinion about the girls' disappearances and who was behind them. I assumed that Tabitha got into her head about it, but I was curious to know what she could have said to do so.

She kept her eyes to the ground, her brows pinched tightly together in a scowl. It was unlike her to not have anything to say. Did she think she could be considered next as a victim?

We paused at the entrance to the hotel, but Blaire walked past me and Tabitha, ripping open the office door and disappearing inside before we could say anything.

"What's wrong with her?" I mindlessly asked, not expecting an answer.

"She's afraid. You should be too," the old woman grumbled.

"Why should we be afraid? Are you saying it *is* the Quarters?"

My thoughts fell to Remy and how none of this made any sense. He wasn't capable of hurting anyone. He didn't even want his powers. In fact, he should be warned that the town was turning against him.

As always, Tabitha didn't show any indication of what she truly felt, and I hadn't expected her to. I figured she'd offer a vague response and leave without an explanation.

Instead, she surprised me by waving her hand and saying, "Come. We need to talk."

She led me into a study down the hall from Blaire's room that I hadn't seen before. When we passed Blaire's closed door, I could hear music blasting through her speakers. I've never seen her shut down like this, though I knew Tabitha wouldn't provide any more insight.

She took a seat in one of the two brown leather recliners placed on either side of the room. A small, empty coffee table separated them, and the walls were lined with bookshelves that nearly reached the ceiling. The leatherbound books that were nestled inside each shelf looked worn down and older than she did.

There weren't any decorations hung. Nothing to show Tabitha's personality or interests. Just the furniture and the books.

"Your family has been a part of Beacon Grove since the town was created," she began.

I remembered Remy telling me the same thing, though I wasn't sure what that really meant in the grand scheme of things. All of my family was dead.

"Your bloodline has deep ties in this soil and many of us fought to keep it alive. That wasn't an easy task, though. People were hunting the original thirteen. They wanted those lines severed."

"Why?"

"So they could make changes to the town and the coven without any consequences."

She reached over to the shelf on her left and grabbed one of the thick, brown leather books. The cover had a layer of dust coating it and when she opened it up, the parchment looked brittle in her fingers.

"As I'm sure you've realized, our coven relies on our four Quarters to protect us while we practice our magic. Blaire has given you the modern version of their story, but it goes back hundreds of years. Since before our ancestors even stepped foot on American soil."

She turned the book toward me, and an ancient-looking drawing covered the pages.

"It's said they were given their gifts from the gods themselves. That Hecate personally blessed them with the tools they required to protect their coven. But as with any gift that comes from the gods, there was a caveat."

She pointed to an amateur drawing of four figures sketched in black with a compass scribbled in the middle. Each one had a corresponding red figure standing beside it, and the compass was missing its center, as if that part had been erased or scratched off the paper.

"The Quarters were each given counterparts. These were entities that they had to share their power with. Their abilities flowed fluidly through the Quarter and the Counter, so that the burden didn't exhaust the Quarter."

"I don't understand. Why was Rayner saying they wanted to hunt their Counters then?"

"Because the Quarters became greedy over time. They didn't understand why their powers had to be shared at all, and they began looking for ways to cut their Counter off from receiving anything."

"So, they want to have their powers to themselves. That's why they hunt and kill Counters," I deduced.

Tabitha moved her head in an irritated negative shake. "You're getting mixed up with the fables that Blaire told you and the propaganda Rayner spreads around. Listen to me and ignore what you heard before."

"Okay." I was so confused.

"You have to remember, Quarters and Counters have been around for centuries. There has been a lot of time for corruption, and nature doesn't like corruption. Nature likes balance. That's why the Counters were created in the first place, right?"

I nodded.

"The Counter issue has been balanced. That was sorted out ages ago. The current issue is generational, but they don't want you to know that. They want to distract you with old problems, so you don't focus on what they're doing."

None of that made any sense.

"Are you telling me this because I'm a Counter?" I finally asked, exasperated with her talking in circles and confusing code.

Tabitha's singular nod sent my heart dropping into my stomach. This was the first time I've spoken those words out loud. I kept these suspicions to myself for so long, they felt wrong to say. I've wanted someone to confirm them since I first heard Blaire talk about it but now that Tabitha had, I didn't feel any relief.

She pointed to the picture and circled her finger around the figures on the west side of the compass.

"All you need to know is that our current Quarters are not the ones who truly hold the power. They're being taken advantage of and villainized in front of the rest of the coven. I know you've been hanging around with the Winters one. You need to stay away. It isn't safe for you."

"Remy would never hurt me." I was speaking to both her and myself. Maybe if I said the words enough, I could feel confident that they were true.

But Tabitha wasn't convinced. "Those boys have been fed lies by men who want nothing more than to retain their power. They've been raised since birth to hunt you. If he knew what you were to him, he wouldn't think twice about killing you. So long as Counter blood runs through your veins, they will consider you a threat to their position."

Her tone didn't leave room for argument. Honestly, there wasn't anything I could say in his defense. She knew more about everything in this town than I could even fathom as a newcomer. Sure, my family may have helped build it from nothing, but they left before I ever had a chance to learn anything about them. She was the closest thing I had to a family at this point.

All the Grangers were, so why shouldn't I trust her?

"Why did my family leave? Not just my parents and Aunt Ash, but the rest of the Graves. Surely, there were more living here before I came along."

"I've already given you the answer to that. Don't waste our time with silly questions. None of that matters anymore. What matters is that you and the other Counters stay alive, so that our Quarters can fulfill their duties and their fathers stay far away from power. Don't distract that boy any more than you have and don't put your life at risk."

This conversation was reminiscent of the one I had with Aunt Ash after Rayner visited our home and she began her downward spiral.

"This is bigger than you and me, Storie. Don't put your life at risk," she'd said when I fought against dropping out of my dream college to switch to an online one.

It was the final step we took before leaving our home. The one that took the most convincing on her end and the biggest compromise between us. I hadn't wanted to end up like her—a lonely spinster with hardly any career to fall back on besides a small homeopathy and massage therapy business that hardly paid the bills. And I didn't understand the risk she was speaking about.

Hearing Tabitha say the same words triggered emotions in me that I wanted to keep repressed. Negative emotions that I'd felt toward Aunt Ash for stripping my freedoms over something I could have never understood at the time.

But now, I understand. I know why she was so terrified. I know what Rayner was demanding when he threatened her that day. I know the sacrifice she made by not obeying. And I know that she was so much more than I ever gave her credit for.

I wasn't willing to give up my free will to this cause again, though. I wasn't going to continue to hide from a faceless enemy. I came to Beacon Grove to find answers, and now that I had some, I was going to fight for myself.

"Do you understand?" Tabitha pushed when I never responded.

I simply nodded. If she knew my thoughts, she would only try to convince me to change my mind, and that wasn't happening. Now that I'd finally been given some answers, I was only hungrier for more, and I knew just where to find them.

Tabitha didn't look convinced, but she still accepted my nod as an answer and slammed the dusty book shut. I watched her slide it on the shelf and tried to read some of the spines beside it but could only make out one of them. It read: Beacon Grove Birth Records 1997. Just as I began making out the title, Tabitha's plump figure stepped into view.

"That's all you need to see. Now, run along and remember what I told you."

CHAPTER TWENTY-SIX

STORIE

I found him at the beach. It seemed as if he was waiting for me there, his pale colors a beautiful contrast to the onyx sand and navy waters surrounding him. I knew better than to let myself believe such lies. Tabitha may have triggered repressed feelings in me from Aunt Ash, but she knew the Quarters better than I did.

I didn't waste any time with pleasantries. Instead, I shoved The Beacon into his chest, front page facing out. He stumbled back a bit, shocked. We both managed to ignore the pain that sliced through us from the quick brush of his fingers against mine.

"Is this your doing?" I heard my voice demand.

He looked down at the paper pushed against him and sighed, turning his face away from mine like it hurt him that I thought he was capable of what was happening to those innocent girls.

"No."

"You need to tell me the truth if we're going to continue whatever this is between us, Remy. I need to trust you."

"It's not us," he insisted, stepping away from me.

I let the paper fall into the sand at my feet, too distracted by him to even notice. He'd fully turned his back to me and began raking his fingers through his hair.

"I have to tell you something," I finally said after staring at him through a few long beats of silence.

The waves crashed across the water, arching and breaking once they hit the shore. They reached out at us, threatening to soak our feet before retreating back into the ocean. I realized it was almost like the water matched his mood each time we found ourselves out here.

His fingers ceased their attack on his scalp and his arms fell to his sides, waiting. As if he knew what I was about to say and had been dreading it for some time.

"I'm a Counter." The words felt thick on my tongue, a disgusting admission that I wished I never had to make.

"I know."

I blinked owlishly. "What?"

Remy turned to face me again, his expression poignant. "I know you're a Counter. I've known since the first day we met."

That gave me pause. He recognized my confusion and his entire demeanor shifted. A smile teased his lips, as if he were pleased by my ignorance.

"In fact..." he added while his feet closed the distance between us before he lifted his arm and let his hand hover over my cheek for a weighted second. Then without warning, he surprised me by grabbing my jaw and tilting my head up just a little.

"You're mine."

He practically growled the words into my face, his hot breath sending chills straight down my spine. His fingers held onto my jawbone just a tad too tight and when I moved to step away, I watched his brow quirk up and excitement flash across his eyes in challenge. His grip tightened even more, letting me know there was no escape.

All at once, the fear I'd felt toward him in the beginning came rushing back. This unpredictable behavior had always been part of his allure, but he never exercised his strength against me.

"Why didn't you tell me? If you've known all this time, why would you let me believe I was holding onto some dark secret?"

"Because of this." He tugged my face closer to him, and I let out a terrified whimper. "Because I had no idea what you'd do with the fear that it would ignite in you."

"Why not kill me, then? Like you were trained to do."

He released me and shook his head with a shrug. I could see the tortured struggle in his expression. He was unable to find an adequate excuse, and that drove him crazy.

"It just didn't feel right."

My mind raced, remembering every piece of information I'd learned from Tabitha tonight. I had to tell him. We were equally entitled to the truth about who we were and what our purpose was.

"You were right. Keeping me alive is what saved your life."

"How? It seems to have only threatened it even further. My brothers are weakening by the day, and the Movement is turning everyone against us. Killing you would have given me the boost I needed to prove I was a worthy Quarter. I just didn't think you'd make it so impossible."

His voice dropped with the last part as he hung his head. *Shame.* He was feeling humiliated at following his instincts and failing to fulfill the one thing he'd been trained to do.

I wanted to kiss him. The urge to climb his body right then and there and hand myself over to him in gratitude was overwhelming. Imagining the power that would flow through us as we connected with this newfound knowledge on a physical and spiritual level had my heart doing excited somersaults inside my chest.

"You've got it all wrong, Remy."

The crazed smile that took over my face was sure to startle him. My body buzzed with anticipation as I finally realized that I shared this unexplainable feeling with someone else. That while it went against everything I'd ever been told, my instincts told me to place my trust in him and they'd been right all along.

"We're not enemies. I'm your counterpart. I've been created to protect you. We share the same energy."

His throat bobbed and I continued, my arms flailing around us manically.

"Can't you feel it? That undeniable force that seems to be pushing us together isn't just in our imagination. It's in our nature."

I could practically see the gears moving inside his head as he considered what I was saying. He knew it to be true, though he was clearly fighting it. It didn't matter how many people tried conditioning us to believe otherwise—our hearts knew each other.

"How do you know this?"

"Tabitha. She's got all these ancient books and records dating back before Beacon Grove was even created. She warned me that you'd hurt me if you found out what I was, but I knew she was wrong. None of the Quarters are as bad as you're made out to be."

"Tabitha Granger?" He shot me with a disbelieving scowl. "Storie, listen to me. You can't let anyone else know about this, okay? Including the other Quarters. If they find out what we are to each other, they'll eliminate you. You *have* to keep quiet."

"No. That's what I'm saying. Tabitha said the same thing about you, and she was wrong. I'm sure if we told them what we knew, they'd understand, and we'll be able to help them."

Why wasn't he as excited as me? This was monumental. Surely, the Quarters would understand, just as he did.

"They won't. They won't understand and they won't hesitate to kill you. They can't feel the connection we feel." He grabbed my arms and the familiar jolt of electric current shot through my body. "Feel that? That's how I knew you were special to me. How I knew not to hurt you. But they've never experienced this before. They won't get it. Please, tell me you understand."

Desperation like I'd never seen before was marring his perfect face. Even though they turned him against his own kind, he believed his words and he needed me to believe them, too. I finally nodded my agreement, hoping he was wrong.

"Just give me some time to figure out how to tell them. This is huge. I've wanted them to know for a while now, but they're growing hopeless with the Movement closing in on us. I can't have them hurt the only thing that's helped us get by. I can't lose you."

"Okay."

"Okay," he breathed. Large hands slid down my arms and grabbed onto my fingers. The scowl from before finally loosened and I could have sworn I saw the ghost of a smile.

"What else did Tabitha tell you?"

We spent the rest of the night together going over every detail of what we knew so far.

T he sun was just making its debut when he reached his hand over and caressed the bruised spot on my face from where he grabbed it the night before to prove his point. We were sitting on the edge of his bed, facing the ocean as the fresh air wafted around us through the open French doors.

"I'm a danger to you," he softly sighed in self-defeat.

I shook my head vehemently. "No. You're the only place in this town where I feel safe."

"Storie, I've got so many people relying on me to make this right. Even the ones who have lost their trust in us. Especially them. I'm afraid you're going to be put in harm's way over a lie that began way before our time just because people want their sense of normalcy back and they think that's the answer."

I had no idea how to make him see that we were in this together. That without the other, neither of us was truly whole. It's how we were created, our fates intertwined long before we were even a blip in the universe. And no amount of time or distance could ever keep us from finding the other again.

My leg swung over his lap until I was straddling him. The move felt more awkward and unskilled than it had in my head, but I pushed through my insecurities and hesitantly rested my hands on his shoulders to steady myself. His palms found my hips, adjusting me until we were perfectly aligned.

"We've managed to defeat the odds together this long," I whispered into his ear.

I thought of the sacrifices my family members made to keep him from finding me. To keep this entire town from learning what I was and hunting me down. Then, I remembered what Lunet said about making a choice based on intuition and standing on the edge of greatness.

My intuition was screaming that this was the way. *He* was the leap of faith that I needed to take into the unknown, trusting the gods and the universe to catch me.

His mouth was on mine before I could say anything else, and I welcomed the warm humming that his touch erupted inside me. My lips opened up to him, our tongues dancing together like old lovers. Large hands tensed against my hips as I rolled them against his jeans, over the growing ridge that sat perfectly between my legs.

This time, my soft moans didn't fluster or humiliate me. They served as a gentle call for him to continue nibbling on my ears and neck. To remove my sweatshirt and place his lips on my milky breasts. They were permission for him to take this further than before.

And he understood every unspoken request.

Before I knew it, all of our clothes were gone, and he had scooted us further onto the bed so his head could lay on the pillow as he gazed up at me in admiration. My naked body was still straddling him, and his manhood was unashamedly on full display between my legs.

I watched his expression closely as I reached my hand out and gently grabbed him. He was too thick for my fingers to fully wrap around. His length was far greater than anything I imagined could fit inside me, but he felt warm and smooth in my grip.

His expression remained stoic while I explored him, never really changing until he let his lips twitch the slightest amount as I applied a bit of pressure and began moving my fist up and down. I liked the way he felt in my embrace. I reveled in the power I held over his body when I added my other hand and his hips moved against me.

I pumped for a few more minutes before gaining the courage to lean down and run my tongue along the back of his entire length, taking him completely by surprise. He tilted his head to the ceiling and let out a string of curse words and I took that as encouragement to keep going.

With one hand still working the base, I moved my mouth up to his tip and wrapped my lips around it, careful not to let my teeth graze his skin. A light, salty drip landed on my tongue as I opened my mouth further and took him into the back of my throat, suppressing a gag when I went a touch too far.

Remy writhed under me as I moved my head up and down, my tongue circling the tip each time it made a pass while my hand still remained on his base. I picked up speed when I felt him twitching inside my mouth and within seconds, his warm, briny liquid was leaking down my throat. Once the pulsing stopped, I pulled my mouth off and cleaned up the remaining mess with my tongue.

"You said you've never done this before," he rasped. I realized he had propped his head on his arm to watch me, and I blushed at how entranced I'd become to not have noticed.

"I haven't," I agreed.

My self-esteem took a dive when I realized he was probably rationalizing why I'd done such a horrible job. Just when I lifted my leg to slide off him, his hand shot out and wrapped around my thigh. He tugged it back into place beside his hip and those menacing, black eyes glared at me.

"Don't." It was a command.

That same dominant look from last night when he grabbed my chin passed through his eyes and I instantly cowered to it. I relaxed back onto him and crossed my arms over my chest defiantly.

"I haven't done this before, either," he admitted after a few breaths.

I don't know why that surprised me. I knew from the start that Quarters were isolated from the rest of the town, though I supposed after Julia's jealous display, it wasn't too far-fetched of a thought for them to have a crowd of girls desperate for their attention.

They were some of the most unique, attractive men I've ever laid eyes on.

Something about his confession gave me the courage to lean forward and delicately take his lip into my mouth. I suckled and teased, and his breathing sped back up. His hands moved up my sides and pulled me forward until he was placed directly at my entrance. A whimper escaped my mouth and disappeared into his as he pressed against me ever so slightly.

He stared up at me expectantly, asking for permission and encouraging me to make the next move. The passionate fire that was burning in my groin made the decision for me. I lifted myself the tiniest amount and slithered my arm between us to gather him into my hand once again. Then, I lined him up perfectly with my dripping center.

He hissed out a breath at the contact, already rock-hard and busting at the seams.

Slowly, I eased down onto him, and my body stretched and ripped to accommodate his. A sharp exhale released between my lips as I began to fear that I would burst before he was fully inside of me.

His mouth was on mine in an instant, absorbing my soft groans until I finally reached his base and realized I wasn't going to break apart in his arms. We stayed still for a brief second, allowing my insides time to adjust to him before he pulled his hips back into the bed and slid out of me.

My body stilled, frozen in place while he thrust himself back inside over and over. Each time he filled me, the pain became easier to bear, eventually melting into white-hot pleasure as my muscles relaxed and my hips began moving in rhythm with his.

Only a few minutes passed before he completely stilled beneath me, and I felt his muscles spasm against my skin. My stomach coiled at the same time he squeezed my hips.

Watching him on the edge of release with the knowledge that my body had encouraged it for a second time sent a wave of heat straight into my core. My thighs clenched around him, and stars appeared behind my eyes as I pulsed around his thick shaft in pure ecstasy. He thrust himself inside me three more times before lifting me from his cock and spilling himself onto his stomach.

I collapsed onto the bed beside him, my body feeling wrung out and weak. It only took a few seconds for embarrassment to flood my chest when I finally glanced at him and saw the crimson mess that my innocence smeared all over him. He reached for the towel hanging on his bedpost to clean up and my hands intercepted him. They snatched the towel up to wipe it away, but he covered them with his own to stop me.

"Never be ashamed of what just happened. It was perfect. You're perfect."

He leaned over and planted three tender kisses on my lips. His hands released mine and wiped away the remaining evidence of my virginity mixed with his release. Once he finished, he threw the towel over the side of the bed and pulled my body closer to his.

We were asleep within minutes.

CHAPTER TWENTY-SEVEN

STORIE

The Quarters had been villainized by the coven. Each day, more people were joining Rayner and the Movement out of sheer terror over what the future held for them if they continued putting their trust into the four men they felt had failed them the most. Remy never shared much with me about the others, but he had insinuated multiple times that our connection was the only thing keeping him going while the others were fading away.

Rayner was now revered by the townspeople. They greeted him with excitement and respect, hopeful that he would be their guiding light out of some of their darkest times. Even if I hadn't been so close with Remy, I knew better than to believe any of the lies he spewed. I'd seen what he was capable of and the fear he instilled in Aunt Ash from one simple visit filled with deadly threats I still wasn't aware of.

Each time we passed on the streets or found ourselves in the same diner or store, I purposely avoided him. He always made a point to pin me down with his pointed stare and creepy smile, but never once bothered speaking to me.

Not yet.

I felt it coming, though. He had plans for me, I knew that much from the sliver of time he'd spent with Aunt Ash. But he wasn't going to reveal them until the time was right.

"Our home is being taken over by dark magic and the people we've relied upon to repel it away have remained silent. They owe us an explanation for allowing this evil to get this far. I beg you, my powerful brothers and sister, to cast your own protection spells and protect your families," he preached from the white gazebo.

A crowd had gathered around to hear, nodding their heads and clutching their hands to their chests as his words sparked more fear. A police officer stood sleepily nearby to ensure peace was maintained while Rayner and his followers rallied. After a few instances where Quarter supporters attacked Movement members during their meetings, the mayor decided to station an officer at every political convention, big or small.

"Those boys were given a gift and they are squandering it. They're no longer deserving of the admiration they've received and taken advantage of from this town. Their fathers promised they can right the wrongs of their sons, yet the darkness continues to linger."

"I can't believe people are falling for this," Blaire mumbled from beside me on the bench we stopped at to enjoy our coffee and listen to Rayner's ridiculous claims. "Fear makes people do stupid things."

"Still, at least half of the town has joined him. I've even seen posters in support of the Movement taped to the walls in The Grind."

It shouldn't bother me that these people were being brainwashed by a man whose ego was larger than the span of the town itself, but I've grown fond of some of them in my time here. To see them being taken advantage of was simply heartbreaking.

Maybe that was a sign it was time for me to leave. Or maybe it was time for me to step in and claim Beacon Grove as my home.

Blaire tapped her foot impatiently against the grass as Rayner continued his speech. "If he's so worthy of the position of High Priest and taking over for the Quarters, why doesn't he remove the black magic spell himself?"

Her mood never lifted to its usual peppiness after the town meeting. She'd adopted a new attitude toward her hometown and the people in it, specifically the Quarters. Instead of speaking against them as she always did, she began sounding like Tabitha, sympathizing with the four men who were being used as scapegoats to complete a larger agenda. She was no longer the naive, doe-eyed girl I met in the beginning of my trip, innocently taking whatever they threw at her and making the best of it. Now, she demanded respect. Her eyes had been opened to the corruption happening around her and she was angry about it.

"Because he can't."

I watched the man in question closely, taking note of his hand gestures and the way his eyes twitched when he was saying something especially ridiculous. It was like he knew the words he was spewing were nothing but hot air, but he enjoyed the way the crowd was so captured by him too much to stop.

"Exactly."

We only lasted on that bench a few more minutes before Blaire stood up in a huff and began walking off. She took the back alley again and I followed. I'd given up trying to figure out the route after trying it a few times on my own and never ending up in the same place twice. Some things in Beacon Grove just weren't worth getting hung up on and the seemingly shifting streets were one of them.

We passed the office and walked straight to my room, where we've been hanging out for the past few days. I managed to avoid Tabitha since the night she told me everything about the Quarters and I ran straight to Remy with my newfound information. Even though there was no way for her to be certain, I could swear she knew what I'd done and wasn't pleased with me.

I didn't care, though. She'd been wrong about him, and when he was ready to tell the others about what we knew, I was sure she'd be wrong about them, too.

Blaire fell onto my bed and laid back, releasing an exasperated sigh into the air above her. I wanted to ask what had gotten into her lately. It seemed like I wasn't the only one avoiding the old woman sitting a few doors down. But I figured if she wanted me to know, she would have told me by now. That was just who Blaire was.

"Where do you plan on going when you leave here?" she asked when I laid down beside her.

We each stared up at the tiled ceiling, me considering my answer while she waited patiently.

"I'm not sure," I admitted.

"I've never left Beacon Grove. Grammy wouldn't ever allow it, and Mom was always too busy to plan a vacation."

"We should plan something. Just you and me," I suggested, turning my neck toward her.

She did the same and her eyes glowed bright even in the dull light the lamp was emitting from beside the bed. They reminded me of the unique shades the Quarters had, almost making her look inhuman.

"That would be great. I want to see the city. I don't care which one."

I smiled at that, remembering how much Aunt Ash loved the city as well. No matter where we went, especially at the end, she made sure there was a major city nearby for her to visit.

"I love the energy of it all. Everyone's too focused on their own lives to care what anyone else is doing. It's the perfect place to hide," she'd said once when I questioned her about it.

I always thought it was peculiar that she spent her life wanting to hide when all I wanted was to be seen. Now, I knew why she felt that way. Beacon Grove felt like an impossible place to hide. Even if no one was looking at you, it always felt like eyes were watching.

"Sounds like a plan."

CHAPTER
TWENTY-EIGHT

REMY

T he Movement was gaining momentum against us by the day. Our coven and town were feeling the effects of the black magic that was being cast around them, and they needed a safe place to turn. Unfortunately, we weren't able to provide them with the same security they were used to having, which made them lose trust in our abilities. They had no choice but to side with the man who was promising them the world and making it impossible for them to resist.

Our fathers were essentially useless. While our gifts were fading away, theirs weren't growing any stronger the way they'd anticipated. Of course, thanks to Storie, I knew it was because they were instead flowing into our Counters to protect them from being abused. But no one else was privy to that knowledge yet. As hard as it was to watch my brothers practically fade away before my eyes, I knew they weren't ready to hear the truth yet. It wasn't worth losing Storie and our only shot at coming out of this alive.

She said Tabitha Granger had loads of history books stored away inside her home. I found that puzzling, considering she was suspected of hiding our Counters from us at birth and forced out of her position. What reason would she have to possess books specifically about Quarters and Counters? With the knowledge she had, it could be argued that in her attempts to keep us from killing our Counters, she actually saved our lives.

So, what was her role in all of this?

Storie seemed to trust her, so I decided to let it go for now. But eventually, I would come for those books. Though Storie wasn't able to confirm, I suspected she could also be in possession of the Quarter Book of Shadows.

"It doesn't make sense," Rhyse grumbled from his familiar fallen log. We were back at our spot in the woods, soundproofing protection spells in place.

This time, I had to lift them myself since the others were too exhausted from the hike in. Enzo and Lux rested on the forest floor at my feet. "Why are we so weak, yet you feel nothing?"

They were growing suspicious of me, as they should. If I hadn't found Storie right before Hell broke loose on the town, I'd be lying in the fallen leaves right beside them.

"I have no idea." The lie was getting harder to maintain, and my lack of explanation only caused more suspicion from them. "I'm grateful that at least one of us has the means to support us, though."

"Of course, you are. Because that one is *you*." Enzo's spite was a living, palpable thing. He was still mad about not being able to lift the protection spell in his own element.

"I hate to say it, but he's right. If one of us is able to hold onto his gift despite the Movement's attempt to weaken us, we should be grateful." Lux leaned back onto his hands.

"We're going to figure a way out of this," I assured earnestly. "You guys are my family. I won't let anything happen to you so long as I can still control my gift."

I meant every word of that. The lies, the deception, it was all going to pay off in the end. It killed me to keep secrets from them, especially one that was so personally significant. I just needed to figure out how to explain it all without them jumping straight to their conditioning and getting them to focus on their instincts instead.

My phone rang, interrupting Enzo's snarky response. Without checking, I silenced the ringer and gave them my full attention again.

"Everyone's starting to turn against us. I went into The Grind the other day and practically had to beg for service. They think we're the ones taking those girls." Rhyse slumped further into his log.

"I wish we could just end this, man. They don't give a shit if we're alive or dead. Why should we go through all this suffering for a bunch of ungrateful—"

"Because, it's our job," Lux cut in sternly. "We've been given these gifts from the gods. It's not up to us or anyone else to decide when we're released from our duties."

"Yeah, well maybe if the gods want us to use our gifts, they shouldn't have made it possible to be stolen from us by people who are obsessed with power and greed. We can't even find our own Book of Shadows to effectively do our jobs."

"There's one person who keeps town records that we haven't looked into yet," I began, tentatively planting the seed. I might not have been able to come out and admit that I knew she was holding some of our secrets, but I could lead them to the trail.

"Who?" Lux was the first to bite.

"Tabitha Granger."

Rhyse scoffed. "Come on, man. I thought you were being serious."

"Yeah, she's already been thoroughly investigated. There's no way she's hiding Quarter information," Enzo agreed disappointedly.

Lux's hand started scratching his beard. I knew he'd be the easiest one to get on my side.

"She was the town's midwife for decades. We know she's always kept her own records of each birth. What's to say she isn't holding onto other records as well? Quarter records," I explained, carefully watching Lux's reaction.

"That's true. Our fathers have never trusted her. Maybe she knows more about us than she should," he thought aloud, slowly working through the possibility in his head.

My phone buzzed again. I pulled it out and swiped to answer.

"Where are you?" my father's deep voice filled my ear.

I looked to the other three, gesturing for them to stay quiet while I put my dad on speaker. "Just went for a walk."

"You need to get back home. The mayor has announced that they're considering cancelling the Samhain ceremony for fear of the town's safety. We've managed to hold him off from his decision for now, promising the elders could handle it if things don't get better, but no one is happy. It's not safe to be downtown right now."

The four of us exchanged panicked glances. This was it, the moment we've been dreading since the start of this nightmare. The town has officially turned.

"I'll be home in a bit," I said, but the line cut out when he hung up without a proper goodbye.

"If the town wasn't against us before, they'll definitely be against us now," Rhyse groaned. He propped his elbows onto his knee and his head fell into his hands.

"It'll be fine. Silas will assure them they've got it under control, even if they don't. They won't let the Quarters fall," Lux attempted to reassure us, but his tone was laced in doubt. Even the king of positivity couldn't believe the lies he was spinning anymore.

When no one had anything to say, he continued, "We'll lie low the way they want us to for now. This is good." He nodded his head, slowly convincing himself. "This gives us more time."

"More time for what? We've hit a dead end," Rhyse complained.

"We can dig more into the Grangers for starters," he said, looking to me for extra encouragement.

"How are we supposed to do that? Tabitha isn't exactly our biggest fan and we've learned the hard way that the crazy librarian isn't on our side." Enzo sighed in defeat. His eyebrows were practically sitting in his hairline.

Lux's eyes swung back to mine knowingly. "Remy has an in."

"No. Absolutely not."

"What are you talking about?" Enzo flicked his gaze between us, confused.

"Storie Graves. She's practically a part of their family now. She and Blaire are best friends and Remy has been spending all his free time with her," Lux explained when I refused to answer.

An uneasy feeling formed in the pit of my stomach. It seemed as if I wasn't the only one who had taken an interest in my Counter. What else did he know?

"Why is this the first we're hearing of this?" Rhyse demanded, his fiery gaze burning into me accusingly.

"Because it wasn't worth mentioning. It still isn't. She's not going to betray their trust after all they've done for her." I knew as soon as the words left my mouth, they were a mistake.

"We've already talked about this. We need to be certain that we can all rely on each other one hundred percent," Lux lectured. He apparently got some of his energy back because he stood from his spot on the ground and stepped closer toward me, his finger pointed in my face. "You're the only one who has even the slightest chance of finding answers right now. You're also the only one who appears to still have his gift intact."

"Yeah, we need to trust that you'll put us before everything else, same as we would for you," Rhyse added.

When I let their words linger in the air between us for a beat too long, Enzo pressed further. "Can we trust you, Remy?"

Of course, they could trust me. That wasn't the issue.

The problem was that I didn't know if I could trust them when the truth came out and they discovered that I've been going against everything we've been taught as Quarters and hiding my Counter from them all this time to keep her alive.

To keep my own gift while watching theirs fade away.

Would they believe in the connection I shared with Storie if they've never felt anything like it themselves? Or would they think I was another force working against them and eliminate me altogether?

Their expectant stares had me answering, "Yes, you can trust me," before the weight of those words could suffocate me.

"Okay, then you'll get into that house and find out what she knows. The rest of us will stay under the radar until then. We'll stay out of town the way we have been until this blows over or Remy finds something that can help us." Lux clapped his hands together as if it were all figured out while Rhyse and Enzo nodded their support.

THE ✳ BEACON

19 OCTOBER 2021

SAMHAIN CANCELED

Mayor Douglas has officially announced that all celebrations for Samhain are cancelled. Anyone who attempts to use magic on the night of October 31st will be subject to fines.

For those unaware, Samhain is a holiday celebrated directly in between the autumn and winter solstices to mark the beginning of the darkest part of the year. Ironically, this festival falls during one of Beacon Grove's most historically dark times. Some even claim that if you look up at the sky, you can literally see a cloud of black magic looming just above our beloved town.

This news comes as another blow to morale after Beacon Grove's Mabon celebration was cancelled just over a month ago.

"This news saddens me as this was an extremely difficult decision to make. Safety remains our number-one priority," Mayor Douglas said in his most recent emergency meeting. Some townspeople remain bullish about the holiday, though, claiming that politics should not get in the way of any more traditions.

"Samhain is the time I get to honor my mother who passed away two years ago. It's when I feel her presence around me the strongest, and I'm not willing to give that up over a silly feud between our town and coven leaders," Beacon Grove local and boutique shop owner, Hazel Rubio, commented when asked on her way out of the meeting.

Others are more willing to comply with the mayor's newest orders, deciding to forgo this year's celebrations and begin moving onto those for the next wheel of the year. Andrew Hart comments, "We, as a community, are going forward. I am now focused on making Yule an event to remember for years to come."

CHAPTER TWENTY-NINE

STORIE

The announcement of Samhain being canceled created an even greater shift in the town's mood. Before, they'd been morose and gloomy. Now, they were angry.

They took their frustrations out on each other, constantly getting into small tiffs with anyone who appeared to look at them the wrong way. I saw it in line at The Grind when the barista got an order wrong, at the diner when Blaire and I met for lunch, and even at the library when I'd stopped in to do some digging on Lunet's family.

The one thing they all seemed to agree on was that this was all the Quarters' fault.

Each day, Rayner's movement gained more followers as people grew tired of the lack of communication coming from their coven's High Priest. It was almost as if the elder Quarters had intended for this to happen. That they wanted the town to rally against their sons and put their lives in danger so that they could swoop in and save the day.

The problem was, they never swooped. It's been weeks since Remy and the others were welcomed into town. They were forced to hide away in their homes and avoid contact with anyone outside of their trusted circles.

In the short moments when Remy would talk openly about the issue, he told me that their fathers expected to gain their gift back as the rest of the Quarters lost theirs. Evidently, that hadn't happened yet, and the Quarters blamed their Counters for it.

"I have to ask you for an incredibly difficult favor," he began one day.

He had been exceptionally glum and more distracted than usual, but I knew better than to ask him about it before he was ready.

"I need to get into Tabitha's study."

"Okay. How am I supposed to help you with that?"

"You've been in that room before. It's likely protected with dozens of spells to shield it from just anyone getting in. But once you've been through those spells, the room is available to you any time, even without her," he explained patiently.

I thought about what he was asking me to do. He was right, it was incredibly difficult, and I was angry at him for even putting me in the position of telling him no. But I had to. There was no way I could do that to the Grangers after all they've done for me.

My head moved in a negative shake. "I'm sorry. I can't betray her like that. She's like my family."

Remy released a loud, frustrated growl, standing from his bed to pace the floor and put distance between us. "I would do it myself, but she's probably got specific spells lifted against us. Especially if she's hiding the information we think she is. This is our last hope. You're all we've got."

"Don't try to put this on me. If you think she has the answer to fixing this mess, I doubt she'd deny you. She wants this to be over just as bad as the rest of us. Just ask her."

The muscles in his neck flexed and his hands balled into fists. "You don't understand. The Grangers have been accused of working against the Quarters for decades. If she's in possession of this book, it's because she *stole* it from us. We can't simply ask her to give up all the information she has on us. She'd never do it." His fists moved up from his sides to work against his scalp, mussing up his jet-black hair.

"So, you want to steal it from her? Is that any better than what you accuse her of?"

"Stop being so naive. There is no right and wrong here anymore, Storie. It's about survival, and we're not going to survive much longer if we can't get our hands on this book and find the truth that no one wants to share. She isn't your family. You don't have a family because of this, remember?"

I couldn't stop the gasp that left my lips at his crass words. I watched him in disbelief as he spun his body around and stared out the balcony doors with his back to me while he gained his composure.

After a few moments, he returned to the room and kneeled down onto the floor before me, gently taking my hands into his.

"I have this obligation to the Quarters. To my coven. I was born into this role and given these gifts without anyone asking if it was what I wanted, and I've felt trapped under the weight of responsibility since birth. But you should know that you're so much more important than any of it. I'd give my soul for you and burn through a thousand lifetimes in Hell as punishment. I never want you to feel like I've forced you into anything against your will. To feel even a sliver of the misery that I've grown comfortable with."

The golden flecks in his eyes shined against the shadows of his black irises. He was looking at me with such devotion, his words rooted from someplace deep inside his soul. I could tell it took great effort for him to admit all of that. To confess that he was willing to betray everything he's ever known for me. To reveal this weaker side of him that struggled with the tasks he was given. To profess such deep, unfamiliar feelings to me.

I was uncomfortable with taking advantage of Tabitha's trust. It didn't make sense that she would be the only one who could provide answers, but I never understood her role in any of this to begin with. She very well could be the one hiding the truth from the Quarters and contributing to the chaos that has ensued since they lost their gifts.

"You don't have to do this. I'm sorry that I even asked. We'll find another way."

"I'll do it."

His brows raised high into his forehead as he blinked at me in stunned silence.

My eyes rolled to the ceiling to hide their growing mistiness. "You're right. She isn't my family. You're the closest thing I've felt to family since Aunt Ash died, and probably long before that. I'll get into the room and see if she has what you're looking for."

"Are you sure? I swear, we can find another way," he started, but I shook my head and stopped him with a kiss.

"I can't lose you, too. And as much as I find it to be puzzling and unwelcoming, I can't let this town burn to the ground over any more secrets and lies," I explained when we pulled away.

It would kill me to deceive the family who has welcomed me with open arms, but Remy was right. The information wasn't Tabitha's to keep, and if he was telling the truth and she was holding onto it out of spite, then she was putting the rest of us at risk for her own ego. I'd make sure to get in and out of there before she even knew and hopefully put an end to the destruction.

Blaire and Tabitha's moods never fully shifted into the same hostility that everyone else had. I'm not sure if it was because they were already generally hostile people or if they had protected themselves with spells strong enough to avoid it. Still, they remained untouched by the growing darkness that loomed overhead.

I realized that Tabitha reminded me of an older, grumpier version of Aunt Ash. Watching her work on her incantations gave me a strange sense of familiarity that comforted me each time I felt my panic rise. I wanted to express my gratitude toward her for taking me in and treating me as her own in a way that I'd never been able to do with Aunt Ash, but Tabitha made that impossible. Each time I tried to offer her anything, she'd swat me away and mumble something crude under her breath. It all made what Remy asked me to do that much more difficult.

She wasn't happy that I didn't heed her warning about him, and she couldn't stand that I kept my faith in the Quarters coming around about their Counters the same way Remy had. I liked to think those feelings were rooted in fear of something bad happening to me, but I knew deep down that Tabitha didn't worry herself with much outside of her family. There was clearly something the Grangers weren't telling me about our pasts, but I wasn't ready to face that reality just yet.

I'd spent nearly a week waiting for the right opportunity to sneak into Tabitha's study. Blaire would be easy enough to get past. It was Tabitha and Callista who made it difficult to find a window of time long enough for me to get in and out unscathed. That was so long as Remy's speculation was correct, and the protection spells were lifted for me. If she put new ones in place, there was no telling what could happen to me.

Tonight, the three of them were at yet another town meeting about the Movement. I faked a stomachache and hung back, grateful that none of them pressed me too hard. Even if they had, the dread I was feeling had put a rock in my stomach so large, my lie wasn't too far off from the truth.

I knew from watching Blaire lose her keys multiple times that they left a spare office key beneath the mailbox hanging beside the door. The entry leading into their home was always open, so after I replaced the spare exactly how I'd found it, I walked right into their dark foyer.

Once I reached the hallway, I was sure the door to the room would be gone again. Remy explained that one of the protection spells she could have used might have masked it, disguising it as part of the wall. I figured that was why I didn't ever remember seeing it before she'd taken me there. But as I rounded the corner, the wood door was still fully visible.

My dread grew stronger the closer I got, nearly paralyzing me in fear when my hand finally reached for the handle. I was shocked to find that it turned with ease, the hinges creaking as I pushed forward into the unlit room. I found the light switch and shoved my fears as far down as they would go, then quickly got to work on reading spines.

Most of them were records of the births she'd assisted, all separated by year. Remy instructed me to look for a black, leather bound book with gold foil lettering titled something along the lines of *Watchtower Quarter Book of Shadows*.

I nearly reached the last shelf, and my hope was all but lost when I stumbled onto the book Tabitha had used to tell me about my role as Remy's Counter. It had been moved to a different spot than where she pulled it from that night, an entire bookshelf over and three rows up. I wondered why she would have gone through the trouble of moving it if she never expected that I'd come back.

Was she just overly paranoid? Or did she know I'd return to find out more? That would explain why she left the spells untouched.

My fingers gently grazed the plain spine of the ancient-looking book, stopping over the small, lonely compass that sat at the top. It was similar to the compass that was plastered all around town and served as Beacon Grove's official logo. This one was slightly different in that instead of the lines simply crossing over each other in the center, there was another circle placed there, same as the one's on each directional point.

I wanted to pull the book from the shelf to show Remy but decided against it at the last minute. If Tabitha had expected me to come back here, that would be the first one she looked for to be missing, since it was the one she showed me. Instead, I committed the logo to my memory and moved on, afraid that I was running out of time.

The Book of Shadows sat on the final shelf I checked. It was set against the wall behind the door and filled with different colored spell books and grimoires. The title was as Remy described, but when I pulled the brittle, cracked leather from the shelf, the cover was nothing like anything I've seen before.

Instead of a four-point compass, the black book was adorned with a silver, five-point star. Each point was labeled with the elements I'd grown familiar with hearing about. Water, earth, fire, and air were represented with their corresponding symbols, with the addition of spirit. It was represented in the uppermost point and was accompanied by a circle symbol. My eyes scanned the cover curiously, wondering if this was the correct one for me to take. I looked back to the shelf I'd taken it from for any other books with a similar title and came up short.

Before I could reconsider, I heard a noise outside the hotel and shoved the heavy book under my arm in a panic. With a quick scan of the room to make sure everything looked as untouched as it had when I arrived, I slipped through the door and closed it quietly behind me. Then, with the same dreadful feeling I entered the house with, I locked the office behind me and ran to my room.

CHAPTER THIRTY

STORIE

I was having dinner with Blaire at the Watchtower Tavern the first time I heard it.

In the beginning, we chalked it up to nasty rumors that would never gain momentum. Then, we heard talk of it while walking past the barber shop and Hazel's boutique. Slowly, the news made it to Maisey's diner where we had lunch two days later, and we knew there was no way it could be false.

The town was planning to hunt down the Quarters.

Each version of the story differed in how they would handle the four men when they finally had them. Some wanted to punish them for failing the coven and allowing the darkness to infiltrate its borders. Others wanted to force them to use their gifts to clear out the black magic and bring normalcy back into their lives. The most extreme plan I heard involved burning them alive and ending the reign of the Quarter families over the coven, similar to what Rayner had always suggested they do.

Every variation left me with an unsettled feeling in the pit of my stomach. I knew that their fathers would do nothing to help them. They'd watch them burn and pray to the gods that their gifts would return back to them. Blaire was hesitant at first, but finally agreed that we had to do something to help them, and we had to do it soon.

I remembered reading about an old cabin in the woods just on the border of the Alden and Easton properties. The Graves owned a sliver of land that was mostly taken up by a large creek flowing through it, rendering it useless for building a decent-sized home like the ones that now made up the town. The cabin was where the Graves lived while they built their family home downtown. Most of the founding families had something similar, but their property was bought up by the Quarter families and the small homes were demolished once the town was officially built.

"It's a crazy idea," Blaire admitted when I first told her about my plans for the cabin.

It'd been three days since I snuck into their house, and so far, they had yet to mention anything being off or the Book of Shadows going missing. I figured Tabitha was still unaware of the stolen book and held my breath every time she opened her mouth to speak in case accusations flew off her tongue and I lost their trust forever.

We were sitting in the library at the crack of dawn with the town's deed records laid out on a table between us. The Graves family was stubborn about their strip of land. According to the records, they never ended up selling it. Instead, ownership was passed down through generations, always left to the oldest heir at the time of the last owner's death.

As the final member of the Graves bloodline, that land technically now belonged to me.

I only hoped that the Aldens and the Eastons didn't destroy the cabin and take over the land when my father and Aunt Ash left town for good.

"It seems to be their only option," I pointed out.

"Why do you care so much about them?" she wondered with genuine curiosity.

I told Blaire about what Tabitha showed me the night of the last town meeting. After what happened with Julia, I realized she was more than trustworthy. She responded with empathy, even when I admitted what was happening between Remy and me.

Blaire may have had her quirks that scared people away, but she was one of the most honest, authentic people I had ever met. Having her around during such a transformational time in my life was a true blessing from the gods and I couldn't stand that I was deceiving her and risking losing the friendship we shared.

"It's not just about them. Rayner and his movement have cost me my entire family. Now, he's coming after the only other piece of me that seems to make sense."

She considered that for a moment before her eyes fell to the spread of parchment before us. "Okay. So, how do you plan to get them there without anyone noticing?"

"First, we have to make sure the cabin is still standing."

The forest on the northeast side of town was far more dense and uncared for than the thinned trails I walked with Remy on his property. Blaire and I hiked for two miles before we found the creek, constantly stopping to find ways over fallen logs, thick brush, and tangled vines. It was clear no one had bothered to come out here for some time. While that made the trek feel impossible for us, it reassured me that there was a chance the cabin remained untouched as well.

"I think it's this way." Blaire pointed to the east, her eyes flicking between the map in her hands and the creek running before us.

The map we were using was a poor photocopy of a slightly outdated one we found in the library that marked property lines. We knew our phones would be of no use this far into the woods, so it was our best bet. I was grateful that Blaire was so capable at navigating through the dense earth because I had lost my sense of direction over a mile back. Where I continuously tripped over random tree roots and ivy, she handled the terrain like a professional, practically floating above the cluttered floor like it was nothing.

We followed the creek for about twenty more minutes before a dark structure came into view just around the bend. It was covered in foliage and surrounded by thick, mature trees that reached far into the sky above. We exchanged an excited glance and jogged the rest of the way there.

"It's really here," Blaire mused. Her hand rubbed against the old logs, and she closed her eyes, soaking it in.

While it was technically still standing, the cabin was in rough shape. Fallen tree branches had punctured a window and weighed down part of the roof, causing it to bow in a way that made me hesitant to walk inside. Vines had taken over nearly every surface outside, suffocating the wood and holding moisture so most of it was rotted and warped.

We broke the rusted lock with a rock and pried open the door, revealing a surprisingly clean living space. It was all one room with a loft built overhead. The roof was curved inward over an area that I assumed was the kitchen. A woodburning stove sat in the back corner beside an old sink and cabinets, and a solid wood table sat a few feet away.

Sure, it would provide them temporary shelter, but it was hardly livable. We'd have to come up with another plan quickly.

"This is amazing." Blaire spun in a slow circle with her eyes wide and mouth hanging open.

I lifted one of the mattresses that was lying on the floor and bugs scattered in every direction. "I'm not sure if this was such a good idea," I admitted dejectedly.

"It just needs some cosmetic work. They'll be able to fix most of this up without even lifting a finger."

I doubted that was true. Blaire seemed to look at this place and see something completely different than me, but I trusted her judgement. I only hoped Remy would feel the same way that she did.

"Should we tell Remy about it?"

She took one last look around and smiled, nodding her head. "Yes."

CHAPTER THIRTY-ONE

REMY

B laire Granger was a strange girl.

She was awkward and unusual, and most people avoided conversations with her because of the odd things that came out of her mouth. Plus, she was a Granger—one of the only families in the coven that proved to be untrustworthy. For some reason, Storie had taken a liking to her immediately.

That was the only reason I allowed her through my front door and into my home. They were both reeking of the woods, their bodies covered in sweat, leaves, and random scratches. Blair wore a look of pure excitement, practically bouncing on her feet as we walked through the foyer while Storie appeared despondent. She chewed on her bottom lip in a way that made me want to grab her up and steal it away.

"We've got a plan, but I don't think you're going to like it."

"That's no way to get him on board," Blaire chastised. Her hand swatted at Storie's arm. "It's actually pretty amazing."

"What is it?"

"Well, as you know, no one's happy about Samhain being canceled. They're blaming the Quarters for everything, and they're getting pretty aggressive out there," Storie began. Blaire's head bobbed in agreement. "Recently, we've heard some concerning things and I thought it might be helpful if you guys laid low for a minute. At least, until the holiday passes."

"Lay low?" I asked, frowning. "You mean, like we've already been doing?"

"No, lower," Blaire said, holding up a very faded map of Lux and Enzo's properties.

"I'm not following."

"My family owns a cabin on the border of these properties. It could use some work, but it should serve as a safe space for you guys to hide out while we figure everything out."

Of course, figuring everything out meant reading through the ancient book of shadows that we stole from Blaire's home to find more answers about why we were losing our magic and how we could stop the dark magic from eating up the entire town.

"I think you're overreacting. We're safe in our homes. There's protections lifted all around the property," I started to say, but Blaire's dramatic scoff stopped me from continuing.

"You Quarters are so hard-headed. Do you think a Granger would be standing in your home right now, offering you safety, if things weren't bad?" She shook her head and looked over at Storie, her brow lifted incredulously. "You guys have managed to screw yourselves so royally, Rayner and the Movement don't even have to lift a finger anymore. Watchtower is crumbling, Beacon Grove is being swallowed by dark magic, and the only people we thought would save us have been holed up in their mansions, refusing to face us."

"You don't understand the politics of it all. Our fathers were supposed to–"

"Oh, please. We all know how greedy and self-serving your fathers are. But *you're* the Quarters of Watchtower, not them. Stop hiding behind daddy and start acting like the powerful men we know you can be." Blaire shifted to cross her arms over her chest, her chin stubbornly jutted out.

Since my father called me home from the woods, none of us had left our homes. We were stuck relying on them to re-lay information from coven and town meetings. According to them, the general consensus was that no one was happy with us.

Of course, our fathers were there to swoop in and save the day, constantly assuring the town that they had us under control. They conveniently left out that they were just as powerless as we were and the darkness was affecting them, too.

We didn't care, though. Now that we finally had our hands on the Quarter Book of Shadows, all of our energy was being poured into finding any piece of information that might be useful in finding their Counters and helping them retain their gifts. We couldn't do anything for the coven if we weren't even capable of protecting ourselves, and whoever was feeding the dark magic appeared to be targeting our powers specifically.

The problem was that the entire book was written in code and every piece of information regarding the spirit element had a redaction spell cast on it.

"Blaire, that was kind of harsh," Storie softly interjected. I had forgotten she was still standing there.

"Am I wrong, though? This is only a taste of what's to come if the four of you keep your heads stuck up your asses." Storie's eyes widened at her friend's crassness, but I wasn't surprised. She was a Granger, after all. "This has to end at some point. Are you going to step in and do your job, or are you going to prove Rayner right and show us how much we really don't need you?"

"It's more complicated than that. Without our Counters, we're essentially useless," I said through gritted teeth.

She was infuriating and overly audacious, just like her grandmother. I didn't think I owed an explanation to anyone in Watchtower after the way they've treated us, let alone one of its lowliest members.

"You've found your Counter; that's enough for now. We don't have time for your excuses anymore. Gather the others and get them out to this cabin."

She held up the faded map again, pointing to the circle she had drawn just between property lines.

I exhaled through my nose and looked to Storie for backup, but she shrugged her shoulders and stepped closer to Blaire, showing that she was taking her side in the argument. "You haven't heard what they've been saying about you. I think this is the safest option until we figure out how to get through this."

"Look, I hate that we're being forced together just as much as you do." Blaire started. She cut her eyes toward Storie, reminding me she was the only reason we were standing in the same room right now. "But even the most diehard Quarter supporters are switching sides. They feel like they have no other choice. This is bigger than both of us."

Blaire tapped her foot impatiently as I digested her words. I kept my eyes trained on the violet-eyed woman who looked terrified to be stuck between the two of us. I would never trust a Granger, but I trusted Storie with my life. If she was willing to back up what Blaire was saying, then it must be true. Things have gotten too dangerous for us, and the time has come for us to fight.

"I can try to talk to them, but there's no guarantee they'll come."

I didn't want to reveal that there was a chance they *couldn't* come. That a hike through dense, uncleared woods might kill them faster than the Movement or Watchtower ever could.

Three hours later, the six of us hiked in a single line through Lux's property until we saw the outline of an old log cabin set beside the creek. It shouldn't have taken as long as it did to get there, though I was sure that if it were just the four of us, we'd take twice the amount of time. Rhyse, Lux, and Enzo stubbornly pushed through their extreme fatigue to avoid allowing a Granger to see them fall.

Pride was apparently a strong motivator. The thought crossed my mind that maybe I should let Blaire go off on them the way she had with me. That might get them fueled enough to actually fight this thing.

"This place is a dump," Rhyse said as soon as we pried open the rotted wood door.

Blaire glared at him and Storie held the same bewildered expression she's had since we met up with the three of them.

"It should be an easy cleanup for the most powerful witches in Beacon Grove," Blaire retorted sarcastically.

The three exchanged glances, a wordless conversation passing between them. They could try to hide it as hard as they liked but anyone who knew them could see how feeble they had become in the past few weeks.

"Why is she here?" Enzo asked me, earning a growl from the feisty redhead.

"Why are any of us here? This rotted heap of wood is way less protected than our homes. If there really is some sort of uprising, I wouldn't want to be caught here." Rhyse purposely turned his body away from Blaire, making it easier to ignore her dramatic facial expressions.

Lux was slowly walking around the space, his eyes assessing the aged home skeptically. Blaire was in the middle of berating Rhyse once again over not being strong enough to lift his own protection spells when Lux finally turned and gave us his attention again.

"She's right, Rhyse. Let's not try to stand here and pretend our gifts are what they once were. The Grangers and Storie clearly know more than we want them to." He pinned Storie down with his intimidating stare, silently accusing her of knowing too much. Of sharing too much.

She shriveled away a bit and my chest vibrated with a deep, soft growl. I surprised everyone by taking a step between them and grabbing her hand in mine. "I don't think this is the time to point fingers. Especially when she's been nothing but helpful."

Lux's brow quirked up in surprise. This was the first time we'd ever been in a disagreement of any sort. Rhyse and Enzo were usually the one's picking fights with everyone. But he couldn't treat my Counter that way and get away with it.

None of them could.

"What aren't you telling us, Winters?" Enzo stepped closer to Lux and Rhyse followed suit, drawing an invisible line between us.

"Oh, for goddess' sake. They don't even know?" Blaire yelled incredulously, her hands waving in the air. "You four need to get it together. Seriously, you're an absolute mess."

She waved her hand between us, ignoring our shocked expressions. "She's his Counter. Not sure how you missed that one since you've supposedly been trained to spot her from miles away," she explained unceremoniously.

Three pairs of eyes swung to Storie as they realized what she said. When my arm lifted across her chest protectively, their stances widened, ready to fight.

I did the same.

Blaire scoffed from the side in jest, rolling her eyes toward the ceiling. "You three don't have a snowflake's chance in Hell against him as long and she's here and your Counters are off in the wild somewhere, hiding from you."

"Does she have an off button?" Enzo growled.

"Someone needs to explain what's happening," Rhyse called out, his glare locked on me.

Lux was the first to relax.

"This is why you've retained your gift," he mused. "Hunting our counters... It was another lie from our fathers. And you've known all this time."

"No, I haven't. I suspected something was off about her and you three blew it off. I knew I couldn't tell you until I figured out how to explain that everything we know is a lie."

"How does it work, then?"

I hesitated for a beat, giving my heart a moment to stop racing and step out of fight mode. When I dropped my arm from across her chest, Rhyse and Enzo followed the lead and relaxed.

"I'm still not entirely clear. But it's like she fuels me. There's this massive amount of power that moves between us every time we're near each other. I couldn't risk losing her if you guys chose not to listen."

When I took a moment to breathe, I noticed the hurt lacing their expressions for the first time. My lack of trust in their ability to listen to me without making a snap judgement crushed them. I knew because that's exactly how I'd feel if the roles were reversed. All this time, I had convinced myself I was only hiding her from them to protect her life, but I think it went beyond that. I didn't want to share her because I was too selfish to consider the possibility that if they knew about their Counters sooner, they wouldn't have lost so much of their magic.

"You could have told us. We don't do secrets, remember?" Lux's glum tone only deepened the knife of guilt twisting in my gut.

"I didn't do it to hurt you," I insisted earnestly.

"This is sweet, but we need to move on. The sun is setting, and this place isn't going to fix itself up," Blaire interrupted.

I'm not sure what her angle was on helping us out to this cabin and making it a livable place to stay. Grangers have never concerned themselves with anyone else's problems unless there was something in it for them. I was sure there would be a catch somewhere along the line involving her and Tabitha, but we didn't have much of a choice but to go along with it. Our fathers have proven to be consorting with the enemy and our coven was now actively working against us.

It took more effort than we'd like to admit, but we were able to use the small amount of magic we had left to clear away the garbage and hazardous materials, fix up the areas that needed immediate attention, and lift a half-hearted invisibility spell to hide the cabin from anyone who might stumble out here. Most of the heavy lifting came from mine and Storie's shared gifts and Blaire's deep knowledge of spellwork.

We didn't finish until well into the following morning. Storie and Blaire chose to sleep at the cabin with us instead of risking the pitch-black woods so deep into the night. Storie fell asleep curled into my chest, and even though the others might not trust me after lying to them, it felt good to share her with them. To hold her out in the open and have the weight of our secretive relationship lifted from my shoulders.

We all awoke with the sun the next morning. The small break in trees overhead allowed light to shine directly onto us through the fogged-up windows. My eyes cracked open to find those beautiful lilacs gazing back at me. A satisfied smile spread across her lips and just as she leaned into me for a kiss, Blaire declared it was time for them to go before Tabitha slaughtered them.

Storie agreed to return with the list of groceries we came up with and then they were gone, trekking back through the woods to a town that no longer accepted us.

CHAPTER THIRTY-TWO

REMY

S amhain is traditionally a time of year for the coven to come together and take advantage of the veil between worlds thinning by honoring those who have passed. It's the midpoint between the fall and winter solstices and marks the time where night grows longer than day. Candles are lit, photos are set out, and prayers are made to loved ones who have crossed over.

The Watchers of the west have always drawn some of their magic from the spirit world, so Samhain is the most powerful time of year for the Winters family. With the veil thinned, even those who haven't mastered the spirit world are able to access and draw from it. In past generations, our ancestors would connect coven members with their loved ones and relay messages as a thank you for their support of us throughout the year. That tradition ended with my grandfather, as he was never truly welcomed into the underworld.

I was explaining this to Storie in the cabin the day before Samhain was set to begin. Lux was on the floor, attempting to read through the Book of Shadows in the dim candlelight, letting out occasional grunts of frustration as he ripped entire pages of notes out of his notebook and crumpled them up before adding them to the growing discard pile. Rhyse and Enzo were lounging on the couches, occasionally offering their input on our puzzling history.

"So, with this veil being lifted, spirits are able to exist closer to us," Storie deduced, tracing her finger on the wood grain of the old table. I nodded my response.

"Then, why don't you try to talk to your Quarter ancestors and see if they'll help you?"

Lux lifted his head from the book for the first time in hours, gaping at her.

"We've never considered that," I admitted, throwing Lux a look of disbelief.

How had we never thought of that before?

"Well, I know if I had the ability to speak to my family and have my questions answered, I'd jump at the opportunity." She dropped her gaze down to her hands and sagged her shoulders dejectedly.

"Let's try it, then. We can call your parents forward, and then try to reach one of our great grandparents. I'm sure Lux can come up with a few trustworthy, pure souls to call forward. They can't all be corrupt assholes."

Storie perked up immediately. I wasn't positive if I could contact spirits the same way my family had all those years ago without any practice, but the warm, wholesome smile that spread across her face was enough motivation for me to figure it out.

"Are you sure we should be wasting time talking to mommy and daddy when there's a real and dangerous threat to the town and coven that needs to be stopped?" Rhyse asked spitefully.

He still wasn't over the fact that I hid Storie from them and he'd been rude toward her each time she came to the cabin to give us updates and deliver food.

"Don't be a dick, Rhyse," Lux scolded without lifting his nose from the floor.

"He's probably right. We can always talk to them another time," Storie conceded, her mood dropping once again.

"No. The only reason you're here is to find answers about what happened to them. I think you've done enough for us to earn a simple conversation with the people who sacrificed their lives for you. We should have time to do both."

I shot Rhyse a warning glare, letting him know he needed to back off her, but he never bothered looking back at me to witness it.

"It'll take me some time to get a list together of people I think we can actually trust. Turns out, the Quarters have never been the most upstanding individuals," Lux said on a sigh.

My hand covered Storie's on the table and squeezed so she would lift her eyes to mine. When she finally did, I stood and cocked my head toward the door, letting her know I wanted to go outside. The sun was setting overhead, though the canopy of trees never really gave it's rays the opportunity to reach us. It was just light enough to see her in front of me, but dark enough where if anyone tried to watch us out the window, they'd barely make out our silhouettes.

"Where are we going?" she asked in a giggle when I tugged her down the stone walkway and toward the creek.

"I haven't had a moment alone with you for days and it's feeling crowded in there with Rhyse's ego."

We neared the edge of the water, and I slid my shoes and socks off, reaching for the button on my pants next.

"Remy, they're right there," Storie hissed. Her eyes grew wide when my pants hit the ground and my boxers followed close behind.

"They can't see us," I assured, tugging my shirt over my head in one movement. "I want to go for a swim."

I stepped down into the creek with a splash. The water was cold at first, stealing my breath away as I sunk deeper into its depths, but my body adjusted to the temperature quickly. The stream was narrow, but the bottom went down further than I had expected it to. The water reached just below my armpits at the deepest point.

The feeling of literally being inside my element was indescrib-able. The creek's constant stream of water flowing against my skin gave me a sense of wholeness I'd never been able to replicate until Storie came along. It was like I'd been plugged into an electrical outlet and was being charged.

Storie gazed at me from the bank in astonishment for a few moments before she swung her head around and looked toward the cabin. Once she was sure no one was watching us, she began stripping her clothes away, revealing the perfect, milky skin I'd grown to love the glow of.

She made quicker work of getting undressed than I had and once she was completely naked, she stood on the edge of the creek for a moment, rethinking her decision. I could see the conflict warring in her irises, and I wanted to pull her in just to prove that I was worth taking the dive for.

Instead, I took the opportunity to look at her body. To take in all of its beauty while she was too distracted to care. Of course, I'd seen it before. She never pushed me away or avoided being vulnerable with me in our most intimate moments. But I could always see the struggle in her eyes—the discomfort it provided her.

Finally, she landed on immersing herself all at once to get the slice of pain from the cold waters over with. In the blink of an eye, she went from this unattainable piece of art standing above me in the open forest air to a warm, soft beacon of hope against my skin. She struggled to stand on the creek bed, so I grabbed her hips and tugged her against me, allowing her to wrap her legs around my torso. I loved the sigh that fell from her lips as our bodies melded together. I became drunk on the sound of her moans when I leaned down and kissed her plump, waiting lips.

In this position, her center was perfectly aligned with my growing cock. She took advantage of our weightlessness, slipping it back and forth between her legs against her clit. Our kiss became sloppy and desperate, teeth clanging against each other, nibbling at the swollen skin of our lips. My fingers dug deep into her hips as she moved against me in rhythmic circles.

When her breathing became erratic and her eyes started to roll to the back of her head, I reached one of my hands around her from behind and explored her slits, massaging her from a completely different angle in the exact rhythm I knew would send her over the edge. Seconds later, with a soft, guttural moan, she came undone against me. I felt the heat of her juices as they moved between us in the water before being taken away with the stream.

"I love you," she whispered into my ear when she was finished.

Those words gave me pause. Outside of my mother, I have never heard them muttered in my direction before. They felt deep and significant and left a weight in my chest that I'd never experienced. I had all but professed my love to her when I asked her to take the Book of Shadows from the Grangers, but I couldn't bring myself to say those three small words. To hear them come from her mouth—to feel the effects of someone as special as Storie saying something so powerful—it was like nothing I've felt before.

"I love you, too," I admitted back, hoping she could tell how difficult it was for me to say.

Her mouth returned to mine in a delicate frenzy, her hot center pressed back against my stretched skin. I couldn't take the teasing torture anymore. My hands wrapped around her bottom as I lifted us both from the water, carefully lying her down onto the padded forest floor. She opened her legs for me, and I rested between them, easily settling into her warmth.

Her lilac eyes peered into mine so innocently, the black flecks danced around her pupils as she awaited what came next. I leaned down and gently caught her lips with mine, slowly easing in. The sun had disappeared somewhere behind the trees, taking most of the light away with it. We were on full display yet blanketed in darkness and I could feel her insecurities about being seen fade away with our kiss.

I raised myself just enough to reach between our melded bodies and massage her mound once again. As always, she was dripping wet for me. When I was sure she was ready, I grabbed my length and lined my tip up with her slick center. Just before I pushed myself in, she wrapped her legs around my back and pulled me into her body, shoving my entire cock inside her in one movement.

A moan erupted from her throat that matched the hiss I released between our lips from how deliciously tight she was. I paused inside her for a moment, pulling away from our kiss to ensure she was still okay. When I saw nothing but ecstasy painted across her face, I began rocking my hips back and forth, savoring every bite and scratch she gifted me as her pleasure built up.

I leaned down and sucked her perky, pebbled nipple into my mouth, taking her full breasts into my hands as my finger played with the other side. Her back arched off the ground and another quiet moan left her as she wrapped her arms around my head and scraped her fingers across my scalp.

I felt the familiar tightening sensation throughout my body and knew I had to bring her over the edge with me. With my tongue lapping against her tits and my cock grinding as far inside her as it would go, I reached my hand between us and rubbed circles around her clit. Within seconds, I felt her muscles pulsing around me and I let go of my own release. We swallowed each other's sounds of pleasure, too caught up in our cloud of ecstasy to care if anyone heard. That same white-hot bolt of lightning from before shot through my body as we became one, strengthening the power that our bond manifested even further.

When we were both finished and all that could be heard in the quiet forest were the echoes of our heavy breaths, I rolled off and laid on the bed of leaves beside her. My arm tugged her closer to me until she turned and nestled herself into my side.

CHAPTER
THIRTY-THREE

STORIE

The prospect of communicating with my parents carried me through the next twenty-four hours in a cloud of oblivion. I left the cabin with a list of random items they needed to perform the ceremony and had Blaire come with me to gather them in town first thing in the morning. Remy didn't go too far into detail about how it works or if I'd be able to actually see them for myself or simply use him as a vessel to talk through, but I was excited nonetheless.

I couldn't wait to see his gifts in action. To share that potent power and know it's what we were made to do together.

"So, do you have a list of questions you're going to ask?"

Blaire and I were standing in the homeopathy section of Granger's Pharmacy, searching the sparse shelves for a bundle of cedar, some dried herbs, and blue and black candles. When I asked her what they could possibly need these things for, she pinned me with a look of condescension and stated, "For protection," as if the answer was obvious.

"Mom says they haven't been able to keep anything in stock lately. I guess everyone in Watchtower is preparing for the worst." She crouched down to rifle through a pile of discarded, wilted herbs that had fallen out of their packages and were left behind. I saw the worry etched across her face before she turned away to hide it. "I just wonder how it's going to go without the Quarters' shield in place."

"Everything is going to be fine, Blaire," I comforted feebly, kneeling beside her. "We're going to get answers and straighten everything out."

She only nodded her response. I could tell she had the same doubts we all had; she was just afraid to voice them out loud. Her hand swiped across the bottom of her nose, and she stood straight, turning toward the cash registers.

"We've got fresh herbs and cedar at home. I'm sure Grammy won't mind if we take a few."

We stopped at the checkout counter and Callista greeted us with a warm smile. She scanned our candlesticks and looked between the two of us skeptically.

"I hope you ladies aren't planning on doing anything irresponsible tonight." Her eyes landed on Blaire and stared for a long moment in stern, silent warning like only a mother could do. "You know how dangerous it's going to be out there."

Blaire held her hands up innocently. "I'm not doing anything."

Callista quickly glanced at me before she turned to the register and printed a receipt that she shoved off to the side. She grabbed the bag of candles and handed them over the counter, casting one last look of caution toward her daughter.

"You're all set," she chirped, never asking for payment.

I grabbed the bag and turned toward the doors, eager to escape Callista's icy attitude. For the first time since I met her, she reminded me of her mother. The Granger insolence was far more intimidating when it came from someone as kind as Callista or Blaire. I had at least learned to expect it from Tabitha.

"She's just worried," Blaire explained when she met with me outside the pharmacy. "After what happened on Mabon, her and Grammy have forbidden me from practicing any magic for Samhain. I think it bothers them that they can't do the same to you."

We walked to the hotel in silence as I considered what she said. I was under the impression that whatever Tabitha and Callista did on Mabon actually helped save Beacon Grove while the Quarters were being attacked. If they weren't planning on practicing any protective spells through Samhain and the Quarters were busy communicating with their ancestors, who would be there to save everyone when the black magic inevitably took over?

I didn't get a chance to ask Blaire before we got to the hotel. As always, the walk from town was much shorter with a Granger there to lead the way. I didn't think that would ever make sense to me.

"What do you think you're doing?" Tabitha barked from her recliner when Blaire began picking off herbs from their back-yard garden just outside the doorway.

"Storie needs a few and Mom was fresh out," Blaire casually explained, throwing random leaves into the paper bag she grabbed on our way through the kitchen.

"Let me guess, you're planning to do something stupid with that boy," Tabitha murmured expressionlessly to me, turning her attention back to the TV.

Blaire rolled her eyes and carried the bag over to the built-in shelves surrounding the TV Tabitha was watching. She opened a few cupboards and dug around before she found what she was searching for. After shoving a thick green bundle of cedar into the bag and folding it shut, she slammed it into my chest and nodded.

"That should be it."

"Are you sure you don't want to come?" I offered one last time while we walked through the house, hopeful that she'd change her mind.

"She's not going anywhere near those boys tonight," Tabitha's startling voice bounced off the walls.

Blaire looked at me and tilted her head apologetically. "It's best I stay here in case they need me. You'll be okay, though."

Remy had a pot of water boiling when I arrived with the supplies. He pulled the herbs from the paper bag, closely assessing each one before unceremoniously throwing them into the water. Rhyse was going through the house and prying open windows, allowing the chilled Autumn air to sweep into the warmed space. Lux grabbed a mop and bucket and waited by the stove for Remy to finish boiling the water.

I watched in astonishment as they each moved together flawlessly through the cabin without speaking a single word. Lux dumped the still-boiling infused water into the bucket and began swiping it around the floor with the mop, starting in the back of the cabin and working toward the door. Enzo lit the cedar stick and waved it around the room as Rhyse followed behind and closed the windows. Remy set the candles up on the table and lit them.

The whole process took less than half an hour. By the time they were done, the sun was setting, and the room was quickly darkening. The fireplace filled the space with a warm, orange glow and the candles flickered on the table, making their shadows dance across the walls as they gathered around the circular table and took their seats.

Remy dragged an extra stool over for me between him and Enzo. Once we were all seated, Remy began to explain the process.

"We're going to draw from our elements as best as we can. Once I've accessed the spirit world, I'll be able to share that energy with everyone and hopefully give you guys a boost. We're going to focus on calling Storie's family forward."

He turned his attention toward me. The flames from the candles reflected perfectly into his black eyes, giving them an odd appearance as he spoke of his ability to access the underworld and manipulate its energy.

"Since we share energy, I'm not sure if you'll be able to enter the spirit world or if I'll have to relay messages to you. Either way, we'll do our best to get answers."

I dipped my head, and he took that as confirmation, his gaze bouncing around the table to be sure everyone else was ready to begin. Enzo grabbed the knife sitting before him and dragged it across his palm with a hiss. I gasped as he handed the bloodied blade over to Lux, who repeated the movement.

One by one, they each drew blood and held their fists over a ceramic bowl in the center of the table, allowing it to spill and mix together with the others.

Remy shot me a reassuring look and they began whispering a chant to fully lift the veil between worlds.

The next few moments happened in a storm of overwhelming thoughts and emotions. The addition of the other three created a far more dynamic experience. One that overtook my entire body to a point of nearly blacking out completely.

My body and spirit were torn apart once again, only this time the dark, dampened wood of the cabin disappeared and I was spit out into a bright, cotton candy sky.

I felt their presence in each of my senses before I could physically see them. It was the oddest sensation, as if they were somehow inside my head and surrounding my body all at once—a deeply rooted part of me.

My father's spirit presented itself first. It felt masculine and familiar and filled my nose with his potent cologne. My eyes opened and he was standing before me with Aunt Ash at his side. When my eyes locked with hers, I was consumed with the taste of her infamous brownies—such an odd detail to remember.

"It's really you," I marveled, my throat thick with emotion.

"You've grown to be so beautiful," my father said through a proud smile. He looked to Aunt Ash and nudged her teasingly with his shoulder. "You didn't mention that."

Aunt Ash shook her head and lifted her eyes skyward playfully. I missed watching them banter. Having them here made me realize that I longed for their presence in my life way more than I was ever willing to admit. It reminded me of the gaping hole I've been ignoring since they've been gone.

"Storie, I'm sure you've had some earth-shattering revelations since coming back home. I'm so sorry I didn't prepare you for this world soon enough." Aunt Ash jumped right in, her face scrunched into her signature look of concern.

"Lighten up, Asher. She's doing just fine on her own," my dad comforted.

"Actually, we've asked you here to answer some questions. I'm not sure how long we have to talk," I explained, remembering that Remy said there might be a time limit on our visit.

"Anything," they both agreed in unison.

I turned toward Aunt Ash, deciding it was finally time to ask the question that haunted me for years, even while she was alive.

"Why did Rayner come to visit us that day?"

She didn't need clarification on which day I was talking about. She already knew. It was the day that our lives changed forever.

The day she sealed her fate.

"He was coming to collect you."

"For what?"

"Rayner was an old family friend," she began, looking over to my father regretfully. "We thought we could trust him with the knowledge of who you were. He was just getting the Movement off the ground and a lot of his ideas in the beginning made sense. But over time, he got more radical. Then, Quarter families were hunting Counters based on false claims, and we were forced to leave Beacon Grove to protect you.

"Before we left, your parents agreed to bring you back when you were old enough to fight the Quarters if need be. By the time you were eighteen, he changed his plans. He wanted to use you as a weapon against them, just as their fathers did."

"That sounds like I should have known what I was much sooner," I accused, glaring at her.

I hated myself for reverting back to my petulant ways, but so much pain could have been avoided if she'd just been honest with me.

"Yes, that was the plan," my father started. He clamped his mouth shut when Aunt Ash held her finger up to stop him.

"When Mason died, I didn't know how to proceed. I thought he would be the one to handle it on his own time, but I was face-planted into single parenthood and completely unprepared. I decided at first to tell you on your tenth birthday. Then, when the time came, I couldn't do it. So, I pushed the benchmark back over and over until before I knew it, you were receiving acceptance letters to colleges I knew you'd never be able to attend. Not when so many witches were hunting you and you had no idea how to protect yourself."

She exhaled a deep breath, the lines in her face only deepening with regret. "I'm so sorry, Storie. I thought we had more time together."

Her face tilted down at her hands and my father wrapped his arms around her shoulders.

"I know your deaths weren't accidents," I began, and then paused.

Was it okay to talk to spirits about their death?

My dad nodded his head solemnly. "No, they weren't. And you know who was responsible. Anyone who stood in his way while he was getting the Movement going was simply eliminated, just like the people he was supposedly fighting against."

All traces of anger or resentment were gone from his voice. He had already come to peace with what was done to him. It was only me who dwelled on it anymore.

That led me to my next question. "Why did you lie to me about my mother's death?"

Almost as if she were waiting to be mentioned, the woman from the photos Hazel showed me materialized on the other side of my father. She wore a kind smile and her purple eyes gazed at me as if I were the most riveting thing she'd ever seen.

"Storie," she breathed. Pale, feminine hands covered her mouth as her eyes misted with emotion.

I felt a tugging in my belly button and my vision flickered between the Graves cabin and the spirit world. Remy was still deeply concentrating on keeping me tethered on this plane, but the others appeared to be struggling to hold their corners. A drop of blood had run from Enzo's nose and over his lips. Rhyse's complexion was faded and gray.

The connection was severing, and time was running out. They wouldn't be able to keep me here much longer.

When the flickering stopped, I pushed away my emotions about seeing my mother for the first time and focused on the reason I was there.

"I don't have a lot of time," I rushed out.

My father stepped forward. "We had to cover your birth up somehow. Tabitha Granger had managed to take care of the others without incident. We should have known Rayner wouldn't let you slip through his fingers."

"I still don't understand what that means. Lunet said you passed five days later." I looked to my mother, then back at my father. "Why did you lie about her dying in childbirth?"

"Because no one was supposed to know you were born twelve hours after Remington Winters. We kept you a secret until it was safe."

"But it wasn't safe..."

"No, it wasn't," my mother agreed soberly. "Rayner knew the truth and he wanted to use you as a pawn to weaken the Winters boy. We didn't know how far out of his mind he'd already become by then."

"So, what exactly happened?"

"He came after you in the same way we feared the Quarters would. They were fighting on opposite sides for the same result: to weaken the future generation of Quarters. Rayner didn't expect me to fight for you as hard as I did. By the time he'd eliminated me as an obstacle, Tabitha found us and stopped him. She wasn't able to save me, though. That has haunted her for years."

Tabitha was weaved deeper into my past than I ever knew, and she kept it a secret from me all this time, pace feeding information as she saw fit. The monster in my chest was roaring to life again, irritated at the deeply rooted lies and deception. Each time I thought I was on the path to finding answers, I learned that I was being led astray by people who didn't think I was capable of handling it.

Who were they to decide?

"So, Rayner murdered all three of you?"

I felt sick thinking of all the times his beady eyes glared at me, knowing exactly what he'd done. Proud of his duplicity and the lives he took for a cause that was just as malicious as the forces he was supposedly fighting against.

All those Movement members were supporting a monstrous murderer. They were feeding him power when he deserved to rot here in the spirit world, where he'd unapologetically sent his own friends.

"Storie, we know how much this hurts, but you have to know that we're at peace. Our purpose was to protect your life until you found your Quarter, and we've done that," Aunt Ash assured, looking to my parents for confirmation. They both voiced their agreements, and she went on.

"It's imperative that you don't dwell on your resentment over what he did to us. Don't let it lower your vibrations and bring you down to his level. You're so much more powerful than he is. Use that power to save your coven and town. They need you right now. We'll be here waiting for you when it's time."

"They aren't my coven," I corrected waspishly.

"Of course, they are. You're a Counter."

My vision fluttered to the cabin again. Enzo was slumped face down onto the table beside me in a pool of blood leaking from his nose. Rhyse was swaying in his chair, his eyes stuck at half-mast, and Lux was collapsed onto the floor. Remy's panicked expression tethered me to the cabin before the tugging sensation in my belly button stopped and I knew it was over. They were gone again.

And once again, I didn't even get to say goodbye.

CHAPTER
THIRTY-FOUR

REMY

S torie's sleeping body was draped across my lap on the couch as Rhyse, Lux, and Enzo lounged on the floor around us. They were too fatigued to make it up the ladder to the loft where our cots were set up. It's been hours since the seance and the three of them were finally regaining their energy.

Energy that they focused strictly on berating me for wasting our one true shot at communicating with our ancestors. I didn't care, though. I'd do it a thousand times over if it meant making the sleeping woman in my lap happy. They'd never understand that.

We would find another way.

I should have known better than to push them when they were already so low. I just assumed it would be easiest on the night when access to the underworld was most available. It seemed as if the moment any of us exerted our power in any way, the looming cloud of black magic that hung over the town syphoned it and used it to grow even stronger. Whoever cast that spell knew exactly what they were doing.

"It seems as if you're completely unconcerned with us finding our Counters and gaining our strength back since you've found yours," Rhyse complained for the hundredth time.

Even Lux and Enzo were growing tired of hearing the same old argument.

"Once we decode the passages in the Book of Shadows, everything will become clear," I reassured in a bored tone.

That had been our biggest obstacle outside of the darkness. It was safe to assume everything our fathers taught us about Counters was spun in some way to benefit them. Lux thought they purposely didn't teach us the Quarter language so that if we ever got our hands on the book, we still wouldn't be able to read it. He spent hours poring over each page and always ended up with nothing to show for it.

The spirit element threw us off as well. We had no idea what it meant or how it affected us. Was there a fifth Quarter? That hardly seemed to make sense, though we were learning that the most confusing things we found were usually closest to the truth.

I didn't want Storie to hear our bickering and blame herself. She was already upset with the abrupt ending to her visit and condemning herself for the condition of the others when she finally came to. I tried to convince her to escape before they woke to spare her feelings, but she refused to leave their sides. She had fallen asleep waiting for them so she could apologize.

These asshats didn't even care.

"With Samhain behind us, we can work at gaining the trust of our coven and taking our positions back so we have full access to town records and our father's studies." Lux was always the voice of reason.

"Their studies have been cleared out," Rhyse whined. He picked at the lint on his pants distractedly.

He was right. Especially now, our fathers were going to keep any information they had about us under lock and key. But it didn't matter. Now that we knew Tabitha Granger had our Book of Shadows, the rest of the information could be anywhere—including her office.

Storie shifted in my arms and her eyes fluttered open. They slowly adjusted to the light and then gazed up at me, a sleepy smile forming on her lips. Just before I leaned down to kiss her, she bolted upright.

"I'm so sorry, you guys. I ruined your chance." She parroted the same words in self-deprecation that Rhyse had been groaning since he woke up. When I looked down at him, all the anger he'd been spewing at me was wiped from his face.

All talk of the events from the night ceased once she woke up. None of them were willing to dig into her as much as they had already done to me, and she wasn't allowing anyone to tell her she wasn't to blame.

We all agreed on one thing: every piece of information we've received from our fathers was completely unreliable and if we didn't find answers soon, we weren't going to survive this war.

CHAPTER THIRTY-FIVE

STORIE

"They know, Storie. They know you're a Counter," Tabitha's panicked tone startled me from across the house. She breezed past me and Blaire lounging on the couches and began gathering candles, crystals, dried herbs, and other random items from the altar, shoving them all into a bag.

"What does this mean, Grammy?" Blaire was the first to stand, reaching out to help Tabitha before she was swatted away by old, weathered hands.

"It means they're coming for you. For all of us."

My mind reeled, my limbs frozen in place as Tabitha and Blaire buzzed around me, grabbing more to shove into the impossibly large bag.

"Your mother's stuck at the Rafferty birth, but she'll join us when she can. Storie, you need to warn Remy that we're coming."

Blaire disappeared down the hallway, mumbling to herself.

"To the cabin?" I shook my head, imagining the horrors that would happen with Tabitha Granger under the same roof as all four Quarters. Even Blaire had been a loose cannon around them, and she's far more timid than the woman who raised her. It had only been a few days since Samhain and they'd barely forgiven me for ruining their chance at finding the truth. They'd never let me live this down.

"No, that's not a good idea. Isn't there anywhere else we can go?"

"Quit worrying and go help Blaire pack a bag. I've gathered your things from your room, they're on Blaire's bed. Only bring the bare minimum," she instructed.

That was an ironic order considering she appeared to be packing everything except the kitchen sink, but I knew arguing would be a waste.

Blaire was already halfway packed by the time I walked into her room. Tabitha had haphazardly thrown all of my belongings into a large pile on the bed. I was about to turn to Blaire to ask what would be considered essential in this situation when she appeared beside me and dumped out my duffel bag. Small pieces of home that I couldn't bear to part with when I left fell into a mess on the floor.

"We need to move fast," she said breathlessly as she threw random pieces of clothing into the bag. I reached around her and gathered my toiletry bag and clean underwear just in time for her to swing the top over and zip it shut.

She turned and walked out of the room without another word, shutting the light off on her way. I followed her into the kitchen where she and Tabitha were slinging their bags over their shoulders. One of them shoved a black tote into my chest so hard, it knocked the wind out of me, but I barely had time to recover before the next one was thrown my way. Once we were loaded up, we walked through the unlit hotel office and headed south toward the cabin.

I had walked this exact path enough times to know that the streets did not line up the way they appeared to do with Tabitha and Blaire.

"How are you doing this?" I panted, struggling to keep up with their fast pace.

We took another turn that should have been a residential street but ended with a path into the woods, instead.

"Hush, girl. We don't have time." Tabitha's signature vague response irritated me more than usual. Where I was hardly keeping up, she didn't even sound out of breath.

She and Blaire had just stepped onto the dirt path when I was dragged backwards by the handle of the backpack I wore. A scream tore from my chest, forcing Tabitha and Blaire to turn around. Their wide-eyed, horrified expressions only made me kick against the cement pavement harder, making it more difficult for my captor to tug me along with them.

"Quit fighting it," Rayner's familiar voice ground into my ear. He jerked my body upwards and slammed me back onto my feet like a small child.

I called out for Tabitha and Blaire to help me, but they hadn't moved from their spot in the mouth of the woods. I watched in terror as Tabitha's lips moved to say something to Blaire, then her back turned to me and she dragged her granddaughter by the wrist behind her. Blaire never took her eyes off me, and the green glow haunted me far after they disappeared into the pitch-black woods.

Rayner hauled my lifeless body through the uncharacteristically deserted streets until another path into the woods appeared. I'd lost all sense of direction along the way and had no idea what side of town we ended up in when he threw me to the ground and kicked at my side.

"You can walk yourself from here. Try to run, and we'll just catch you," he warned. His hands brushed against the lapels of his suit coat, then tugged at them to straighten it out.

I tripped and fell multiple times on the messy forest floor, slipping on wet leaves as my hands got stabbed by pine needles. Rayner appeared to float over the fallen branches and tangled vines, hardly stopping to wait for me to gather myself or wipe the caked dirt away from my only pair of jeans before he moved on.

I knew based on the maps I'd studied of Beacon Grove that all the woods surrounding the town belonged to the Quarter families, save for the Graves' sliver of land. This part appeared to be even more untouched and uncared for than the portion that led to the cabin. Still, Rayner navigated the twisted, darkened path with ease, as if he'd walked it thousands of times.

Just as my legs were nearly about to give out, a large bonfire came into view. The soft light reached deep into the forest and illuminated the area enough for me to see the obstacles in front of me and dodge them. There were several silhouettes standing in a silent circle around the tall flames, waiting.

"We've arrived!" Rayner called out, throwing his fist into the air.

The group turned in our direction at once and cheered back. Others came from around the opposite side of the pit and joined in the celebration as soon as their eyes landed on me.

I was able to identify numerous familiar faces in the growing crowd of people. Maisey from the diner, my regular barista from The Grind, Esther from the library.

"It's finally time! We've hit many roadblocks on the path to gathering our missing piece, but the gods have rewarded us for our patience."

Roadblocks.

He meant my family. The people who stood in his way and were bulldozed over as if they didn't ever matter.

My monster awoke from his slumber, lighting a fire in my chest that burned ten times hotter than the one that blazed before me.

"What are you going to do, Rayner? Kill me? Remy and the others will never let that happen," I provoked, hoping my words were right.

I just needed to buy some time.

Rayner's roaring laughter made me jump, which encouraged the crowd of people surrounding us to chuckle at my expense. I gritted my teeth and staved off the monster for a little while longer.

"We'll get to that in a little while. For now, I want to savor this moment."

He turned toward his sickening group of followers and lifted his arms in victory. For a long while, he just stared at them in contentment. It was creepy and confusing and made a few of them nervously shift on their feet.

"For almost all my life, I've strived to take down the Quarters and end their reign on our coven. To strip them of their power and transfer it to someone more deserving."

A few cheers interrupted his speech, but he ignored them and went on.

"I watched as their grandfathers slaughtered my father in the street and stole away my brother, tearing apart my family limb from limb. I later learned that my brother was taken prisoner by the Quarters and forced to work as a Counter slave for them to protect their precious gifts."

Rayner paused to hear the surprised gasps erupt from his audience. He nodded in approval, then continued speaking. He paced the ground before me with his hands clasped behind his back.

"That knowledge sparked the beginning of the Movement. You see, these families have done nothing but lie to us and take advantage of our generosity toward them in order to hold onto their own gifts and capitalize off our fear. The Quarter elders have convinced us that Counters were to be killed to strengthen their powers, even though the exact opposite is true. They knew they needed their Counters alive to continue protecting the coven, but they've put us all at risk by convincing us to kill our own people so they could weaken their sons and hold onto their power for a little while longer."

He shook his finger in the air and tilted his head to the side, a smirk tugging at his lips.

"But our Quarters have figured out the truth."

He stopped pacing and looked off into the crowd, allowing this newfound information to marinate with them for a brief second. I found Silas in the sea of faces, noting that his expression remained stoic through Rayner's attack on his integrity. He knew it was coming.

"Thanks to their fathers, Watchtower's current generation of Quarters is weak and defenseless. And we've been able to prove it. We tested their gifts by casting a simple black magic spell on Mabon, when their shield should have been impenetrable. Not only were they unable to stop the spell from being cast, they have even gone as far as allowing it to grow and flourish while they remain absent. They've hunted down our daughters for their own personal gain. They've hidden away in their mansions that were paid for with *our* hard work and left us to fend for ourselves."

A few angry shouts sounded from the back of the crowd, cursing the Quarters for their inability to protect them.

"I know, I know," Rayner agreed, his eyes twinkling mischievously in the firelight. "It's time for a change. That's why I've gathered you all here tonight... why I've brought this girl here. She is Remington Winters' Counter."

Two large men came up from behind me and grabbed my armpits to hoist me out of the dirt. The tip of my Converse barely touched the ground as they held me up for the crowd to see my face.

"We're going to send a message to these boys about how the new Watchtower is going to run without them being a part of it."

The men lifted me higher, and the forest boomed with the Movement member's raucous cheers.

The monster clawed at my chest as fear took over. He was desperate to break free and show these people the ancient magic they were really dealing with. The Quarters may be able to control the power, but I had full access to it as a Counter. I just needed to figure out how to do it without Remy near.

Before I could manage to make a plan to break free, the men began walking me toward a cross that sat beside the fire with a pile of potent, gas-soaked wood surrounding it.

My heart nearly beat out of my chest as I realized what was about to happen.

They were going to burn me at the stake.

I writhed in my captors' arms, finally recognizing one of them as Beau. I pleaded with him to show mercy as he had before. To remember that we were neighbors, and he knew I wasn't a threat. But just when his eyes began to soften and his grip loosened the smallest amount, Rayner slapped him across the face.

"Don't listen to her, Nephew. You've already failed me once. Do it again, and your body will burn right beside hers." I heard his low voice mumble into Beau's ear threateningly.

Beau's eyes hardened once again, and he looked away from me to begin helping the other guy tie me up to the wood.

The icy burn of panic ripped through my core as the leather straps were tightened on my wrists and ankles. When they released me from their grips and left me to hang, the pressure from my weight made the straps cut deep into my skin. My throat burned from the gasoline and the desperate screams that were tearing from my mouth, begging these people—my friends and neighbors—to save me.

Not one of them stepped forward. They just watched in complete astonishment as my body was left hanging from the wooden cross and Beau and the other man sloshed more gas around my feet. Rayner was saying something in the background, but all their attention was on me and my cries of terror.

Realizing that I'd stolen his audience, he stepped over to me and whipped a thick branch across my face, stunning me into silence. The bark tore at my skin and within seconds, hot blood poured from the wound and down my neck. The pungent air and my salty tears stung against the raw flesh, and I wanted to wail even louder just to spite him but decided to reserve my energy for an escape plan.

When he was sure I wouldn't interrupt him again, Rayner continued his twisted speech. I blocked him out, concentrating solely on the crackle and pop of the flames beside me. I slowed my breathing to the sounds and escaped deep into the bowels of my mind, just as I had with the wails coming from the hotel. I imagined Remy's face and prayed to the gods that it would work.

Within seconds, my eyelids fluttered closed, and everything went black.

CHAPTER THIRTY-SIX

REMY

"What's going on?" I asked as Tabitha busted through the door with Blaire in tow. I craned my head, expecting Storie to come stumbling in behind them, but Blaire slammed the door shut.

"What are they doing here?" Rhyse pointed at the Grangers, his face twisted in a nasty scowl and the flame in the fireplace grew and licked at the top of the hearth.

Tabitha growled at him—actually growled—and dropped her bags onto the floor. "Watchtower is falling. They've got Storie and they're hunting anyone else who will get in their way."

"Why would they hunt one of our Counters? They think eliminating them will make us stronger. Don't they want to keep us weak?" Enzo propped himself onto the arm of the couch.

"The darkness has taken over the town. Everyone is feeling violent and restless. Rayner has convinced them that she's the final piece of the revolution." Tabitha surprised me with her candid answers. She was usually so selective of the information she shared.

"Where did they take Storie?" I called from the kitchen. I was already reaching for my jacket when Tabitha's words stopped me.

"Rayner took her to the woods on the south end of town. He knows that killing her will make you weaker."

Enzo let out a string of curse words and Rhyse paced in front of the fireplace. His family owned the woods on the south side. Was it possible his father had crossed us once again?

"What did you find about locating your Counters?" Tabitha asked, her eyes bouncing between us fervently. We each exchanged confused glances until we directed our attention to Lux, who had been studying the book for days.

"You mean to tell me you stole the Book of Shadows and didn't bother finding the most critical piece of information?" she asked incredulously, huffing out a sigh of frustration when no one had any defense.

"You knew we took it?" I asked her, daring to take a step closer with my stomach twisted into knots. We were wasting precious time. I could feel Storie's fear growing in my chest.

Tabitha's eyes briefly closed as she took a few deep calming breaths. "Of course, I knew. Why do you think I allowed her into that room in the first place?"

"What were you doing with the Quarters' Book of Shadows?" Lux's eyes narrowed. He crossed his arms over his puffed-out chest.

Blaire took a defensive step toward Tabitha, but the old woman still appeared unfazed. In fact, she rolled her head from side to side and stared at the ceiling as if she couldn't believe she had to deal with any of this.

"There's not enough time for this." She let out another frustrated growl and balled her fists, scanning the room for the aforementioned book. "I should have known better than to rely on a group of children," she grumbled, walking right past Enzo on the armrest of the couch to lift the cushions.

Lux rolled his eyes. "The book is useless. None of it makes sense."

"It's written in Quarter code. Didn't your fathers teach it to you?"

Standing from her assault on the couch, she moved to rifle through the bookshelf that Lux filled with books he thought might help us.

"Where is it?!" she shouted, amplifying the panic that was growing in my chest. I wasn't sure if it was Storie's or my own, but we needed to stop wasting time on nonsense and get to her.

I climbed the ladder to the loft and swiped the book from the floor where Lux had left it, ignoring their betrayed scowls as I walked across the cabin and shoved it into her hands unapologetically.

"Here. I can feel her anxiety growing stronger. I think we can use it to find her. We need to get to her soon."

"You can feel her?" Blaire ran up before me, her eyes widened in alarm.

I nodded, fear gripping my throat. It was growing stronger by the second.

Tabitha sat down at the table and began flipping through the Book of Shadows. Enzo and Rhyse were having a quiet argument off to the side when Lux gave in and pulled up a chair beside her and attempted to decipher the coded text on the pages.

It happened in a blink. The terror was all-consuming, locking me into one spot with no choice but to stand there and allow myself to feel it. If I was so overcome with these feelings, she must have been going out of her mind. I figured that as long as I was feeling *something*, I could assume she was alive.

Then, everything stopped.

Panic surged through my veins. Somehow, the lack of emotions was worse than anything else and as soon as I opened my mouth to warn the others, her translucent form appeared before me.

Blaire gasped from somewhere behind me, then Lux and Tabitha finally looked up from their impossible task, and Enzo and Rhyse's arguing ceased.

"They're going to burn me," Storie breathlessly rushed out. Her violet eyes remained on me, ignoring the rest of the room.

"Who? Where are you?"

"Rayner took me somewhere in the woods with a huge clearing for their bonfire. Silas is here. Remy, practically the whole town is here and they're going to kill me to weaken you and prove a point." Her voice quivered as she rattled on, her eyes slowly moving around the room as if she were just now noticing everyone else.

I looked to Tabitha for advice, my throat clogging with raw fear like I've never known before. They were going to kill her because of me.

"How are they planning to kill you?" Tabitha calmly asked.

It seemed like such an odd question. Who gave a fuck how they were doing it? The point was we needed to get there and stop them.

"They've got me tied to a cross and surrounded by firewood. They keep pouring gasoline on me while Rayner talks about sacrifice. I don't know, I can't listen to him. I need your help!"

Her words were igniting a storm inside of me that shook my entire being. My physical body was here, but my spirit was off somewhere, searching for its other half before it disappeared forever.

"We're not going to make it to you in time. Storie, you need to listen to me. You have to save yourself," Tabitha was explaining while Storie shook her head in denial. Tears were falling down her cheeks as she begged for us to come find her.

"What do you mean? We can make it there; we just need to go now. Enzo can shift the streets to get us there faster," I yelled out, though no one was listening.

Everyone had their attention focused on Storie, who was slowly fading in and out as she was being pulled back to her physical body. Each time she disappeared from sight, the anguish she was feeling sliced through my chest like a knife.

"You need to call Remy's magic to you. Storie, can you hear me?" Tabitha was shouting at the flickering manifestation of the woman I loved. "Focus on Remy and draw the connection. You don't have to be near each other for it to work. Call his gift to you and use the water from the earth to put the fire out..."

Tabitha's words faded off when Storie disappeared for good.

"We need to get to her," I said to no one in particular.

I wasn't listening to anyone's response as I reached for the handle on the door and stepped out. Lux grabbed my arm and tugged me back into the cabin, pointing to Tabitha.

He turned my body to face him and placed both hands on my shoulders, forcing my attention onto his icy blue eyes. "We'll get you there. But you need to listen to her to figure out how to transfer your gifts to Storie and help her get out of this herself. Otherwise, there won't be anything left to save."

I considered him for a moment, my chest burning again with the same fear that had overtaken me before. He was right. There wasn't time. With a stiff nod, I walked back into the kitchen and stood before the old woman, peering down at her expectantly.

"Tell me what to do."

CHAPTER
THIRTY-SEVEN

STORIE

R ayner was wrapping up his speech when my connection with Remy was severed. I was pulled back to consciousness by Beau and his partner carving into my skin with small pocketknives. They made cuts along my arms and legs that formed into odd, wicked looking symbols. The pain hardly phased me as my body had gone numb when I left it to visit Remy.

My head spun as thoughts swam around my mind, circling too fast for me to land on one. I tried to recall what Tabitha told me, but the gasoline fumes were jumbling everything up. Remy's face appeared before my eyes and the monster in my chest roared to life, reminding me what I was fighting for.

I couldn't give up. I wouldn't allow them to use me to hurt him.

Closing my eyes to block out the massive flames licking the sky beside me and the orange-tinted faces it danced across, I focused inward. I imagined myself pulling power from the ocean miles away.

From the damp ground below me that I'd stumbled on during my trek through the woods.

From the living trees in the forest surrounding us.

Even from the gas-soaked wood at my feet.

I pictured tiny drops of water evaporating from my surroundings and gathering into the air until they formed large splashes that fought the flames down into a tamed pile of embers glowing on the blackened forest floor. Those same splashes doused the wood pile at my feet, diluting the gasoline and clearing my senses enough to form a real, coherent thought. Next, my mind had the water lift my body and loosen the ties around my wrists and ankles, so I could slip out of them with ease.

All of this was an illusion. Something my mind chose to focus on as a survival tactic instead of giving my murderers the satisfaction of watching me writhe around in fear as my final moments approached. I'd managed to block out their chants and the deep rumble of Rayner's voice while he droned on and on to his crowd, too conceited to give up their attention for a few minutes to watch me burn.

Instead, I went to a place in my mind where Remy and I were together without the complications of these supposed gifts that were bestowed upon us by the gods. We were regular people, living a regular life in our tiny bubble of love. Our families never lied to or betrayed us, and our friends were happy and accepting. Everything was perfect, and for a moment, I could breathe.

Those are the daydreams that carried me off into the sky and floated me away.

Up, up, up.

Gone.

CHAPTER
THIRTY-EIGHT

REMY

W e were able to find them deep in the woods of the Forbes property based on the vague description Storie gave us. Even without them, I would have hunted her down. Our souls were intertwined and hers was practically screaming for me to come find it.

Rhyse sensed the fire before anyone else and he led the way through the last of our hike. Tabitha managed to walk through the tangled foliage on the forest floor as well as the rest of us, despite her wobbling and limping any other time. I was growing more suspicious of her and Blaire and I sensed they were hiding something from us. There were just too many unexplained co-incidences when it came to them, and it was time Tabitha shared everything she knew about Quarters and Counters.

After we got to Storie, though.

That throbbing fear I'd felt before had faded into a dull ache. I wouldn't allow myself to consider what that meant for Storie. Instead, I used it as motivation to move forward and get to her as fast as possible.

"What the hell?" Rhyse whispered as we came up to a large clearing of trees.

Bonfire smoke was wafting all around us and people were mulling about across the charred earth. Large embers sat in the center of the blackened circle, providing the only source of light in the blackened abyss.

"Where's the fire?" Blaire asked, tilting her head quizzically.

"She did it," Tabitha breathed out. She hung her head and allowed herself a moment to feel the same silent relief that I had at that revelation.

She did it.

But where was she?

Enzo pointed to a large pile sitting off to the side. That must have been where they had her slung up. My feet were taking me there before any rational thought could stop me. I opted to take the heavily wooded area surrounding the clearing instead of exposing myself to whoever was lingering about. Halfway there, something reached out to my left shoulder and hissed.

"Remy," her broken voice called out.

I turned and watched as she fell onto her knees. Despite the darkness surrounding us, I could see her clear as day. Her skin appeared to be glowing and I wasted no time kneeling before her and taking in her ragged appearance.

Officer Abbot was sitting on the ground behind her. He had been supporting her weight and attempting to wrap bandages from his first aid kit around her arms.

Dried, brown blood was caked all over her skin, concentrated in certain areas of her arms and legs where she appeared to have been cut. I couldn't make out the symbols they formed before our touch began healing them. Officer Abbot's eyes widened, and he leaned backward, shifting his weight so he could stand before us.

"Thank gods you're here," he breathed, bowing his head to Tabitha and Blaire.

"Where is Rayner?" Tabitha's gravelly voice asked from somewhere behind me.

Storie's heavy breathing filled the thick silence as we all waited for their answer.

"I only got here at the end of it," Abbot began quietly. He looked out at the small crowd of people that lingered behind and dropped his voice even lower. "I heard about something going on in the woods and that he'd taken her. I couldn't stand by while another Graves was harmed by Rayner's agenda. By the time I got here, the fire was gone, and she was just getting out of her restraints. I brought her over here out of sight to tend to her wounds."

I never looked away from Storie. My hands remained on her while he spoke, and she allowed my touch to heal her more before attempting to move or speak again.

Her legs pushed off the ground once they were strong enough to hold her and propelled her into me. Soft arms wrapped themselves around my neck as she buried her face into my chest, breathing me in. My own arms held her tight while I did the same.

Finally, she turned her head toward our audience and rasped, "He ran."

EPILOGUE

STORIE

The weeks following Rayner's bonfire were a frenzied blur. He managed to somehow disappear into the wind that night, and no one had heard from or seen him since.

His actions divided Beacon Grove into two separate sides, although most who followed the Movement had quickly shifted their loyalty back to the Quarters once news got out about the fateful events that happened. In the days after, the most loyal Movement members were taken in and questioned regarding everything they knew about the man who led them, including those who were confirmed to have been present for the bonfire. No one knew where he had gone, and if they did, they weren't sharing. The police had no choice but to let everyone go and allow the town to come together and attempt to find some semblance of normalcy.

Remy and the other Quarters returned to their homes early that morning. They each confronted their fathers about the lies they've been fed about their gifts and bravely reclaimed their roles as Quarters of their coven. Some resisted, like Remy's father, but even in their weakened state, they were no match to their sons. It was as Tabitha had said before; nature liked balance. It didn't reward those who tried to manipulate their way around it. And the elders certainly made every attempt to manipulate the natural order of things.

Since I was able to personally identify Silas as an active part of the Movement and the bonfire was held on his property, he was immediately stripped of his title as Watchtower High Priest and placed on house arrest. In a town full of magic and angry witches, that was a little different than anything I'd seen in the past.

Rhyse had him thrown into the cellars below their house and imprisoned him there with various incantations that Tabitha guided him through until they could come up with a proper punishment. They found his Counter down in the cellars as well, and it turns out that Rayner's crazy ramblings that night were correct—his brother had been taken from his family and forced to spend his life as a prisoner, feeding Silas his powers any time he needed them.

I learned that my parents were correct when they insisted I was already a part of the Watchtower coven. Now that everyone knew I was a Counter, they had no choice but to allow me in without initiation, and I had no choice but to accept. It would take a while for me to heal from what some of them had done to me when they were following Rayner, but it was nice to be a part of a community after a lifetime of missing that.

Once I recovered, Remy and I were able to remove the black magic spell that Rayner allowed to fester and grow for nearly two months. It had taken us a few long hours and a lot of guidance from Tabitha—who was not the most patient teacher—but we managed to disassemble the dark cloud lingering over Beacon Grove and release its inhabitants from the control it had over their minds and moods. The shift was instantaneous for Rhyse, Enzo, and Lux, who were finally able to access their gifts again.

Tabitha, Blaire, and Callista were still battling the tarnished reputation their family had suffered from helping Counters all those years ago, though they were welcomed amongst the coven members more easily with the knowledge that they were friends of the Quarters. The others attempted to force Tabitha to identify their Counters, but she adamantly refused, explaining that it wasn't her place as that wasn't how nature intended for them to be reunited. The argument continued each time they were in the same room as the other, which happened more often as the coven attempted to right themselves after the fall of their High Priest, and the Quarters vowed to attend every meeting.

"Is this everything?" Remy asked, holding up the last of my belongings that were scattered around Blaire's room.

I decided to make my stay in Beacon Grove indefinite now that I had managed to form my own little dysfunctional family here. There wasn't much for me in the real world anymore and being here made me feel closer to the people I missed the most. I also had this overwhelming feeling that I still had a lot to learn about the people and place I came from.

Beacon Grove wasn't going to share its secrets with me easily, though. This place doesn't follow the same rules as the rest of the world. That much was obvious.

Remy refused to allow me to rent a home downtown when I brought it up with him.

"I've got a mansion with tons of empty rooms," he had said when I mentioned it, exuding a new confidence that I hadn't seen in him yet during our short time together.

I attributed it to the fact that his father was finally unable to abuse and mistreat him daily anymore. Once we discovered that Julia's mother and the Housekeeper, Marta, was his father's Counter, she was immediately fired from her position and she and Julia were removed from the grounds. There was no use for her to be so close now that her Quarter had lost his gifts, anyway. He allowed his parents to keep their room, but Rowan was forced to hand over the keys to his study and every piece of information he had on the Quarters and the coven.

I was hesitant to take our relationship to that level at first but realized what a ridiculous thought that was when I reminisced on our past two months together. Nothing about us was tra-ditional. It only made sense for us to stay together when there were so many unknown threats still looming in the shadows of Beacon Grove.

When I finally confessed to Blaire that the screams and moans in the hotel were too much for me to bear, she released a loud cackle and made me wait in mortified silence as she caught her breath before explaining, "Those are Mom's clients. You were hearing the raw and excruciating realities of labor. I understand why that would freak you out, though."

It made sense that all along, the only thing that allowed me to discover my connection to Remy were the sounds of women escaping the physical realm to collect their child from the spirit world and bring them back to her. It was the purest, most self-sacrificing form of love there was. Once I learned the truth, I was able to laugh right along with Blaire at my ignorance and self-consciousness over simply asking them from the beginning.

"Let's go home." His whispered breath sent tingles running down my spine after I did one last check around Blaire's room. With hundreds of promises to be back as soon as possible, Blaire released me from her embrace and sent me off.

The inside of the Winters home looked similar to the dark, bland style I'd seen in Remy's room. The space lacked any personality, and while the windows were open and the fresh ocean breeze was wafting through the air, it all felt dark and suffocating. I didn't have much time to dwell on the state of my new home before Remy's hand was wrapping mine up into his and tugging me over to a large sitting room.

"It's yours now. Do whatever you want with it," his deep voice mumbled into my neck after he pulled me down onto the stiff, velvet couch with him, somehow giving voice to my concerns as if I had said them aloud.

I cast a nervous glance around the room, positive there would be a set of staff eyes watching us, or one of his parents would meander down from their living quarters. I didn't end up finding anyone, but the fears remained in the back of my mind as his lips trailed along my jawline, pausing at my ear lobe to lightly nibble and send a wave of goosebumps over my entire body. Long fingers made their way to the hem of my black sweater and slowly tugged it up over my head, exposing me to the open air.

This was the first time we'd been together without the weight of the world hanging on us. No life-altering revelations, no crazed staff members, no Quarters standing on the threshold of life and death. Just us taking this exhilarating step into our future as a couple.

My reservations and self-consciousness melted away with every stride of his tongue down my bare neck and shoulders. My hands fumbled around his waistband until they freed the button of his jeans and allowed me access to his full erection. Remy shifted just enough for me to wrap my whole hand around it and pull it out. A quiet groan left his lips and he leaned back, slowly inching his hand into the waistband of my leggings to return the favor.

Our intimate bliss was short-lived, though. Just as soon as I began working my hands up and down his shaft, the doorbell rang. I paused, wide eyes staring into his for guidance. The doorbell sounded again and the intruder on our intimate moment rapped against the hardwood impatiently. Remy released a loud, frustrated growl and stood from the couch to button his jeans. He helped me back into my shirt, muttering under his breath about someone else coming to answer it.

When he swung the door open, we were met with Rhyse, Lux, and Enzo's wide-eyed, teasing stares.

"We need to talk," Lux greeted with a restrained breath, ignoring the snickers from the two men standing behind him.

Remy led us all into the kitchen, brushing off their requests to have a Quarter-only meeting, which only made me feel even more out of place in the enormous space that was now supposed to be mine.

"She's my Counter. She knows everything we do," he stubbornly explained to them as he reached into the fridge to grab bottled water for each of us.

I kept my gaze cast downward, barely able to meet any of their eyes through my embarrassment.

"Fine," Lux relented on a sigh, ignoring the huffs of disapproval from Rhyse and Enzo.

"I've finally managed to override the redaction spell on the Book of Shadows."

Remy raised his brows impatiently and circled his hand into the air in a motion that said, "Get on with it."

Lux nodded and slowly inhaled a deep breath when Rhyse stepped forward and blurted, "There's a fifth Quarter."

The muscles in Remy's arms tensed as he completely ceased movement. Rhyse and Enzo returned his stunned expression with bewildered smiles while Lux just nodded his head in confirmation.

"As it turns out, the spirit portion of the star marked on the Book of Shadows is a completely separate element than the rest of ours. Whoever possesses that gift has access to all of our elements combined and can control each one with ease."

His icy blue eyes watched unsurprisingly as we took in this new information and considered what it meant for them.

"Who possesses that gift?" Remy wondered and the rest of them shrugged in response.

"Honestly, it could be anyone," Lux admitted. Where Rhyse and Enzo were practically bouncing with excitement, he appeared more irritated than anything.

My hand flew to my mouth as the realization dawned in me. Every odd and confusing encounter came rushing back to me in tiny, fleeting memories as my new revelation grew legs and ran wild in my mind.

I knew exactly who it was.

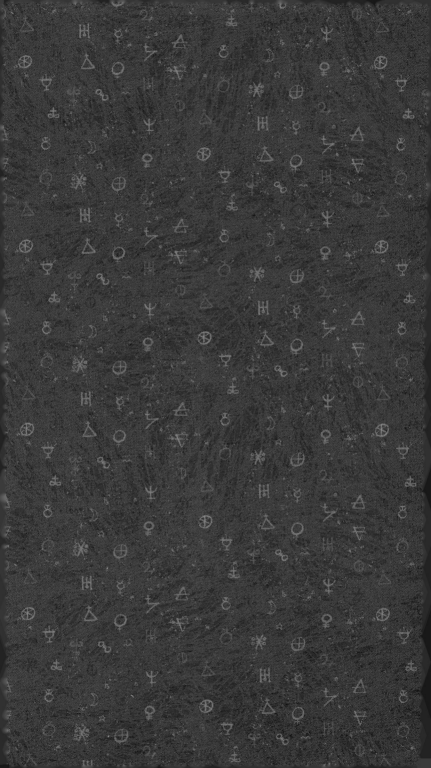

A PREVIEW OF COUNTING QUARTERS

Ready to find out what happens next in Beacon Grove? Flip ahead for a sneek peak into Counting Quarters!
You can read book two for free in Kindle Unlimited today!

BLURB:

My quiet little coven town has never accepted me. I've been branded with the reputation of outcast since the moment I was given the Granger name.

It isn't until I inherit my family's secret ancient gifts that rival those of the town's beloved Quarters that I realize how small my bullies really are.

But these gifts come with a centuries-old resentment that has overtaken my entire being, making it increasingly difficult to be around those closest to me. Add in the dead girls who now haunt me at every turn, and I've become an isolated shell who needs to break free.

When ▢▢▢▢▢▢▢ ▢▢▢▢ ▢▢▢▢▢ posts an ad about his empty apartment, I see an opportunity to get out from under my grandmother's suffocating thumb, and I take it.

I never expected that a man twice my age would be the one I could relate to best, yet being around him felt like reuniting with the other half of my soul. It's not long before we start giving in to our temptations while uncovering more truths about our town... and ourselves.

PROLOGUE

I come from a place most have never heard of and many wish to forget. Nestled deep in the woods, surrounded by steep mountains and dark waters. My hometown follows its own set of rules, laid out centuries ago by the original thirteen families who built it into what it is today. Run by a coven with powers that defy all logic and a government with corruption embedded into its very foundation.

It had always been a stale and unchanging place.

Until it wasn't.

My monsters walk beside me each day, in a town filled with secrets and corruption—with bullies and liars.

But what happens when the most bullied person here ends up being the most powerful? When fury burns through generations and reaches its boiling point?

Catastrophe.

Beacon Grove is all I've ever known.

And I've never wanted out more.

About Jen

Jen Stevens was born and raised in Michigan, where she enjoys the weather of all four seasons in a single day. After obtaining her Bachelor's degree, she quickly realized the corporate world wasn't for her and instead took on the daunting role as her children's snack maid. Reading has been an obsession for a long as she could remember, while writing has always been an escape. Jen could quote The Office word-for-word and proudly refers to herself as a romance junkie. She could live off anything made of sugar and has recently obtained the title of Lady. Most of all, she loves connecting with readers!

Check out Jen's website and socials for the most up to date publishing information: www.jenstevenswrites.com
Socials: @authorjenstevens

JOIN MY COVEN!

Join Jen's Coven of Wicked Little Sunflowers on Facebook today for early looks, exclusive content, and to just hangout!
Scan this code:

Also by Jen Stevens

Check Out All Jen Books!

Dark Romance:
- Ugly Truths (Grimville Reapers Book One)

- Untold Truths (Grimville Reapers Book Two)

Contemporary Romance:
- Advice from a Sunflower

Urban Fantasy Romance:
- Calling Quarters (Beacon Grove Book One)

- Counting Quarters (Beacon Grove Book Two)